Secrets of Lostmor

ANN SMYTHE

CRANTHORPE
— MILLNER —
PUBLISHERS

First published by Cranthorpe Millner Publishers (2025)

ISBN 978-1-80378-284-3 (Paperback)

www.cranthorpemillner.com

Cranthorpe Millner Publishers

For Mona

‘Don’t believe what your eyes are telling you. All they show is limitation. Look with your understanding, find out what you already know, and you’ll see the way to fly.’

– *Jonathan Livingston Seagull*, Richard Bach

Prologue

Thursday 17ᵗʰ June, 1971

Soft laughter floated up from the sisters' hiding place in the tall grass. They lay on flattened, dark green blades, arms and legs spread wide from making grass angels. Above them, puffy clouds scudded across a bright blue summer sky.

'You can't always see them,' said Lily, 'except for a tiny dot, but you can hear them.'

'How do you know that?' Alice asked, squinting upwards.

'Joe told me. He knows everything about birds.'

The skylark's twittering abruptly stopped as the unseen bird swooped on an unsuspecting snack before ascending, bobbing and singing somewhere overhead. For the girls, the rest of the afternoon slipped by in a haze of chatting and laughter.

'I wish it was tomorrow,' sighed Alice.

'Hmm, and how old will you be?' Lily teased her younger sister, who had spoken of little else for the past two days.

'Six, silly!' she giggled. 'Remember? I'm having a party, and all my friends are coming.'

'Oh yes, I forgot!' she grinned. 'Come on, we should get going. I promised Mother we wouldn't be too late.'

They picked their way along the edge of the field, heading towards a familiar gap in the hedgerow which opened into a large meadow. The girls ambled through a mass of swaying oxeye daisies and buttercups. Earlier, bees hovered and flitted among the flowers, the air vibrating with their soft drone, but now the sun lay low on the horizon, and the only noise was a gentle breeze whispering through the grass.

At the upper end of the meadow, flanked on the left by dense woodland, lay their home, Penwyth House. Beyond lay unseen cliffs and the sea below, its waters calm and subdued. The Gothic mansion loomed up in front of them, grim and silent, its silhouette dramatic against the pink-tinged sky. Oddly out of place in such a setting, it was still a wondrous curiosity. Tall, leaded windows towered either side of the heavy oak front door like royal sentry boxes. From its vaulted roof, numerous spires rose shambolically, casting long, thin shadows which crept across the lawn, beckoning to the girls like fingers. As they drew nearer, Lily looked for her father's car in the driveway – not there.

Relieved, she turned to Alice. 'Come on! I'll race you!'

They half skipped, half ran the rest of the way home, screaming and laughing as they collapsed against the door.

Lily banged on the big brass knocker as hard as she could. 'Mother, let us in!'

Their mother greeted them with open arms before shooing them upstairs to wash and change for supper. Outside, an unseasonal cool breeze blew in from the sea, whispering down the house's old chimneys like a warning.

The journey was no quicker than taking the busier A road, but Maggie preferred the more scenic route. She followed the country lane that wound down the hillside through dense woodland to West Hill Primary School in the valley below. She glanced at her granddaughter, Ellie, who was humming along to tunes on the car's cassette player. Disney characters *Ariel* and *Flounder* smiled benignly up at her from the *Little Mermaid* backpack resting on her lap.

'Will you be picking me up from school, too?' Ellie asked, twisting a strand of long blonde hair around her finger.

'Yep. Your mum's home a bit later. Macaroni cheese all right for tea?'

She nodded. 'I love macaroni cheese. Can we have ice cream for pudding?'

Maggie laughed gently. 'If you promise to draw me your best picture ever at school today, then yes, it's a deal.' She straightened the car, which had strayed a little to the right as they approached another bend in the road. Not that her slight lapse in concentration would have made any difference. The motorbike appeared from nowhere, hurtling towards them, its curve too wide. It had no time to brake, smashing headlong into the car. The collision threw Maggie first backwards then forwards, just shy of the windscreen. The force fractured her spine in two places; two seconds that guaranteed her chronic back pain for the rest of her life.

Ellie sat stunned. She had hit her head on the dashboard but was conscious and otherwise unhurt. The bike buckled on impact; its rear end arced high, propelling its rider onto the bonnet before he dropped to the ground. Helmet Man, as

Ellie later named him, struggled to his feet. The effort caused a searing pain to shoot down his left leg, his jeans turning a deep red beneath his hip bone. Using the car to steady himself, he shuffled along to the front passenger door and peered through Ellie's window, his face obscured by a dark visor. He didn't speak nor try to help them. Instead, he staggered back past his ruined bike, its engine still droning and back wheel spinning relentlessly. He swung around wildly like a drunk man, seemingly searching for something.

From inside the car, the dazed little girl watched. Helmet Man slowly looked back in her direction, then upwards. Ellie was distracted by leaves fluttering onto the windscreen. At that moment, the sycamore gave up its new weight. The girl, who had been riding pillion, followed, smashing onto the bonnet with a sickening thud that rocked the car. The impact had catapulted her headlong into the tree, snapping her neck and suspending her within its branches. She lay prone, splayed booted legs hanging over the side of the car, one hand resting at an impossible angle against the windscreen. Her visor was partially ripped away, revealing one dead eye that stared blankly at Ellie. The cheery notes of *Flounder* singing *Under the Sea* started playing just as she began to scream.

PART I

Chapter 1

Friday 13th January, 1995

Windscreen wipers working overtime, the young woman strained to see the narrow lane ahead. Above, storm clouds converged into a marauding grey mass stampeding inland, while an off-sea gale pummelled her little red Ford Fiesta. It was only 3:00 p.m. but it felt more like midnight.

The car's tyres struggled to find traction as she tentatively drove down the cliffside track, and sheet rain ricocheted off the bonnet. Panic threatened to well up inside her. Not because of the poor driving conditions – something more intangible was unsettling her. Her stomach constricted like a tourniquet slowly twisting ever tighter.

To her relief, the lane began to widen, leading her into a small parking area. At the far end, she could make out a farm gate and, beyond it, through a few scrawny trees, Kleger Cottage emerged. As confirmed, a dark blue Land Rover was waiting for her with *Seaward Lets* painted white on the rear door. She pulled up next to it, feeling slightly foolish driving such an urban car in the near off-road conditions. She waved at the man in the driver's seat, barely visible through the torrential rain. The figure waved back before pulling his hood up and entering the downpour. Taking a deep breath, she grabbed her denim jacket off the back seat, raised it above her head, and took the plunge.

'Hello!' the man shouted through the storm. 'I'm Adam, from *Seaward Lets*. You must be Miss Sanders.'

'Yes, we spoke on the phone.' She offered a soggy hand while struggling not to lose her coat in the gale. 'Pleased to meet you,' he grinned. 'Shall we get inside?' He shoved the aged wooden door open and gestured for her to go ahead. The traditional low-beamed kitchen had a broad, slate-tiled floor, and to the left, a large inglenook fireplace dominated the room. As stated in the Seaward Lets brochure, it was 'a quintessential Cornish holiday home'.

'Welcome to Kleger Cottage,' he said, stooping slightly to enter.

'It's lovely – very cosy, especially right now,' she smiled, glancing at the kitchen window where fingers of rain tapped insistently.

Adam pushed his spectacles up his nose. 'I'm glad you like it,' he said in a soft West Country lilt.

Lily trailed behind him as he showed her around: a cosy nook which could be used as an office and a charming lounge with a small working fireplace. All the rooms had low-beamed ceilings and slate floors covered with thick, warm-coloured rugs. She peered out of one of the deep-silled windows, snatching a glimpse of a dark, volatile sea.

'Why don't I leave you to look upstairs?' he suggested. 'I'll wait in the kitchen for you.'

She nodded and climbed the steep, narrow stairs leading to a cosy bedroom in the loft. While a furious wind rattled the eaves, she watched in awe through a tiny window, as a writhing black mass of water crashed into the cliffs – land versus sea.

'Everything's great,' she said, back in the kitchen.

'Good. This is for you,' he smiled, giving her the front door key. 'Oh, and there is some local info and details about the cottage.' He nodded at the Seaward Lets folder on the table. 'If there's anything else I can help you with, just give me a call.'

'Thanks, I'm sure I'll be fine; I'm only here a few days.'

'You just down from Bristol for a bit of a break, then?'

His question threw her slightly. 'Yes,' she lied, fiddling with the key. 'Hopefully tomorrow I can do a bit of exploring.' She smiled weakly as the wind whipped even harder.

'Storms do come and go quite quickly around here. Fingers crossed for a bit of sunshine,' he grinned. 'Oh, and if you want to try a nice traditional pub while you're here, there's always the Black Dog Inn at the far end of Tresor Bay. Most holidaymakers head for the newer bars near the beach, though this time of year things are pretty quiet.'

'I'll bear that in mind. And thanks for braving the weather to come and meet me.'

With Adam gone, her initial relief at finding Kleger Cottage began to wane. She dragged her case from the car and got wet all over again. Night descended and the temperature quickly dropped. After a few practice runs and half a newspaper later, she lit a fire using the generous stack of wood and kindling left in the inglenook. She pushed the old couch nearer to the flames and curled up with a glass of local wine from the welcome pack. Fatigue finally set in from the day's events. She felt herself relax, submitting to the fire's warmth and the numbing effect of the wine, while outside, the storm continued relentlessly into the night.

Chapter 2

Lily awoke suddenly from a dream in which a giant, aqueous claw wrenched Kleger Cottage clean off the cliffside, plunging it deep into the black water below. She blinked the images away. Silence (the storm had blown itself out), and pale sunlight filtered through the window. Quickly throwing on some old jeans and a sweatshirt, she ventured outside. Yesterday's roughshod sea had transformed into a panoramic expanse of shimmering calm water. To her right stretched uninterrupted coastline; to her left, hidden behind the headland, lay the seaside town of Lostmor. She closed her eyes, enjoying the winter sun on her face. Seagulls spiralled overhead. Their familiar sky-call spiked childhood memories of her and her sister, Alice, laughing, running through sand dunes, and eating fish and chips by the sea. She watched the gulls disappear over the cliffs, heading for richer pickings in the bay.

Unexpectedly, a low-pitched, guttural sound made her swing around. A huge seagull was perched on a rickety old table, inches away from her. She hadn't seen or heard it land. Mean-looking yellow eyes observed her as it shifted closer. Taken aback, but fascinated by the bird's sheer audacity, she stayed very still, and for a few moments they eyeballed each other. Then the gull lifted its head skywards and made a long, undulating call. It took flight on powerful wings that raised it high over the cottage, still hollering as it wheeled out of sight.

'Nice of you to drop by!' she shouted after the errant bird, half expecting it to swoop back down for another look, but it had gone as quickly as it had appeared.

Back inside, Lily sat at the kitchen table, rereading the letter that had instigated her return to Lostmor for the first time in twenty-four years. She took a deep breath, then dialled the solicitor's number at the top of the page. 'Mr Walker, hello. This is Lily Sanders, Elizabeth Sanders's daughter. We spoke on the phone a few days ago.'

'Ah yes, Miss Sanders. I've been expecting your call. Once again, I am so very sorry for your loss.'

'Thank you.'

'Thank you for travelling to Lostmor – I think it is in your best interest to be present for the reading of her will.'

'I admit, all this has come as something of a surprise.'

'It's probably easier if I explain in person. When would be a good time for you to drop by?'

'As soon as you like.'

Since leaving Lostmor as a child, Bristol had been Lily's home. Now, just days after her mother's funeral, she had received a letter from an unknown solicitor, informing her of a will she knew nothing about. As far as she knew, any money her family once had was gone.

When her mother was first diagnosed with early-onset Alzheimer's, she had talked openly with Lily about what was to come. Ever pragmatic, she wished to plan ahead – whilst she still could. After visiting several care homes together, they were impressed by a place called Meadow Heights. The staff were friendly and sincere and the home set in the most beautiful grounds. Reluctantly, Lily agreed that should the time come when she could no longer care for her at home, she would make the necessary arrangements. Sadly, the disease quickly progressed. In a few short years, Lily was left with a mere shadow of the woman she loved so much. Eventually, she made the difficult decision to admit her to Meadow Heights. She sold the family home to cover nursing home fees and moved into rented accommodation. Four years later, her mother passed away at the age of sixty-four.

And now this.

She was glad her meeting with Mr Walker was that afternoon. The sooner this was over, the sooner she could leave.

Taking the coastal path to Lostmor was much more appealing than driving, but she needed a few supplies. Once again, she tackled the cliffside. To her surprise, manoeuvring back up proved easier. The views previously hidden by a wall of grey were stunning; lush pasture dotted with yellow gorse rolled inland, and the sea, still bathed in sunshine, was a golden strip below clear pale blue. After a few miles, the coastal road descended and widened, revealing the whole of Tresor Bay. A tumble of houses spilt down the hillside, bejewelled windows sparkling in the low sunlight. Residential homes popped up on either side before gradually giving way to restaurants, shops and pubs, all crowded together and jostling for a prime position on the seafront.

Lily parked a few streets back in the bay area. Still a little early for her appointment, she meandered through the quaint cobbled streets, glad of the distraction. The place was quiet, just a few couples and dog walkers enjoying the winter sunshine.

The small inlet was a hundred-metre stretch of sand dotted with canvas-covered rowing boats. She sat on a bench and gazed out; the bay looked different to how she remembered it. Its narrow horizon very nearly enclosed by looming headland on both sides, it seemed smaller and, strangely, less colourful. To her left, she and her family had sometimes climbed the steps hugging the cliffside that led to Stoney Point, a favourite picnicking spot. Beyond that, about four miles east, was her childhood home: Penwyth House. She wondered who resided there now, or maybe it was a country retreat or hotel. She had lived there with her family until Alice's sixth birthday.

Then, her world had fallen apart.

A familiar knot formed in her stomach, her hands trembled, and a cold sweat prickled her forehead. She closed her eyes and saw her – Alice giggling, her fair hair golden in the sunlight; the two of them, hidden in the long grass, whispering little girl secrets. But the images swiftly dissolved, giving way to a blackness that cleaved through her consciousness. Some part of her mind tried to reach her, to force her to look at something, something she did not want to see.

Lily's eyes sprang wide open.

Chapter 3

Mr Walker's office was in a terraced, Tudor-style house above a souvenir shop at the far end of the bay. He buzzed Lily in. Her thoughts raced as she climbed the narrow spiral stairs. What if there were outstanding debts she knew nothing about? She prayed it was just a matter of signing some overlooked documents. She wasn't sure how these things worked.

A man stood in the doorway, smiling congenially. 'I'm Timothy, Timothy Walker. It's so nice to finally meet you, Miss Sanders.'

They shook hands, and he gestured for Lily to take a seat. Originally an attic, the sloping ceiling and book-lined walls made the space even smaller. An ornate wooden desk and aged leather-studded chair were positioned beneath a skylight – she wondered how he'd got the furniture up the stairs.

Mr Walker, who looked to be in his early sixties, squeezed his generous paunch behind the desk and unbuttoned an ill-fitting suit jacket. 'It's a little snug in here,' he apologised, searching for his glasses among the paperwork before him.

'It's fine,' she smiled. 'As I said on the phone, your letter did come as something of a shock. I didn't know my mother had made a will. She had Alzheimer's for many years, so I assume she wrote it some time ago.'

'It was written when you were still a child. Miss Sanders, I hope you don't mind me asking, but is this the first time you've returned to Lostmor since moving to Bristol?'

'Yes. A long time ago, our family suffered a terrible loss. Perhaps you know?'

The solicitor nodded.

'Well, my mother wanted us to start again somewhere new.' She stared at her hands, her voice no more than a whisper. 'It was a very difficult time.' *And I don't want to talk about it – not now, not ever.*

'Indeed, indeed,' he said, regretting having asked. 'I am sorry, I do not mean to intrude. I'll get to the point. You are here because I was instructed by your mother to keep this document safe.' Mr Walker unfolded the will, which had remained a secret from Lily for so many years. He peered at her over the rim of his glasses, knowing the life-changing impact his following words would have. 'Your childhood home here in Lostmor, Penwyth House, was never sold.'

Lily looked up, eyes wide in disbelief. 'But it *was* sold! Mother was too upset to come back here, and we needed the money from the sale to buy a house in Bristol.' She twisted her hands in her lap, wishing she was back in her art studio, surrounded by her beloved jumble of canvasses, paints and brushes.

A few weeks after her father's and Alice's funerals, Lily and her mother left Penwyth House for good. Still reeling from her loss, Lily did not understand why they had to leave. She was only nine years old, and to her young mind, it seemed like they – no, *she* – had done something wrong, made worse by her mother's refusal to talk about what happened.

To this day, she could not recall the exact events of that

tragic evening, those last moments of Alice's and their father's lives, just before they fell from the roof of their home.

The same images come to her on nights when sleep is impossible, teetering at the edge of her thoughts, snapshots of a scene, replaying in her mind a million times...

A wild storm is raging; her father stood on the roof amongst Penwyth's strange spires, statue-like in the darkness, his face drained of all colour. Behind him, flashes of lightning scuttle like spiders across the sky. Lily is at the doorway, afraid, watching Alice, so little, running barefoot through the rain to their father. He sweeps her up in his arms just as Lily hears her mother calling from below. She goes to the stairs, but a man is blocking her way. He has a mean face with pinched features and narrow eyes.

Then, as always, she wakes, gasping for breath, her heart racing.

Now, Lily tried to focus, to listen to the words coming like white noise from Mr Walker's mouth, instead of the voices in her head.

He was looking at her with concern. 'You look a little pale, Miss Sanders. This must be a lot to take in. Would you like a glass of water?'

'No. No, thanks. Please carry on, I'm fine.'

He smiled sympathetically before continuing. 'I don't fully understand why your mother wanted to keep the house on all these years, but she left the estate in the care of the groundsman, Joe Newman. Perhaps you remember him?'

She nodded, trying to take in this further revelation. Joe – of course she remembered him. But she had not thought of him for many years, another lost face from her childhood.

'I believe she took him on not long after she bought

Penwyth House, and he's stayed ever since. You will see he has taken good care of the estate, but the house has stood empty for over two decades – nobody knows the condition of the interior. Your mother left strict instructions that no one should enter.'

'Why?' Lily asked, feeling beyond shocked. 'So, you're saying that the house I've always been led to believe was sold, remains as it was when we left twenty-four years ago? And to cap it all, the same groundsman still works there!' It was too much.

'When we were little, Alice and I...' She realised it was the first time she had uttered her sister's name in years, and a sudden wave of emotion threatened to surface. At that moment, she knew she had never really escaped this place. Struggling to keep her voice even, she continued. 'We used to follow Joe around the grounds. He was kind to us. He kept us busy in the summer holidays and gave us little jobs to do. He taught us about the plants and herbs growing in the old Victorian glasshouses. And he knew about birds. Mother had an aviary – he took care of that, too.'

'I'm glad you remember him so fondly. Shortly after you left Lostmor, at your mother's request I asked him if, in return for lodgings at Edhen Cottage and a modest income, he would stay on and tend to the grounds. He agreed. Months passed, and I waited to hear from your mother, but she never contacted me again. During the following years, Joe did not ask me why she wanted him to stay on. I can only guess he was continuing the job he always loved. In the early days, I used to drop in at the cottage now and then for a chat; see how he was. Now, I think he prefers his own company; he rarely answers the door anymore. Occasionally, I see him in town coming in for supplies, and he'll give me a nod.'

'I don't know what to say. I thought this meeting might be about some final request, but this... Why? Why did she do it?'

'It was not my business to ask. I know that before you left, back in 1971, Elizabeth granted me power of attorney over her affairs regarding Penwyth House until you inherited. As requested, an account was set up to pay Joe a monthly wage and an annual sum towards the general upkeep of Penwyth's twenty-acre estate, including Edhen Cottage. I was contacted by Meadow Heights upon your mother's passing and, as her appointed solicitor, it now falls to me to notify you of the contents of her last will and testament.

'It is what she wanted, Miss Sanders, for you, her daughter, to inherit Penwyth House.'

'But if Penwyth was never sold, how did she afford our home in Bristol? I was still a child, and she, a single mother working part-time at the local kiosk.'

'That may be so, but your mother was once wealthy. Back then, many people around here presumed your father owned Penwyth House. But it was hers.'

'How much do you know about her parents?'

'Not much – they died in a house fire before I was born. Mother was only in her twenties when it happened. She didn't like to talk about them; I think it upset her.'

'It must have been a terrible time in her life,' he agreed. 'She first contacted me when her offer for Penwyth Estate was accepted, and she needed a solicitor to handle the purchase. When we met, she mentioned the fire. She told me she had considered one day taking over the family business. But after tragically losing her parents, all she wanted was to make a fresh start somewhere new. Her parents' business was insured, and she received a considerable sum of money when they passed. She paid in cash for Penwyth Estate.'

'I still don't understand how they accumulated so much money – I mean, for Mother to buy Penwyth Estate outright, even back then it would have cost a small fortune. Her parents made a living as farmers; they can't have been that wealthy.'

'Originally they were farmers, but at some point they diversified. They wanted to be the first Cornish family to produce a single-malt whisky in over three hundred years. Elizabeth told me they built a distillery, and even grew their own barley. It started small, but over time became a hugely successful company. I don't think your mother realised just how profitable the business was until she inherited its proceeds. So you see, although she suffered a terrible loss, she also became rich, more or less overnight. After buying Penwyth Estate she still had a large chunk of her inheritance, which she invested wisely.

'She married your father just a few years later and opened a joint account that she regularly paid money into. But she also kept several other accounts in her name only. In addition to this, she set up a trust fund for you, the details of which you can read for yourself.' He handed Lily her mother's will.

She tried to focus on the words before her, not the thoughts ricocheting around her brain. Her newly discovered trust fund was worth over five million pounds. She placed the document on the desk and leaned back in the chair, meeting Mr Walker's eyes with a steady gaze. 'I think I really could do with a drink, after all. But maybe something a bit stronger than water?'

'There's a nice little pub called the Black Dog inn just around the corner.'

'Believe it or not, I have heard of it. That would be splendid. It's been a strange day, and I still have so many questions. If you have time?'

'You're my last appointment, Miss Sanders, and it would be my pleasure.'

'Please, call me Lily.'

He smiled affably. 'Lily it is. Then you must call me Timothy.'

Chapter 4

Marcus Cole, the manager of the Black Dog inn, nodded and smiled at Timothy and Lily as they entered.

'Hello, Timothy. What would you like?

'I'll have my usual, please, Marcus. And for you, Lily?'

'A glass of Chardonnay would be great.'

'Coming right up. Why don't you find yourselves a seat and I'll bring your drinks over?'

They had just sat down when a black Labrador sloped up. Timothy gave the dog a friendly pat.

'He's lovely,' she commented. As if in response, he wandered over to her side and rested his head on her lap. 'Well, you're friendly,' she laughed, giving him an ear rub. 'Does he come with the pub?'

'No, he belongs to Marcus,' Timothy replied, sipping from a welcome pint of ale.

'I was joking. Black dog, get it?'

'Oh! Black Dog inn. Yes, I see what you mean.'

'That's Horace,' Marcus added, placing their drinks on the table. 'Soppy thing. Not much of a guard dog.' He smiled at Lily before returning to the bar to serve another customer.

She sipped her wine. 'This place has great views of the bay.'

'It has,' Timothy agreed. 'How are you feeling now, Lily? Your inheritance has obviously come as a huge shock.'

'It's going to take a while to sink in. You must have known my mother reasonably well. Have you any idea why she kept so many secrets from me? Did she not leave me a note, a letter, anything?' Timothy shook his head. 'I'm afraid not. As well as acting in a professional capacity for your mother, our paths crossed from time to time – you know, weddings and funerals. In fact, she kindly invited me to her own wedding.

'Lostmor is a small place; I am often privy to sensitive information – confidential matters. Understandably, your mother wanted to keep our relationship purely professional.'

Lily looked around and then lowered her voice. 'Five million pounds? Most people would be extremely pleased to be in my position right now, but it just doesn't seem real, any of it.'

'Well, it is real. And you are now a very wealthy woman. Perhaps you may find some answers when you go to the house.' He regarded her with kind eyes. 'How long do you plan to stay?'

'I only rented a cottage for the weekend, but clearly I will need more time now. I'll have to go back to Bristol first and sort out a few things – close the art gallery for a week or two.'

'You're an artist?'

'Yes. I'll speak to Adam at Seaward Lets. When I booked the cottage, he mentioned there were no other lets for a while so I can't see it being a problem to extend my stay.' Of all the scenarios she could have imagined – perhaps a last request to scatter her mother's ashes – being bequeathed the family estate and millions of pounds were not amongst them. 'As far as the estate is concerned, I don't know where to start. Before I can even think about selling it, I'll need to go through the contents of the house. I've no idea what to expect.' Her stomach lurched. The thought of returning to Penwyth, especially knowing it was untouched since she had left as a child, filled her with dread. It felt like something almost ethereal was creeping up on her, as if she had glimpsed a dark shadow or movement in the corner of her eye. She drained her glass. 'And what do I do about Joe? Edhen Cottage has been his home for decades – since he was young.'

'I'm sure he will be pleased to see you after all these years. He's a good man. Talk to him. If you plan to sell the estate, maybe consider keeping Edhen Cottage. It does lie near one of the estate's borders. Perhaps you could come to some arrangement with him.'

'It's more a matter of *when* I sell than if,' Lily smiled weakly. 'What would I do with it all? My home and my work are in Bristol.' She was going to add 'friends', but that wasn't strictly true. Patsy, her best friend and one-time roomy at art college, now worked as a theatre set designer in London. And Archie, a former flatmate, had fallen in love with a French man and moved to Nice three years ago. Over time, other friends, including several disillusioned boyfriends, had drifted away. She was always so busy building up her gallery (and loving every minute) that her personal life had fallen by the wayside.

She suddenly felt weary. Grateful though she was to talk things over with Timothy, all she wanted to do now was get back to the cottage, curl up in front of the fire and try to process the day's bizarre events.

'Well, if I can help with anything else. If you need financial advice or someone to talk things over with, you know where I am,' he joked, gesturing around the pub's cosy little bar. 'Sorry,' he frowned, noting the young woman's tired expression. 'I'm being insensitive. I didn't mean to be flippant.'

'Not at all. I'm grateful for your time but I should probably go. I have a lot to think about.'

'Here, please take my card. In the meantime, these are yours.' He fished out a large, padded envelope from his briefcase.

Lily looked quizzically at him.

'The keys – for Penwyth Estate.'

Chapter 5

Lily drove towards Kleger Cottage under a bleached white sky, the day's brightness stultified. Her thoughts drifted from her mother to Alice to her father, then to Joe and Penwyth House.

Up ahead on the side of the road was what looked, at first, like a small white boulder, but as she drew nearer, she saw it was a dog – a Jack Russell. She slowly pulled up. He sat quite still, his head slightly cocked, the tip of his tail moving from side to side. She got out and hunched down in front of him.

'Hello! What are you doing out here?' She scanned the remote horizon, hoping its owner might appear. Pleased she had come along, he trotted around the car, jumped in and sat on the passenger seat, as if he'd been waiting for a bus. Lily got back in and dialled Adam's number. He answered promptly.

'Hello, Adam. It's Lily Sanders here. I am sorry to bother you.'

'How are you, Miss Sanders? Is everything all right?'

'Yes, okay thanks. I wonder if you could help me with something. I'm driving back from Lostmor and have found a dog sitting by the roadside. I can't see anyone around, and there are no houses in sight. You wouldn't have any idea who he might belong to, would you? He's a Jack Russell. Doesn't look like a stray, but he's not wearing a collar.'

'Where are you?'

'On the coastal road, a minute or two away from the cottage.'

'There aren't many places along there, apart from another of our lets, but that's empty. There is a farm about half a mile past Kleger – the Bligh's place. You could try there. If not, maybe the local vets on the high street could help. Dr Morgan might be able to hazard a guess. Do you want me to find her number for you?'

'Well, the farm's closer. I'll try there first. Oh, and I need to talk to you about something else. I was hoping I could extend my stay?'

'That shouldn't be a problem. How long were you thinking.'

'A week, maybe two.'

'Well, there's no one booked in for another month. If you like, I can drop by later to discuss it.'

Having agreed on a time, and with the dog riding as co-pilot, Lily followed the meandering road as it headed inland. Grazing pasture soon gave way to agricultural fields. The turning for Bligh Farm was signposted. She drove up the track that led to a low stone farmhouse. Several battered corrugated barns stood further back. As she got out of the car, the dog leapt past her, scrambling over a tumble-down wall and into the front garden. He seemed at home as she pushed the rusty gate open and tentatively knocked on the front door. The door slowly opened at her touch. She peered inside.

'Hello! Is anyone home?' She looked around the low-ceilinged room. On either side of a stone fireplace were worn leather sofas. The dog flopped down on a rug in front of the hearth.

Lily sighed. 'Well, 'bye then, fella.' She smiled. 'Be good now.'

The Jack Russell looked up briefly before closing his eyes for a well-earned snooze.

'Can I help you?' said a gruff voice behind her.

'Oh!' She jumped. 'I'm sorry for the intrusion. I'm Lily. Lily Sanders.'

The man who filled the low doorway ignored her proffered hand.

'Um, is this your dog?' she asked. 'I found him about a mile away, up on the coastal road.' She presumed the man was a Bligh. He wore dirty old jeans and a faded checked shirt.

He looked her up and down, unimpressed, then nodded toward the dog, who looked as if he'd been asleep for hours. 'That's Flynn. He knows his way around; he doesn't need rescuing.'

'Well, I didn't like to just leave him—'

'I really am very busy, so if you don't mind,' he said, cutting her off mid-sentence whilst guiding her through the door with his hand. Outside, he swung round to face her, his dark eyes studying her. 'Look, I know you're trying to help, but I must get back to work.'

'I'm going!' she exclaimed, raising her hands in exasperation.

The man yanked the door shut behind them and marched up the path. He then tramped around the side of the house, wiping his brow with one sleeve. He didn't look back.

Later that day, Adam stopped by Kleger Cottage and arranged

to extend Lily's stay by two weeks. He didn't seem particularly fazed by her weak excuse of wanting to explore the area more. Having already told him she was there on a weekend break, it was easier to continue the pretence. *Lies beget lies*, she thought, hoping the extra time would be long enough for her to at least clear her family's belongings out of Penwyth House.

She wondered how her mother would feel about her selling the property, having gone to so much trouble to keep it. On the other hand, the will did not prohibit her from doing so. Lily could only assume that her mother perhaps intended to return home one day and tell Lily the truth. But as more time had passed, and they became settled in Bristol, it was too hard to go back. Now, as the family's only surviving member, what happened to the estate was down to her.

And something else had occurred to her: what if returning to the house finally helped her recall what had taken place on the night of Alice's birthday?

Chapter 6

Lily always felt restless when she was away from painting for a long time, so she was relieved to be back in Bristol, if only briefly.

Her apartment was on the first floor of a big Georgian house in Clifton, a leafy and affluent part of town. The rooms were large and airy, with traditional corniced ceilings and tall sash windows.

She checked the answering machine and sorted through the mail before walking the short distance to her gallery, The Blue. Her studio was her haven, and art was her passion. Every painting she worked on was treated with equal care and attention, whether it was commissioned or not.

Collecting her palette, paints and easel, she carefully packaged a small, unfinished seascape to transport back to Lostmor. It would be a welcome evening distraction since her days would be spent at Penwyth Estate. Before leaving, she recorded a message on the landline, apologising for the gallery's temporary closure, and left a note on the door. This made her uneasy; she'd never closed for more than a few days before.

The following day, she packed a suitcase and set off again for Lostmor. During the three-hour drive, she tried not to dwell on her imminent return to Penwyth House, but with every mile that passed, she felt more anxious.

It's time to move on, to close this chapter of my life, she told herself, gripping the steering wheel so hard her knuckles turned white.

Later that evening, back at Kleger Cottage, she sat at the kitchen table, picking at a ready meal and scanning a local paper she'd picked up. She flicked through various news items. In one, Lostmor's council acknowledged complaints from locals regarding the dangerous condition of the coastal road in several locations. Proposals were in discussion, but repairs would inevitably result in council tax increases. Turning the page, she saw an advertisement for Lostmor's first luxury dog kennel – 'Fern Retreat – a home from home for dogs' – was soon opening on the outskirts. Beneath that, a minor heading read: *Parrot Pandemonium!* – a curious story about three green and yellow birds spotted by a surprised family while eating fish and chips in their car at nearby Penny Cove.

'Time to stop distracting yourself,' she sighed. The thought of being solely responsible for such a large estate was a daunting prospect.

She reluctantly turned her attention to the classifieds. Casting her eye through the various local traders, she circled a number for Lostmor Antiques, offering appraisals and house clearances. It was a start.

Lily listened to the fat raindrops splattering the kitchen window. She cupped her hands on the glass and peered through; it was inky black outside. The rain began beating harder, and she heard the first low rumble of thunder in the distance. Drawing the flimsy gingham curtains against the brewing storm, she lit a fire, quicker this time having learnt how. She pulled up a seat in front of the easel set up in the far corner of the kitchen and tried her best to ignore the menacing wind which shook the front door so violently, its hinges rattled. Instead, she familiarised herself once more with the half-finished seascape before her. Waves of deep royal blue rolled into soft silver sand; the sky was ablaze: a spectacular sunset of coral, violet and turquoise. She worked the colours in from her palette, smudging the edges of the fading light into a fiery orange, creating a stunning scene.

She painted late into the night, losing track of time and paying no attention to the altogether different setting outside, where the ocean raged, fierce and unforgiving.

Chapter 7

The next morning, Lily stood looking out to sea. Pale sunlight filtered through static clouds, giving her the sudden urge to paint the ever-changing scene before her. The raging sea of just a few hours ago was now benign. But she had no time to paint. Today, she had other plans.

A short time later, Lily was driving along the coastal road east of Lostmor. On the passenger seat of her car was the large envelope Timothy had given her. Lips set in a hard line, she was for once oblivious of the changing landscape.

Could returning to Penwyth explain her strange nightmares? Were they actual memories, distorted and fragmented over time, or just childhood imaginings, a reaction to the trauma of losing Alice and her father?

She recognised the turning when she saw a large, rusty iron gate that looked to have been wedged open many years prior. Tall grass had grown through the gate's fretwork, which hung off one of two lichen-covered stone piers. These were topped with fierce-looking eagles, their weathered wings raised, dark expressions watchful.

The drive up to the house was long and meandering. She passed through lush green meadowland and apple orchards, where rows of cropped trees stood dormant, patiently awaiting their spring revival. The narrow road levelled out, and the familiar lawns and side view of Penwyth House, with its foreboding spires, came into view. Lily's stomach took a nosedive. She held on to the wheel as if lost at sea, clinging to a lifebuoy. She pulled up on the drive, her heart pounding. Glancing around, she saw no other vehicles and no sign of Joe Newman. She got out and gazed at the familiar meadow. Then she turned to look at the old house. It dawned on her how out of place the building looked.

Built in the 1800s by an eccentric gentleman who spent over a decade creating his Gothic vision, he then sold it two years after its completion. Nobody knew why, but locals suspected his romantic ideal had not entirely lived up to the harsh reality of long, bitterly cold winters in a draughty mansion. In time, it was updated with running water and mains electricity. When Elizabeth finally viewed the property over a hundred years later, she instantly fell in love with its Gothic design – its point arches, stained glass windows and prominent chimneys, not to mention its proximity to the sea.

Lily took a deep breath. The keys were labelled, and she slid the largest one into the lock, turned it and pushed. Her legs felt heavy and rooted to the floor. Surprisingly, the old oak door swung open easily. As her eyes adjusted, she could see the grandiose staircase which rose majestically, sweeping up either side of what was once a formidable hallway. Dust particles, suspended in long, thin shafts of light, filtered down from a glass dome in the ceiling above. The house was dull and airless. She stepped across the threshold, and a slight breeze – the first in decades – sent dust swirling around her. She pushed the door shut, the noise echoing around the large space.

Through the gloom, she could see the eerie shapes of

furniture covered in sheets. She gazed at the swaths of cobwebs hanging from the ceiling which clung to the arched walls like draped curtains. More tendrils criss-crossed a once beautiful French crystal chandelier.

As she entered through the double doors to what used to be known as the breakfast room, another layer of dust swamped her. Lily imagined her mother sitting at the long breakfast table, young and beautiful, her blonde hair swept up in a loose ponytail. She smiled and beckoned for Lily to join her and Alice, who was sitting on her lap, grappling with a piece of toast.

Lily shook the memory away and stared at the vaguely familiar shrouded shapes of dressers and shelves lined with dust-covered books. Leaded windows with cracked, stained-glass panels ran floor to ceiling; thin rays of light seeped through chinks in the once richly coloured panes, now blunted by years of neglect and weathering. Beyond lay the gallery room. The door was locked, so she dug into her envelope and found the correct key. Inside, the windows were boarded up, presumably to prevent looting. In the dim light she could make out the large, heavy-framed paintings that still hung the entire length of the galleried wall. Someone – perhaps Joe – had managed to cover them up with more sheets. She walked towards the painting mounted above an imposing wrought iron fireplace in the gallery's centre. Lily gingerly pulled at the edge of the mildew-spotted material covering it. This picture she remembered well. She had been a little afraid but also intrigued by it as a child. The sheet fell more quickly than she expected, and she only partly escaped the cloud of dust that came down with it. Coughing and blinking hard, she slowly raised her head. Her eyes met those in the painting.

Her father sat in an armchair in front of the same fireplace she now stood in front of. One ankle rested on the opposite knee, whisky in hand, while he stroked a pale-coloured Labrador. She remembered the animal. Much to the girls' disappointment, he was a gun dog that was never allowed in the house. Instead, he was kennelled near the old stables with several other harshly treated hounds.

The painting had darkened with age, but still those fierce eyes looked down at her, angry and accusing. As a little girl, it seemed his intense gaze had followed her wherever she stood in the room. Seeing her father's face again brought back uncomfortable memories, memories of his drunken behaviour and violent temper. But his portrait was also a sad reminder of everything she had lost.

Walking from room to room, she familiarised herself with her childhood home. Most of the downstairs windows were boarded up although there were signs of attempted break-ins. In places, the walls and rugs were weather-damaged; furniture was knocked over and ornaments smashed. All around were the dusty artefacts of lives lived then hastily abandoned: books, dolls, a chess set laid out for a game never played. The dank basement kitchen was a time warp of long-forgotten brands neatly stored in cupboards; piles of once gleaming porcelain plates were stacked on units, now covered in fragments of damp plaster.

There were two ways of getting to the first floor: the central staircase and the narrow stairs in the west wing, used mainly by the staff. She climbed the latter that led to the upper hallway and abruptly stopped. For a moment she felt like a child again, playing hide-and-seek with Alice. She visualised her sister, clear as day, standing halfway down the landing, beckoning her to follow. She giggled and waved at her before running away, disappearing into the east wing.

Lily's vision swam and the passageway seemed to stretch into eternity, distorting the doorways and stone-arched windows. She fell against the wall in a panic and slid to her knees. She squeezed her eyes shut then opened them again. Gradually, everything stopped spinning. It was just a memory, nothing more; being home was playing tricks on her mind. After a few minutes, she felt recovered enough to get to her feet. Determined not to give up, she walked on, pushing open bedroom doors to long-forgotten rooms. Rooms that were never used apart for occasional guests. In some, dark stains spread across the ceiling where water damage had seeped through from the porous roof above. The rotten attic space had dripped unfettered onto the carpets and furniture, turning once richly coloured damask wallpapers into peeling strips of brown.

Luckily the east wing, where the family bedrooms were located, had fared better. She hesitated when she reached Alice's room. She couldn't face it, not yet. Instead, she slid into her bedroom opposite. Most of the furniture was covered up. On the shelves, between storybooks and a faded pink jewellery box, was a neat line of teddies and dolls, patiently awaiting her return. A few comics and clothes were scattered on the floor; a child's pair of silver sandals thrown hastily in the corner. Lily looked around her old bedroom. How sad, her childhood room frozen in time. She felt sorry for the little girl she had once been. Twenty-four years ago, not only had her family been ripped apart by tragedy, she and her mother had completely abandoned their home. They had fled, as if this familiar old house was to blame for everything.

The door to her parents' bedroom opened with a sigh that made her shudder. Like hers, it looked to have been left hastily. She felt as she always had when she'd entered this room: an intruder. She remembered hearing terrible arguments coming from behind this door, her father's raised voice, usually in a drunken rage, her mother crying, begging him to leave her alone.

She lifted the sheet covering her mother's dresser and ran her fingers over the cool glass of scattered perfume bottles. A faint smell of jasmine permeated the air. Even as a little girl, Lily had noticed how men behaved around her mother. She had emanated an aura of femininity yet seemed unaware of her effect on people. The atmosphere would lighten whenever she entered a room; men and women wanted to be around her (unless her father joined them, then the atmosphere would often sour and lie heavy with an unspoken mood).

She was struck by another vivid recollection: herself sitting on her parents' bed, watching her mother brush her hair, her reflection smiling back. Her mother and Alice had the same heart-shaped faces framed by long blonde hair, unlike Lily, whose face was narrower with higher cheekbones, and dark brown, wavy hair that refused to frame anything.

She was brought sharply back to reality by the wild reflection staring back at her; spiderweb threads were trapped in her hair, and dust plumed off her when she tried to brush the filth away.

She realised then she had been wandering around the house

for hours and not noticed the light beginning to fade. She felt weary and in need of a hot shower, and was hit by the sudden urge to run out of the house and never come back.

As she turned to leave the room, she noticed her mother's wardrobe. The door was hanging slightly open under its shroud, and she remembered it never quite shut properly. She pulled the sheet down, revealing shiny, dark ornate wood. Inside, a few of her mother's long, floaty dresses, now timeworn and musty, still hung on padded wooden hangers.

On the upper shelf was a large cardboard box. Lily struggled to lift it out and onto the floor. Inside were books – at a glance, mostly detective novels. On top of the books was a small silver-framed black-and-white photo. Lily studied the grainy image. Alice sat on her father's lap; Lily sat next to her mother, everyone smiling. She decided to take the box with her and go through it later. Maybe there were more photos, even an album.

She locked the front door and stored the box in the car boot. She knew she should try to see Joe, even though she was no longer in the mood for conversation. Coming home had left her emotionally drained, but her conscience got the better of her. She left her car and walked through the woods to Edhen Cottage.

The small, thatched house looked the same as she vaguely remembered – low-slung with tiny windows. To the side of it was a large pile of logs neatly stacked in a wood store. She knocked on the door several times and shouted Joe's name, but the place looked empty. The curtains were drawn, and there was no vehicle anywhere in sight. Perhaps he was in town or working somewhere on the estate. In hindsight, she realised she should have come here first; she had been so anxious when she had pulled up at the house that she hadn't thought things through. She needed to let him know about her mother's passing, explain her inheritance, and thank him for staying on so loyally all these years. She didn't want to leave a note as it seemed too flippant: *Hi, it's Lily. Just thought I'd drop in...*

After waiting ten minutes, she returned to the car and vowed to return to Edhen Cottage on her next visit. If Joe still wasn't home, then she would have to track him down, even if she had to search the entire estate.

Chapter 8

Lily drove home as the low winter sun released its tenuous grip on the day, descending fast behind a grim line of foreboding clouds. She hoped there wouldn't be another storm that evening. Up ahead, she spotted movement – a small animal, lying motionless on the grassy verge. As she drew nearer, she saw it was Flynn. She slowly pulled alongside him and got out.

'Hi, Flynn. Hi, fella.' Lily spoke softly as she knelt before him. He was shaking, whether due to the cold or through shock she wasn't sure. Flynn raised his head slightly and whimpered. At a guess, the poor dog had been struck by a car. She opened the rear passenger door, then gingerly lifted him in. Next, she drove very carefully to Bligh Farm as it was only minutes away. 'Hang on, Flynn,' she said gently.

This time the farmhouse front door was locked, and there was no reply when she knocked. She walked around the side of the house and shouted hello. Still no reply. She wandered around the yard area and barns but there was no sign of him. Returning to her car, she contemplated what to do. Obviously Flynn wasn't her responsibility but as a life-long animal lover she couldn't bear to see him suffering. She remembered Adam mentioning the veterinary practice on the high street and made the decision to drive him there to get help.

The veterinary waiting room was small, with a few dog-eared posters advertising worm treatments and reminders for pet vaccinations.

'Oh my goodness,' said a woman in a white coat upon seeing the forlorn dog Lily had cradled in her arms.

'Please can you help?! I found him at the side of the road.'

'Of course. Follow me.'

In the treatment room the vet gently took Flynn from Lily and laid him on the examination table.

'I'm Dr Morgan,' she smiled reassuringly at her, whilst carefully examining the dog. 'I believe this is Flynn.'

Lily nodded. 'You know his owner?

'He's a family friend, yes.'

'I'm not from around here but I knew Flynn was from Bligh Farm. I took him home but there was no one there.' Lily watched as the vet continued her examination. 'Is he going to be okay?'

'I think he's fractured his front left leg. I'll need to do some x-rays. Poor fella, may have a concussion too. Did you say you found him by the road?'

'The coastal road. Near Bligh Farm and not far from where I'm staying at Kleger Cottage.'

'Oh, that's the one perched on the cliffside, isn't it?'

'That's right. I have to say that this is actually the second time I've found Flynn out on his own. I returned him once before to the owner.'

'I'm sure Mr Bligh will be very grateful to you for bringing Flynn in and you've no reason to worry about this little fella anymore. I'll put him out back in a nice quiet bed and give him some fluids and medication for the pain. There's an on-call nurse who can monitor him here overnight and I'll let the owner know what's happening. I can pop in and see him on my way home.'

'Thank you. I'm not sure what I would have done without your help.'

'That's my job. Oh and in the owner's defence, he has been through a difficult time lately. He recently lost his mother. And I happen to know that Flynn is a bit of an escape artist!'

Lily thought of her own circumstances and wondered if she'd judged him too harshly.

'I understand. I'm only in Lostmor because my mother recently passed away. In fact, I've just come from my old home.'

'Oh, my condolences. I'm sorry for your loss.'

'Thank you. Well, I'll be on my way then,' she said turning to leave.

'I'm sorry. I didn't catch your name,' said Dr Morgan.

'It's Lily. Lily Sanders.'

Dr Janet Morgan had known Oliver Bligh and his late mother, Megan, for many years. She missed dropping in for a cup of tea, regaling stories from her practice, while Megan, in turn, would recount the latest happenings on the farm. It was only a year ago that she'd been diagnosed with terminal cancer. Her health had quickly deteriorated, during which time Janet had become a frequent visitor.

Megan always greeted her with a smile, and never complained of the pain she was most assuredly in. Nonetheless, the brutal disease continued to unfurl inside her. Towards the end, Janet and Oliver took turns sitting with her, holding her hand or reading to her from her beloved book of Charles Causley poems. She slipped quietly away in her sleep just a few months later.

Now, Oliver Bligh stood at the window, watching Janet's station wagon pull away. She had explained how the woman staying at Kleger Cottage, found Flynn lying injured and brought him to the surgery.

In truth, he regretted his rudeness towards Lily Sanders, especially as she may have saved Flynn's life.

The day Lily had turned up at Bligh Farm, Oliver had just been in an altercation with a farmhand he'd recently taken on. (Douglas Holt had replied to his advert in the classifieds for casual labour.) He'd explained to Douglas that he needed someone reliable who would turn up on time. The young man assured him he was and had experience working on his uncle's farm. So, Oliver took him on, and things worked out okay for the first week. The lad didn't seem to know as much as he made out, but he was punctual and followed instructions. He didn't talk much and kept to himself. No different to other farmhands he'd previously hired.

However, by the second week, Douglas started turning up late, jobs were half finished, and farm equipment left lying around. On this particular day, Oliver had found him smoking behind the barn. He angrily asked why he wasn't working and why he had left the tractor out the night before. Douglas had become sullen, glowering at him, tight-lipped and unapologetic. When Oliver told him he was letting him go, Douglas had grabbed a pitchfork and hurled it at him. Oliver had easily dodged it, but he was shocked at the farmhand's hostility, especially when Douglas then launched himself at him, swinging a punch that luckily completely missed its target. The young man was powerfully built but easily outwitted. As Douglas lunged at him again, Oliver restrained him from behind before pushing him away, causing him to stumble and fall.

'You'd better get out of here right now before I really lose my temper,' he warned.

Douglas struggled to his feet and spat at him; his eyes filled with inexplicable malice. Oliver watched him swagger towards his van, slam the door and accelerate away, deliberately kicking up a cloud of dust as he left.

Chapter 9

Having showered away the grime she was covered in from her visit to Penwyth House, Lily sat at the kitchen table sorting through the forgotten box of her mother's books. It made her feel closer to her seeing the old Agatha Christie and Nancy Drew mysteries. She smiled at the memory of her sitting on the front lawn reading, dressed in her trademark floppy hat and oversized sunglasses, while she and Alice played in the meadow; back when their days were long, sunny and carefree, before it all went so wrong, and things became so dark.

She was disappointed that she couldn't find any photos apart from the framed one of the family, although she did uncover a book she instantly recognised: *The Enchanted Wood* by Enid Blyton. She wondered how her book had ended up with all her mother's novels. On the inside cover she had proudly written: *Lily Sanders, 8½ years old, 2 September 1970.*

Her favourite childhood story was full of charming characters who inhabited a vast, magical tree. How she had loved reading about the incredible lands waiting to be discovered at the top where its branches disappeared into the clouds! She had often walked with her mother in the woods, secretly hoping to find such a tree, wishing she too could visit some fantastical world with fairy tale castles and mythical creatures. Turning the book's pages, she felt something bulky inside its jacket. She pulled out the folded pieces of paper and spread them out on the table. Most were grubby, the paper torn, and the writing smudged in places, but each had a partial date scribbled on the outside. She flipped open the earliest, dated 2 May: *Please, I must see you again tomorrow. 6:00 p.m., same place x*

That was it – no signature and no clue as to why 'they' needed to meet. It sounded like a secret liaison. Perhaps her mother had kept this note and the others for sentimental reasons?

The letters were dirty as if left outside – outside in an arranged place where only her mother would find them. They surely couldn't be from her father? Unless it was before he lived at Penwyth House; perhaps a game they had played. Her mother had once said how romantic and utterly charming her father was when they first met. (He would have been a younger and more sober man back then.) Even so, she couldn't imagine him playing such a game, and she was proved right when she read the following note dated 12 May: *Dear Elizabeth, I will watch for his car leaving and wait for you here. Please come if you can x*

She had to concede the fact that the notes implied her mother had had an affair. Lily could hardly believe it. All the messages were deliberately brief, arranging a meeting time and place only. The dates became further apart, some separated by several months. She had no way of knowing in what year they were written, but the sequence of months indicated they'd been penned over the course of a single year.

Lily couldn't remember her mother's friends, only social gatherings; evenings where people milled about in the downstairs rooms, drinks in hand, swaying to music by the likes of The Rolling Stones and Bob Dylan, albums stacked up on the record player. During the summer, she and Alice would sit on the upstairs landing, secretly watching as gatherings spilt outside. Groups of people had sat on the lawn, smoking, drinking and chatting, their mother amongst them, flicking her long hair off her shoulders, happy and at ease. They must have been good times for her, before her husband's drinking took hold.

The last note was dated August; she supposed the following summer. It was another meeting at an agreed place, probably somewhere on the estate. Lily was frustrated. Now she knew of her mother's affair, she had even more unanswered questions. She understood why her mother may have strayed – her father had not treated her well – but who was this man? Were they in love? She sighed. Perhaps it didn't matter anymore.

A loud knocking at the door shook her from her thoughts. It wasn't that late, only seven o'clock, but if it were Adam or Timothy, they would have phoned first or dropped by during the day. She tugged open the door only to be confronted with Oliver Bligh, stooped on the porch, smiling and proffering a bottle of wine.

'Oh, hello. You're the last person I expected to see,' she said.

'I'm sorry for disturbing you like this. I just wanted to thank you for rescuing Flynn and... apologise for being rude to you the other day. My name's Oliver Bligh, by the way.'

'I know who you are.' She hesitated to invite him in but felt obliged. 'Um, you'd better come in for a moment. How is Flynn?'

'He's fine, thanks to you,' he smiled. 'He has a cast on his front left leg and Janet – Dr Morgan – has given me strict instructions. For now, he has to rest. Not too much activity. Meanwhile, I plan to build a bigger wall and fix the gate.'

'He does seem to be a bit of a Houdini.' She laughed nervously, feeling awkward sharing the small kitchen space with a stranger.

'You look busy,' he commented, glancing at the scattered books on the table.

She hastily pushed the notes to one side to make way for the wine he'd brought. 'Oh, it's just some stuff of my late mother's I've been going through. She passed away not long ago.'

'I'm sorry to hear that,' he said uneasily.

'Thank you. That's why I'm in Lostmor. I've been at my old home today for the first time since I was a child. It's a long story,' she sighed

Oliver sensed a fragility about her that he had not noticed before (probably too busy shouting at her). 'Well, I don't want to impose, ' he said, reaching the door. 'I am sorry for my rudeness the other day; that too is a long story. I'm not usually quite so obnoxious.'

She smiled. 'Your friend, Dr Morgan, said as much.'

He laughed before pacing towards his battered old Land Rover, raising his hand and disappearing into the gloom.

Chapter 10

Penwyth House loomed large as Lily stood staring at the roof turrets fifty feet above, at the place from where Alice and her father had fallen.

Her memories of that night were vague. She recalled Alice going to bed, tired after her birthday party, and her father coming home drunk. Her mother had later explained to the coroner that she thought her husband, Vincent, had gone to bed, as was usual, after one of his drinking sessions. But it was later surmised that he had inexplicably gone onto the roof in the foulest of weathers. Alice must have awoken, perhaps hearing her father or the sounds of the storm raging. She left her room, saw him climbing the narrow stairs to the roof, and followed him. Outside it was dark, wet and windy. She may have wandered too near the edge of the roof; her intoxicated father could have slipped trying to save her. Tragically, they had both fallen, and no one knew exactly what had happened. At the coroner's inquest, a verdict of accidental death was recorded.

'It was a terrible, tragic accident, Lily. Now we must try to put it behind us,' her mother had placated her after her return from the inquest. 'We have a new life in Bristol now; a new home.'

So, Lily had put it behind her, or at least tried to. The

nightmares became less frequent over time, but like a festering wound that won't heal, they always returned, spewing forth the same terrifying images over and over. *Inescapable*, she thought, *a bit like this place.*

She turned away from the house and went through the woods to Edhen Cottage. This time, an old Ford Ranger truck was parked in front of the wood store. She tentatively knocked. The door opened a fraction.

'Who are you?' The man looked dazed. Lily imagined she was the first person to knock at his door in quite some time, maybe even years.

'Hello. I am sorry to intrude like this, but you are Joe, aren't you? Joe Newman?'

'I don't know how you know my name, but you're trespassing. I think you'd better be on your way.' He started to close the door.

'Mr Newman, my name is Lily – Lily Sanders. Do you remember me?'

'Lily?' He let the door fall open. 'I don't believe it... Look at you! Come in.'

She sat while Joe made them both tea. He returned from the kitchen with two steaming mugs. Neither had said a word since he'd invited her to sit.

'Mr Newman—' she began.

'Joe. It's just Joe,' he said. 'Look, I'm sorry, I didn't know who you were at first. You took me by surprise. I didn't think you were ever coming back.'

'It's been a long time, Joe, for both of us. Thank you for seeing me.'

'I always hoped one day you and your mother might return.

How is Elizabeth?'

Lily felt tears pricking her eyes. 'She's gone,' she whispered, suddenly overwhelmed. 'She was ill for quite some time. I'm afraid she died a few weeks ago.'

'I see.' His voice trembled and he looked visibly shaken. 'Your mother was a lovely lady.' He had a kind face etched with deep lines, and the most startling green eyes which now shone with tears.

'She was. I miss her very much.' Lily hadn't intended to upset Joe. I'm sorry to bring you this sad news. I should explain that although my mother and I were close in many ways, I only recently discovered that she kept things from me – some important things.

'I thought Penwyth House was sold decades ago. Mother said we needed the money to buy a house in Bristol. I had no reason to disbelieve her. And I knew nothing about you staying on to look after the estate.

'After she passed, I received a letter from a solicitor, Timothy Walker, asking me to come to Lostmor. Until a few days ago, all I knew was that he thought it wise for me to attend the reading of my mother's will, a will I didn't even know existed. That was when I found out Penwyth House had never been sold, and that my mother had left the entire estate to me.' Lily looked apologetic. She felt guilty; guilty for not wanting to keep the estate, and guilty for the upset she was causing Joe. She looked away from those piercing eyes.

The old man placed one weathered hand on hers. 'It seems another lifetime ago, doesn't it?' he smiled. 'You and Alice playing in the meadow and following two steps behind me round the gardens; you girls, laughing and chasing each other around. They were good times.'

'Yes.' Lily was still struggling to meet his eye. They were talking about things she had tried hard not to think about most of her adult life.

'I was shocked when I realised you and Elizabeth had left. But you had suffered a terrible loss. Then that solicitor bloke, Timothy, came to the cottage and told me about a letter he'd received from your mother, asking if I would stay on. It just seemed the right thing to do; to carry on doing what I'd always done – look after the estate as best I could – which meant I could stay here.' He gestured around him. 'Edhen Cottage is my home, Lily. I've never thought about leaving.'

'Of course,' she replied. 'I understand, and I want you to know that you don't have to leave. Edhen is yours, as far as I'm concerned.'

'That's good to know, thank you. What about the house? Will you move back in?'

'I'm afraid not. In time, I shall probably sell most of the estate. My life is in Bristol now. I run a small art gallery there.'

'You're an artist?'

She nodded.

'That doesn't surprise me. You always loved drawing. You would pick wildflowers, collect stones, feathers – anything that caught your eye, including a few things smuggled out of the house! Then you'd pick a spot and lay out your scene, kind of like a, what do you call it? A still life, that's it, you'd sit and draw, sometimes for hours, or until Alice came looking for you.' He smiled, pausing. 'The pair of you were good at keeping yourselves occupied. You were either helping me in the gardens or off on some adventure, armed with a bag of sandwiches from the kitchen. Now look at you, all grown up, a beautiful and talented young woman. I'm sure your mother was very proud of you.'

Lily felt a warmth for this man who had always been so kind to her and Alice.

'I hope so. I'm afraid she was lost to me in the end. She had dementia for quite a few years before she died.' He shook his head, visibly upset by the news. 'When we left, mother always remained positive about our new life together and said what an adventure it would be. But I hated Bristol at first. I didn't want to leave everything I'd ever known. She hid it well, but I understand now how much she must have been grieving. Gradually, we picked up the pieces of our lives. She never remarried, although I think she had a few proposals. And she had a lot of friends. I believe she was happy.

'I had a pretty normal childhood; went to school and then college. As I grew older, it was easier not to think about how life was before. I started to forget Alice's and my father's faces. Everything became kind of fuzzy and vague.' She shook her head. 'I'm sorry, I don't know why I'm telling you all this. Perhaps because there is no one left to remember except you and me.'

Though happy to see Lily again, Joe felt overwhelmed. The news of Elizabeth's death had stirred long-buried memories – of a stormy night and her running towards him screaming, her face full of fear. A scene he had tried hard to forget for decades had risen sharply back into focus.

He rose slowly to his feet. Lily took his cue, standing also.

'I'm so glad you came back, Lily. It's good to know you are okay. I've often wondered about you both. And I'm sorry to hear of your mother's passing. Excuse me but this is a lot to take in. Maybe you could come back another day, if you have time?'

'I'd love to.' She wanted to hug him, but offered her hand instead. He looked a little unnerved. 'I'm so grateful to you for looking after the estate all these years.'

As she headed for the door, she noticed a black-and-white photo on the windowsill. It was a close-up of a beautiful young woman, her head thrown back laughing. She looked so carefree and happy.

It was unmistakably her mother.

Chapter 11
Thursday 17ᵗʰ June, 1971

A loud crack of overhead thunder awoke Alice, dragging her from a deep sleep. Frightened, she sat up, pulling the blankets tightly around her. She wanted to find her mother, but at the same time was reluctant to leave the safety of her bed. She heard her father shouting. Lightning flickered across the bedroom, transforming a row of dolls into pale little ghosts whose shadows flashed across the wall. There was another huge explosion of thunder. She grabbed Hoppy (her favourite blue bunny), jumped out of bed, and ran into the hallway, just in time to see her father disappearing up the stairs that led to the roof.

'Daddy, I'm scared! Where are you going?' she called, but her voice was lost in the storm's chaos. 'Wait for me! Please!' Barefoot, she ran to the bottom of the narrow stairs.

Her father had already flung the door to the roof, wide open to the elements. By the time she reached the top, he had vanished. For a moment, Alice could not see anything in the driving rain. But then, as lightning streaked across the night sky, she saw his silhouette. He stood amongst the turrets, staring over the edge.

'Daddy!' she screamed, dropping Hoppy.

Vincent, shaken from his dark thoughts, turned to see his daughter standing in the doorway. He watched in a daze as she

ran through the storm towards him, wearing nothing but a
thin nightie.

Chapter 12
January, 1995

At first, Lily's bequeathment of Penwyth House seemed an onerous burden. However, as the days passed, she found herself surprisingly pragmatic about going through her family's things. She was so busy, she realised she no longer dreaded entering the place. Instead, she felt strangely drawn to it.

Mr Carne, the owner of Lostmor Antiques, had visited the house several times to label and record the more valuable pieces of furniture and *objets d'art*. In happier times, her parents brought back many antiquities from their travels through Africa and Asia. Mr Carne suggested an auction in the local community hall, and Lily thought it a splendid idea. She decided that all proceeds be donated to local charities. Not one to miss a business opportunity, Mr Carne also offered to organise the clearance of any unwanted items and soft furnishings from the house, which was no small task. Lily realised how naïve she had been to think Penwyth House would be ready to sell within a few weeks and gladly accepted his offer. Even with professional help, the size of her newly acquired home meant emptying it would still be a massive undertaking.

The more time she spent at Penwyth, the more attached to it she felt. Somehow, airing rooms and packing and labelling boxes became strangely cathartic. She sorted through her childhood possessions and cleared out her parents' bedroom.

Her mother must have disposed of her father's things before they left Lostmor. If it wasn't for the framed photo she found and his portrait still hanging over the fireplace, one could almost believe he had never existed. Almost... Yet during restless nights, images of him standing amongst the roof turrets, gaunt and pale-faced, still haunted her.

Lily had stopped outside Alice's room several times but couldn't face going in. Instead, she threw herself into the task of packing up the contents of the house as best she could. She promised herself that one day soon she would explore the grounds. She should check the condition of the glasshouses, the old kennels and stables. For now, she had more pressing jobs.

One particularly blustery day, she listened as the wind moved through the building, whistling down the chimneys and rattling windows. Just like her mother, she too liked the sounds their home made; she could hear its strength, feel its spirit. Even though it desperately needed repair, it felt solid and safe, standing proudly defiant against the harsh sea winds and winter storms that had battered and tormented it for decades. Gradually, a thought was forming in her mind. What if she were to do more than clear the house? What if she restored it to its former glory? She now had the resources to try. Perhaps by stripping away the decades of neglect, she could somehow purge the place of its terrible past.

Joe continued to be busy around the estate, doing what he had done for decades: tending to the grounds and gardens; an endless list of jobs, a bit like the house. When his and Lily's paths crossed, their conversation remained light.

She often stopped at Edhen Cottage for tea, telling him about her day. Sometimes he would reminisce, regaling her with stories of some of the more flamboyant characters who attended her mother's famous parties.

One day, he seemed particularly thoughtful.

'Is everything all right today, Joe?'

He gazed steadily at her, his emerald-green eyes as intense as ever. 'I wondered if you'd been to visit Alice's grave since you'd been home?'

Alice was laid to rest under a cedar tree on a secluded hill overlooking the sea, five minutes' walk from Joe's cottage.

When Lily shook her head, he looked at her sadly. She couldn't easily explain it to him, but she wasn't yet ready to visit her sister's grave. It was important for her to recall what happened that night first.

After what turned out to be nearly three weeks of daily visits to Penwyth, Lily finally climbed the central staircase and walked towards Alice's room. Would seeing her childhood things help? Even though she was frightened by the possibility, she had to try. And she wanted to see her sister's room again; to feel closer to her. In the end, there was no sudden recollection, just another child's room frozen in time, much like her own. But there had been no second chance for Alice, no new start.

Gazing around in dismay at the hastily abandoned doll's house, and the dusty pink chest of drawers with teddies and dolls piled on top, Lily felt herself crumble. She sank to her knees and wept, overwhelmed by sadness. Poor, poor Alice – *her* Alice.

She lost track of time, sitting there surrounded by the remains of her sister's short life, but when she left the room, she felt strangely calmer. She found herself heading for the stairs that led to the roof. But as she put her foot on the first step she was hit by a sudden wave of nausea, and felt gripped by panic. She heard voices, as if she was trapped in one of her nightmares. At first, her father shouted her name. Then, up close, she heard him again, whispering in her ear as if he was standing right next to her:

'Why did you run away, Lily?'

Shocked to her core, she walked quickly down the main stairs and through the hallway, pulling open the front door. Outside, she fell to her knees, gasping for air. She looked back at the imposing entrance hall and sweeping staircase. She had heard her father so clearly. She was afraid to go back in. This wasn't like any dream; it had been real. She shut the heavy oak door and walked to her car, then drove off at speed, watching the spires and chimneys recede in her rear-view mirror. Turning the corner, she breathed a sigh of relief that the house was no longer in sight.

Back at Kleger Cottage, shaken by the day's events, Lily had second thoughts about her plans to renovate. What was she thinking? She wasn't sure she could face going back at all. She called Timothy and asked him to help manage things in Lostmor while she returned to Bristol. He had offered to help, and she knew she could rely on him to oversee any essential repairs. Besides, Adam had another booking for the cottage soon. It was time for her to leave.

Chapter 13

After a restless night's sleep, Lily packed her newly finished seascape. It was 9:30 a.m. Usually she would be on her way to Penwyth but since yesterday's frightening episode, her plans had changed.

A loud knock at the door startled her. *Maybe it's Adam,* she thought. 'Oliver. This is a surprise. How's Flynn?'

'Recovering well. He's still not allowed to over-exert himself so we're just going for short walks on the lead for now. Oliver smiled wryly. 'And he's a little put out by the newly repaired wall and secure gate he now has to contend with.'

'No doubt a new challenge for him soon.'

He laughed. 'I hope you don't mind me dropping by. It's just that last night I drove past you on the coastal road and you looked straight through me. It was like you'd seen a ghost. Is everything okay?'

'Oh, I'm sorry, I was just tired. I must have been on autopilot. I was on my way back from Penwyth House.'

'I see. Well, as long as you're alright. I don't mean to be a nuisance.' He studied Lily's face. She seemed different – downhearted. 'It can be lonely here, especially in the winter.'

'I'm fine, honestly, and you're not a nuisance.' She took a step back. 'Why don't you come in? I'll put the kettle on.' She could do with some company. Other than Joe, she had hardly spoken to anyone in weeks.

'Okay great, thanks.'

She pulled a kitchen chair out for him and moved her newly packed painting off the table.

'Did you say Penwyth House?'

'Yes.'

'I've heard of it, I think. Is that the place where there was a tragic accident years ago?'

Lily instantly wished she hadn't let the house name slip. Now he would be curious and want to ask questions. Since her hasty exit from there, she felt uneasy about things again, and a familiar creeping dread had taken hold of her. Oliver was right: she had been scared driving back to the cottage. Then, last night, she had dreamt about her mother calling out to her through rumbling thunder...

'Do you mind if we don't discuss it? Sorry, it's just that it's been quite unsettling for me returning home after all this time.'

'No, of course not. I honestly didn't mean to pry,' he said, accepting a mug of tea. He glanced at the box of brushes and easel on the kitchen floor.

'You're an artist?'

'Yes,' she replied, relieved at the change of subject. 'It's my passion and, luckily, my job.' She smiled. 'I have a small gallery in Bristol called The Blue. I'll be heading back there soon.'

'That's a shame' – he looked disappointed – 'I mean that you're leaving.' He leant forward slightly. 'Why don't you let me take you out for a drink before you go?' He spoke softly, his face close to hers.

Perhaps it was the emotion of recent events, but he stirred

something within her. Despite their awkward first meeting, Lily found herself liking him. He was his own man; that much was obvious. There was something exciting about his self-assuredness, but at the same time, she sensed he had a gentler side. 'Why not.' she replied. 'Yes, I would like that very much.'

Oliver thought her stunning. She had a delicate, almost ethereal quality. Her almond-shaped eyes were green, but close up he could see they were flecked with gold, and her hair fell in waves over her shoulders. He longed to touch it. 'Great. How about tonight?' he said. 'I know a nice traditional pub near the seafront.'

'Tonight?'

'Why not?' he grinned. 'No time like the present.'

'It wouldn't be the Black Dog inn, would it?'

'Ah-ha,' he joked, 'so you haven't been working all the time!'

She laughed. 'Timothy, my mother's solicitor, has an office near to it. We went there once after a meeting.'

'Oh, I see. I'm sorry if I upset you a moment ago. I always seem to be saying the wrong thing to you.'

'It's not your fault. Being back in Lostmor has been strange for me. It's complicated.'

'I lost my own mother not long ago. She was ill for some time – cancer. I knew the end was coming, but it didn't make it any easier.' His dark eyes filled with concern. 'I understand how difficult it is to lose a parent. She and I were close. It was just the two of us for a long time.'

Lily felt guilty that he was opening up about something so personal, while she had just instantly shut him down at the mere mention of her family.

'I'm so sorry to hear that.'

'It's okay. I'm getting used to being alone at the farm. It was strange at first. It's the family home. I was born and raised there. How about you? Do you have any remaining family in Lostmor?'

'No. No family anywhere. I guess I'm on my own now.'

'Look. I know you're leaving soon, but whilst you're here you don't have to be alone.' For a second, his hand lightly touched her shoulder. 'Not if you don't want to be.'

She nodded. 'Thanks. I think I could do with a bit of company.'

'Me too,' he smiled. 'How about I pick you up at eight?'

Chapter 14

'Sorry to hear about your mother,' sympathised Marcus, pouring Oliver a pint of ale.

'Thanks. How are things with you? Where's Horace?'

'Upstairs asleep. Saturday nights are too noisy for him. He prefers lunchtimes, when there's food around!'

Oliver laughed and carried the drinks to the booth where Lily sat. The pub was low-lit and cosy, with couples stowed away in various nooks and crannies. The melodic tones of *Fields of Gold* played in the background while people enjoyed their evening, most happy in the knowledge they had no work tomorrow.

Oliver sat opposite Lily.

'Thanks,' she smiled, sipping her Chardonnay. 'This place has a different vibe at night than in the day – more welcoming.'

The inn was beginning to fill up, mainly with couples, but a crowd of young singletons had gathered around the bar too.

'So, what's all this about you leaving?' he grinned, unable to help himself. She looked more relaxed than earlier and more radiant than ever. She was dressed simply in jeans and a plain white cotton shirt, her hair loosely plaited to one side. She smelled good, too.

'No pressure then!' she laughed.

'How long have you lived in Bristol?'

'Twenty-four years.'

'A long time.'

She nodded. She knew it would be difficult for them to chat without mentioning Penwyth House; after all, it was why she was in Lostmor. Besides, she found herself wanting to. So, she talked, and Oliver listened. She told him about her mother's illness and the surprise letter from Timothy Walker. Before she knew it, she'd explained her surprise inheritance, and that Joe Newman still looked after Penwyth Estate.

Oliver was captivated, not only by her incredible story but by her. She was articulate and engaging, and despite the recent upset she'd been through, still managed to find humour in her strange circumstances. He remembered his school friends talking about the terrible accident which had occurred at Penwyth House. Rumours that the place was haunted had led to a couple of them daring each other to go there at night, but he had refused to join them. He was too busy helping on the farm. In truth, he was afraid to go. The loss of his father a few years earlier and the shock of finding his body had left him feeling vulnerable – death was unpredictable. 'So, have you nearly finished clearing the house?'

'As much as I can. Most of it is being collected this week. I'm going to auction a lot of it off.'

'What will you do with the place?'

'Well, it needs renovating, which would take months.' Lily sensed he wanted to ask more but appreciated that he didn't. Why spoil a charming evening discussing her family's dark past? 'How about you? How are things at Bligh Farm?'

'Well, nothing I have to say will be half as interesting. But if you're ready to be bored, how about I get us both another drink?'

'Yes, please.' She smiled. The wine had taken the edge off her earlier low mood. She sneaked a peek at Oliver, who had his back to her and was laughing amicably with the barman. Maybe she had become a bit too set in her ways in Bristol; too much work, not enough play.

A curl of dark hair skimmed the collar of his navy shirt. She liked how he looked. He was a striking man – she guessed over six-foot tall – the type you noticed when he strode into a room.

Just then, a thick-set, muscular-looking guy walked in. Oliver glanced sideways at him and then leaned over the bar and said something to Marcus, his body language now less relaxed. When he returned, he looked thoughtful, his mouth in a hard line.

'Thanks. Everything okay?' she asked.

'Yes, sorry,' he said, sliding back into the booth. 'No big deal. I just saw someone I wish I hadn't – a young farmhand I hired not so long ago. Turned out to be a big mistake.' He took a swig from his pint glass. 'Not only was he lazy and unreliable, but when I asked him to leave, the little hothead took a swing at me!'

'And you said you had nothing interesting to say. What happened?'

'I was tempted to retaliate in the moment, but I refrained. He's just some lowlife. The type who thinks everyone owes him something. I threw him out, he drove off. That was that. I doubt he'd start anything in here. He's sloped off to the pool room in the back. Marcus, the landlord, said he'd keep an eye on him for me. I had just come from dealing with him when you and I first met at the farm.'

'So, I caught you at a bad time.'

'Still no excuse for being rude. I shouldn't have let him rattle my cage. Anyway, enough about him. I'd much rather be talking to you than thinking about him and you are way more attractive.'

She laughed, and the conversation came easily. He told Lily about the farm and how he had taken it over, with his mother's help, when still a teenager. His father had collapsed and died having suffered a heart attack. Afterwards, Megan managed to keep the farm going, with his help. Over the next five years, she taught him everything she knew about farming and how to run the business. By the age of sixteen, he was driving and maintaining farm vehicles and harvesting and storing the crops.

It occurred to Lily they had both lost a parent in childhood, and in sudden and dramatic circumstances. 'It must have been terrible finding him that way.'

'It was. Looking back, we helped each other get through it. My mother was a strong woman. The farm kept us both busy, and I grew up fast.'

'Tell me about your art. What do you like to paint?'

'Landscapes and seascapes. I do quite a lot of commissioned work too. Got to keep the pennies rolling in! That can be anything from local landmarks to portraits to people's pets.'

'I confess, I know nothing about art, but they do say the light here is perfect for painting.'

'Do they?' she smiled, leaning in towards him. 'I may be leaving soon but I will be back.'

'I'm glad.' His steady gaze met hers. 'Thanks for coming out this evening. I'm enjoying myself.'

'Me too.'

He seemed momentarily at a loss for words, his dark eyes locked onto hers. 'Do you think we could meet again before you go? If you have time.'

'Okay,' she said, feeling more relaxed than she had in ages. 'I'd like that.'

'Tomorrow?'

She looked away, contemplating. 'I have to go to Penwyth House. There are still things to sort out. I need to track down Joe and let him know I'm leaving soon.'

'Well, I've the usual chores but nothing that can't wait. Why don't I come with you?'

'To Penwyth?'

'Why not?'

She looked concerned.

'I might come in handy. If you need help lugging things around, I'm your man.' He gently squeezed her hand. 'Wouldn't you like a bit of company?' his eyes implored.

Lily studied his face. She had the feeling he was not a man to be easily dissuaded. Besides, it would be nice to have him there, especially since her hasty departure from the house yesterday.

Maybe it was time to stop trying to deal with everything on her own.

Marcus nodded and smiled at Oliver and the woman as they left the pub. His friend looked smitten with her. He recognised her; he was good with faces. His previous career in the military meant being observant was second nature. The woman, Lily, had been in a few weeks ago with Timothy, the solicitor.

Marcus had only lived in Lostmor for a year, but he made it his business to know who was frequenting the Black Dog. Last summer, there were so many tourists he couldn't possibly keep track of everyone, but things were quieter now.

He had no idea what the man he was searching for looked like, just that he liked motorbikes. Not a lot to go on. But after a few drinks and a little persuasion, it was amazing how easily customers confided in him about their friends, neighbours, and even family. He watched anyone who seemed out of place, especially bikers. Since managing the pub, he had discreetly investigated a few individuals, but so far, his efforts had led nowhere. That was okay. He had nowhere else to be. The advantage of being in a coastal town was how easily you could stay under the radar

As Marcus watched the young farmhand leave the pub, he wondered if his initial impression of the lad was wrong. Douglas Holt had been in once or twice before, always on his own. Going by his physique and general appearance, he surmised he did some sort of physical work. Following a few brief conversations with him he had ruled him out from his search. But from what Oliver had just told him, he was something of a misfit and a troublemaker. Maybe he did fit the mould. Could this stranger be his daughter's killer? Marcus balled his fists on the bar top and resolved to find out.

<h1 style="text-align:center">Chapter 15</h1>

Marcus sat in his apartment above the Black Dog inn, whisky in hand. During the day, he could be busy and distract himself; the nights were the hardest to bear. He thought back to 1972 when he was a sixteen-year-old army rookie. He had met and quickly fallen head over heels in love with a girl called Rebecca. Knowing he would be away for extended periods of time, he had wanted to show his commitment to her. Unsurprisingly, their parents had disapproved when they married at Bristol Registry Office four months later. They had little money and spent their honeymoon in his aunt's caravan in Devon. To them, young and in love, it was perfect, and when a year later Rose was born, they could not have been happier.

Their marriage lasted longer than he deserved. While he was away overseas and Rose was still young, Rebecca had plenty of support from the other army wives, many with young families. Meanwhile, he was quickly promoted through the ranks. Military life suited him, but long absences from home meant his daughter inevitably grew up without him.

He was deployed to Northern Ireland many times. On his fourth tour of duty, during a particularly violent shootout with an IRA unit holed up in a house in County Antrim, Marcus lost a good friend – a fellow soldier, Jack, who had enlisted at the same time. They knew each other as man and boy and had previously been assigned together on special ops missions. On this occasion, the IRA unexpectedly opened fire just as his team approached the front door. Jack was shot in the chest at close range by armour-piercing bullets fired from an insurgent's M60 machine gun. Despite Marcus's efforts to save him, he died almost instantly. Rejoining his unit, they returned fire, killing everyone in the house.

As a result of his actions that day, he was awarded the Military Cross and promoted to major. It was a hollow victory. As a mark of respect, he had the medal inscribed with the words 'Jack Caldwell – for bravery in the field' and presented it to his widow.

In 1982, while stationed in the Falklands, Marcus was seriously wounded during a bloody encounter at Goose Green. The bullet split his right femur. He spent three weeks in a military hospital before being sent home to convalesce. In time, the bone healed, but not perfectly. His options were medical discharge with full honours, or the offer of another promotion, this time to colonel in a non-active role as staff officer. He chose the latter.

Looking back, he could see somewhere along the line the fighting had become personal, perhaps after Jack's death. If he hadn't been injured, he was certain sooner or later he would have died in battle.

It was while recovering at home that his marriage started to crumble. When he told Rebecca of his plans to return to the army on non-active duty, she accused him of putting his family second. Rose pleaded with him to stay, telling him how much she loved him. He hugged her and told her he loved her too but that he couldn't leave the military. He was still only thirty and didn't know anything else. As soon as he was deemed medically fit, he left, promising to see them both soon.

For the next decade, he was stationed in operational commands worldwide. Although he missed the camaraderie of a tight-knit troop, he didn't miss the killing. He had lost too many good men; seen bodies blown to bits and minds damaged beyond repair.

It was no surprise when Rebecca asked him for a divorce. He was half expecting it. She'd met someone else, some white-collar guy called Roger – reliable hours, reliable life. Marcus signed the divorce papers without argument.

He had let the military become his whole life, to the extent that the outside world seemed chaotic and pointless. After the divorce, he and Rebecca kept in contact for Rose's sake. He learned their once happy little girl had turned into an angry, confused teenager. She showed no interest in school or exams, dropping out at sixteen. Despite Rebecca's efforts to enrol Rose on a course at the local college, she refused, instead taking casual jobs working as a waitress or in local bars. She merely shrugged when questioned about her choices, saying she was saving up to travel.

Marcus was by then permanently stationed abroad, but he kept calling Rose's mobile. On the rare occasion she did answer, she was quiet and sullen, yes and no answers, as befitted an absent parent.

Chapter 16

Flynn was sat on a makeshift bed between Oliver and Lily in the Land Rover, eyes fixed on the road ahead as they drove towards Penwyth House. The sun was a golden globe hanging low over an ocean of sparkling water. Once they were past Lostmor town, the coastal road widened, gradually turning inland across rolling pasture. Another mile on, Lily pointed out the moss-covered iron gate to their right. They followed the road that wound its way through the estate.

As the house came into view, Oliver stared in disbelief at its size and dramatic façade. He slowly crunched to a halt on the drive. 'Wow, I knew the place was big, but this is very imposing.'

Lily was distracted. She tried to force from her mind the image of herself fleeing from the house like a mad banshee the last time she was here.

'Come on' – he gently grabbed her arm – 'let's go inside.' A minute later, Oliver stood in awe, gazing around the vaulted hallway. 'This place is incredible, Lily. I don't know what I was expecting, but not this.'

'A creepy Gothic mansion, you mean?'

'Well, kind of, but in a good way.' He put his arm reassuringly across her shoulders. 'Ready to show me more?'

Lily had given Mr Carne copies of the house keys so he

could remove the boxes she had already packed. Looking around, she felt sad to see her home gradually stripped of its past, but it was for the best.

Downstairs, they roamed from room to room. Flynn had grown used to his leg cast and walked alongside them eagerly, sniffing every nook and cranny. As they walked, she reminisced about happier days and soon forgot her fears of earlier. She spoke of days spent with Alice, playing hide-and-seek or building dens in one of their home's many rooms. When they reached the basement kitchen, she was struck by the memory of the cook, a large, jolly lady called Margaret. She and Alice had sat for hours in the kitchen with her, shelling peas collected from the vegetable garden.

'This room could use some air. Shall I open a window?' he asked.

'I have tried. It's jammed fast.' The sash window frames were rotten and blistered, enabling the rain to seep through and permeate the walls.

When he tried to budge it, the cord broke, and pieces of wood came away in his hands. He frowned then placed a warm hand upon her arm. 'I can't believe you've been trying to cope with all this alone. I'm sure you're a very capable woman,' he quickly added, 'but it's not a one-person job!'

He was right. She was crazy to think she could empty the house in a few weeks and give it a quick tidy before leaving.

He reached for her hand. 'Shall we sit outside on the front lawn for a bit?'

They managed to unlock the kitchen door without it breaking. Oliver then fetched a flask of tea, some shortbread, and a rug from the car. Flynn stayed close, snoozing in the sun.

'I was thinking – I could stick around and help this week if you like. If I'm not overstepping the mark?'

'That's kind, but aren't you busy?'

'Not until it warms up a bit. That's when I start preparing the land for crops. Right now, it's more general maintenance – cutting back hedgerows, machine repairs. It's nothing that can't wait. And much as I enjoy farming, there's really no competition between winter chores and spending time with you.'

'Okay, that would be nice.' She smiled. 'But things will be hectic around here. I have a team of people coming from Lostmor Antiques to strip out the soft furnishings, and a surveyor to assess what work needs doing.'

'You could sell it as it is – cut your losses and run?'

'That's what Timothy said. I might; I'm not sure yet.'

'You must have a lot on your mind,' he empathised, gently brushing a wisp of hair from her face.

His touch made her skin tingle. 'Ever since returning to Lostmor, my world has been turned upside down.' She looked into his kind eyes and smiled. 'Thank you for coming today. Dealing with all this seems less daunting with you here.'

The following day, the removals team arrived at Penwyth House en masse.

A thin man in blue overalls and greasy hair tied back in a limp ponytail stuck his hand out in greeting. 'I'm Richard. Quite some place!' he said, looking around the vast hallway.

'Hi, I'm Lily, and this is my friend, Oliver. I'm afraid you've got your work cut out.'

'We've come prepared,' he grinned, revealing uneven, nicotine-stained teeth. 'Mr Carne did explain it was a big job. Don't you worry, me and my men like a challenge!'

'That's a relief. Shall I give you a quick tour, so you know your way around?'

'Yeah, great. That'll help me figure out how long things might take. I've got some men tasked with loading up the remaining furniture and others stripping out all the soft furnishings. Am I right in thinking all the stuff for auction has gone and everything left is for our disposal?'

'Mostly. I've got a few things labelled up that I'm keeping. I'll show you as we go around.'

Just then, they heard another vehicle pull up outside.

'That must be the skip arriving,' said Richard. 'I should warn you, there will be a lot of noise for the duration.'

'No problem. It's to be expected.'

While Lily gave Richard the tour, Oliver went outside to watch for the surveyor. Two large removal vans were parked at the far end of the drive, and one of Richard's men was guiding a flatbed truck closer to the house. A wiry man jumped out of the passenger side and watched a large skip being lowered onto the drive. He gave the driver a thumbs up when he unhooked it on the ground.

'Quite a place,' the man said to Oliver as he climbed back into the cab.

As the truck pulled away, he caught sight of the driver, who looked equally surprised to see him.

'You're not going to believe who I saw earlier.' Oliver glanced at Lily as he drove them home that evening. 'Douglas

Holt, the man I told you about.'

'Where?'

'At the house. He was one of the men delivering the skip today.'

'Really? Well, he is a jack of all trades, isn't he?'

'Hmm, more like the master of none.' Oliver felt uneasy about Holt being anywhere near them or Penwyth Estate.

He dropped Lily off at Kleger Cottage and arranged to pick her up early. Richard and his team were also due back the following day, as was the surveyor, who had disappeared for the entire day investigating the house and its grounds. Tomorrow he was bringing a colleague to assess the structural damage to the roof.

As he drove back to Bligh Farm, he couldn't stop thinking about Lily. She was undoubtedly a beautiful woman, and a successful artist too. But she was also complex, which he found fascinating. On the one hand, she seemed to possess a quiet inner strength, a strength she may well have needed to draw upon in the past. Or maybe because of her past? But she was also guarded at times. Losing half her family in such a dramatic way would leave its mark on anyone, and he sensed a carefully hidden vulnerable side to her.

Penwyth House held secrets that still troubled her: he would have to wait to see whether she chose to share that part of her life with him.

'You like her too, don't you?'

Flynn, who was sat in Lily's vacated seat, barked once in agreement.

The following afternoon, Lily dropped by Edhen Cottage to let Joe know she was finished for the day but would be returning next weekend.

While she was at the house, Oliver packed the car boot with some family belongings she had salvaged. Only a few paintings were left behind, including the one of her father which needed packing more carefully before they moved it.

Richard and his men finished loading the last of the furniture, and Oliver glanced at the flatbed truck arriving to collect the final skip. He was relieved to see the other guy there instead of Douglas.

On the drive home, he asked Lily, 'Why don't you come over to mine for dinner later?'

'That sounds lovely. I can tell you about my conversation with Joe. He's agreed to keep some of the surrounding land and Edhen Cottage.'

'That's good. I've heard so much about him, it would be nice to meet him sometime.'

'Of course! How about next weekend?'

They were momentarily distracted by a pick-up as it crossed the T-junction in front of them. Oliver tooted his horn and laughed at the black labrador hanging out of the passenger window.

'Isn't that the landlord from the Black Dog inn?'

'Marcus, yeah. He's probably taking Horace out for a walk – he likes the coastal path.'

'How do you know him?'

'Just from chatting in the pub. Nice bloke; quite private, but a decent sort. You okay to come over about seven?'

'Great. I'm starving already.'

'What sort of thing do you like to eat?'

'I'm not fussy. I'm embarrassed to tell you what I exist on in Bristol.'

'Cheese on toast?'

'More or less. With baked beans when I'm feeling ambitious.'

'I've nothing to beat, then,' he teased, pulling up in front of Kleger Cottage.

'Well, thanks again for your help,' she said, getting out of the car.

'My pleasure,' he smiled. 'See you later.'

Chapter 17

Marcus pulled up in a layby close to the cliff tops and let Horace out. Earlier, at the T-junction, he was momentarily shaken from his pensive mood when Oliver tooted his horn. Usually, he found walking the coastal path cleared his head. But as Horace ran enthusiastically ahead of him, even a bracing sea breeze couldn't stop him from remembering the day of the phone call.

Rebecca, normally so even-tempered and calm, was hysterical. He couldn't make out what she was saying, but he didn't have to – he knew Rose was dead. He heard the word 'accident' and let the phone slip out of his hand. His ex-wife's wailing faded from his consciousness as he slid into a very dark place.

He couldn't recall much about the funeral or the months that followed. He tried to help Rebecca with the arrangements, to be helpful in some way, but she didn't want him around. She had Roger now: Roger the Reliable. Marcus watched as Rose's coffin was lowered into the earth, Rebecca softly weeping. Rose's friends hugged each other, teary-eyed and disbelieving. He had drifted through the wake like a ghost. When the unbearable had been borne, he caught the first flight back to Croatia, returning to his duties as staff officer.

For a few months, Marcus managed to function. But soon,

even the war in Croatia could not detract from his personal battle. In his spare time, he spent hours looking at photos of Rose, images Rebecca had sent over the years. Rose as a baby; Rose as a toddler, giggling, looking unsteady on her feet, clutching a teddy bear by its foot. On her first day at primary school, Rose wore a red jumper, an oversized grey pinafore dress, and a big grin on her face. She was not nervous about her first day. He smiled, then stiffened. How would he know? He wasn't there: not for her first steps, school, or the many birthdays and milestones he had missed. Guilt and an overwhelming sadness had engulfed him. Everywhere he looked he saw Rose, and when he closed his eyes, he saw her face even clearer.

Marcus knew he could not hide behind his commission anymore. He had to face what had happened; to allow himself to grieve.

For the first time, army life was no longer enough for him. After twenty-two years of service, he informed his superiors of his intention to resign and gave the required twelve months' notice. However, his commissioning officer, who knew Marcus well, permitted him an early release due to his tragic personal circumstances.

Six months after his daughter's death, he advised the UK police of his return and new contact details in Bristol. And, as he had numerous times before, asked to be kept abreast of any news or progress made in finding Rose's killer. But it was clear her murderer had vanished into thin air.

Months went by, and the grief he had been running away from finally hit home. Waves of despair overcame him so fast and relentlessly that he could hardly breathe. He rarely left his rental apartment, only venturing out when he was forced by days of hunger or to buy more alcohol to help numb the pain. Losing Rose was worse than any physical injuries he had endured, and more frightening than any combat situation he had faced. He wanted to lash out, to scream, and to shout at anyone he encountered. How could people casually walk past him, smiling and laughing as if nothing was wrong? Did they not know how dark a place the world was?

Before his daughter's death, Marcus had always been the type of guy everyone wanted around in an emergency: calm, confident, in control. Now... he was teetering on the edge of an abyss and contemplating jumping.

It was his training that stopped him in the end. To take his own life went against everything he was ever taught. In the military, you were trained to survive in dire circumstances. To take his own life felt cowardly, like a failure. But the only way he could cope with being alive was to drink himself into a constant state of oblivion. Old army friends tried to reach out a few times, but he ignored their messages, eventually pulling the phone out of the wall. He existed on the couch, either half unconscious from drinking or staring unseeingly at the television, surrounded by empty bottles and half-eaten meals.

One morning, he awoke with a thudding head, the effects of the previous night's bottle of whisky. The television was muted, but he half registered a familiar stretch of road being discussed by the newsreader. Marcus stared blurry-eyed, in disbelief, as a picture of Rose appeared in the corner of the screen. He struggled to find the remote control buried under the debris on the floor, just managing to increase the volume in time to catch the end of the news item:

He blinked, for a moment doubting his sanity. Was he dreaming? The shock of seeing Rose's face, and of being told by a news reporter that it was a year since her death, gave him a massive jolt. He looked around his apartment at the one-person chaos he had created. Could it really be twelve months to the day? He staggered into the bathroom and dared to look in the mirror. He barely recognised himself. Usually close-shaven, his face was covered in a layer of matted hair; the once sharp, observant eyes which took in every detail had dark shadows etched beneath them. He looked haunted.

That was the moment – the moment he decided to live again. He splashed cold water on his face and grabbed a razor from the cabinet.

Now, another year on, he wondered: would he have stayed in the army if his daughter were still alive? Probably. A few hours later, he returned to the Black Dog with Horace. Soon, the staff would arrive for the start of another long evening shift. In the upstairs accommodation, he fed Horace, then took a shower, ready to start work. Since losing Rose, he had sunk deeper than he thought possible, but coming to Lostmor was helping him refocus. Now, he had a new purpose in life: revenge.

PART II

Chapter 18

At Bligh Farm, Lily sat in the warmly lit kitchen overlooking a courtyard garden as Oliver took a bubbling lasagne dish from the oven.

'Hmm, that smells wonderful.' She was trying not to sip too much of the large glass of wine before her, conscious of her rumbling stomach. It was easier said than done when she felt relaxed, glad to be somewhere other than Penwyth House or Kleger Cottage.

'It's the least I can do to repay you for all the flasks of tea and shortbread this week,' he smiled, placing supper on the table.

Lily breathed in the aromas of mild spices. 'Wow, this smells amazing.'

'I'm not just a pretty face, you know.' He passed her a plate.

They ate hungrily and enjoyed good red wine while chatting about the day's events.

'So, it went well with Joe today?'

'Yes. He's agreed to keep a small parcel of land surrounding the cottage, including the glasshouses. I'm going to ask Timothy to draw up the necessary papers but it's just a formality. I don't want any confusion about his ownership when I come to sell the house and the rest of the estate.'

'A generous gesture on your part.'

'I think he deserves it after thirty-plus years of service, don't you?'

'He does. I don't know how he's managed it all alone.'

'I've offered to get him help, but he wants things to stay as they are until I find a buyer.'

'I guess it's hard for him to let go after all this time.'

'I think so. He could easily retire now.'

'Did you say he was keeping some glasshouses?'

'Yes, two big old Victorian structures. He says he still uses them. Alice and I used to love to play in them when we were little. Mother grew orchids in one, and the other was used for growing kitchen produce.'

'Being in Lostmor must have brought back memories of Alice.'

'Yes,' Lily sighed. 'At times, I've felt overwhelmingly sad, but returning to Penwyth has also brought me great comfort. Mother and I were in Bristol for so long. She didn't like to talk about our lives in Lostmor. She said it was best forgotten. I understand she was grieving, but she was wrong. This is where Alice and I spent our childhood. It may not have been perfect, but we did share many happy times together.'

'How old was she when the accident happened?'

'Six. It was her sixth birthday. If she'd lived, she would have been thirty this year.' She paused before adding, 'She's buried here on the estate. Not far from Joe's cottage – under a cedar tree overlooking the sea.'

'And your father? Is he buried there too?'

'He was cremated. We scattered his ashes at the cliff's edge just beyond the house. Apparently, he once told mother that's what he'd like if he should go before her. It wasn't much of a ceremony. It was just us – he had no other family or close friends. I remember it was a warm summer evening. Afterwards, mother said a few words. I cried; she didn't.' Lily shrugged. 'Then we walked home again.'

'How old were you?'

'Nine.'

'So young. Have you had a chance to visit Alice's grave since you've been back?' he asked warily.

'No.' She quickly rose and started gathering plates. As always, an unthinkable question lurked at the back of her mind: what if she was somehow to blame for her sister's death?

Oliver stood too. 'Come on,' he said softly. 'I'll clear up later. If you like, we could sit by the fire. Why don't you go on through, and I'll pour us some more wine.'

Lily joined Flynn in the lounge, who was curled up on the hearth rug. Oliver came in with fresh drinks and sat beside her. Orange flames crackled and danced, sending light and dark flickers across their faces. He took hold of her hand.

'I hope you don't mind me asking, but have you ever talked to anyone about that night?'

She shook her head, trying to ignore the faint rumble of thunder which stirred out at sea. 'As a teenager, I had many unanswered questions because I couldn't remember exactly what happened. I still don't. But as mother would never discuss it with me, eventually I gave up asking. I grew up and tried to put it behind me. I just wanted to live a normal life.'

'Would it help to talk about what you *do* remember?'

She looked into ebony eyes that radiated kindness. 'Why spoil a lovely evening?'

He smiled. 'You couldn't possibly do that.'

'You've only known me for a matter of weeks. I don't want to burden you with my problems.'

'Why don't you let me decide that?' he said, putting his arm around her.

They sat gazing at the fire, and to Lily, it felt right, like the most natural thing in the world. 'All right, if you really want to hear.'

Lily fought to contain her emotions as she spoke about her family and that fateful evening for the first time since childhood. 'My father, Vincent, was an alcoholic, which caused problems in my parents' marriage.

'Mother told me they were happy once. When they were younger, they travelled all over the world and visited some amazing places. But his drinking got steadily worse. I used to hear shouting coming from their bedroom and things being thrown. I would hide in my room with Alice, praying they would stop.' Lily's hands trembled as she took a large sip of wine.

'On the night of Alice's birthday, father had been out drinking all day. He missed her party and came home late. Mother claimed I was in bed asleep, and that it wasn't until after the accident she woke me up and took me downstairs to wait with her until help arrived. But I still have nightmares where I see my father standing on the roof amongst the spires in the middle of a raging storm. It's always the same thing: Alice is there in just her nightie, running to him through the rain, then mother calls to me from inside the house. I try to go to her, but there's this man, a scary-looking man, stood in my way. He has a strange face, almost mask-like.' Lily shrugs. 'I sound crazy, but these dreams have haunted me for years.

Mother said I was mistaken, confused. It was just the four of us in the house; there was no stranger. It's true, it doesn't make any sense. Now I'm not sure if my flashbacks are actual memories or traumatised imaginings.'

'Can you think of any reason why your mother might lie to you?'

'No. I understand her avoidance – it was her way of dealing with the pain – but she had no reason to lie.'

'Forgive me for asking, but do you think she could have unintentionally been involved?'

'I have thought about that. I can't be sure, but I don't think so. She would have died rather than put Alice or me in harm's way. She always tried to protect us.'

Oliver looked thoughtful. 'Maybe that's it.'

'I don't understand.'

'She lied to protect you. What if you were on the roof, and she knew it? She realised you'd somehow blocked out what happened and did what she thought was best. She refused to discuss it, and denied you were even there in the hope you might forget something so terrible.'

'So, she could have lied?'

'I can't say for sure, but it's possible.'

'What about the man I saw?'

He shrugged. 'All I know is however well-meaning your mother was, you've had to carry this weight ever since. It must have been daunting for you coming back to Lostmor.'

'At first, yes. When I discovered Penwyth Estate belonged to me, I was terrified of returning there. I don't know what I expected, but in the end, it wasn't as bad as I imagined. Once I overcame that initial fear, I felt strangely connected to the place.

It started to feel like home again because I was visiting the house daily and sorting through my family's things. Not long ago, I finally plucked up the courage to go into Alice's bedroom. That was a very sad and poignant moment. Afterwards, I felt compelled to go up on the roof. I hoped it might somehow jog my memory if I stood where they had stood. But when I reached the steps, I thought I heard my father's voice. It was as if he was standing beside me, whispering in my ear. I completely lost my nerve; I freaked out.'

'What did he say?'

'He said, "Why did you run away, Lily?" I panicked. He was speaking about that night. I was so scared. I ran straight out of the house and thought I would never go back. You must think I'm crazy.'

'Of course I don't. And whatever it is you experienced you did go back – you faced your fears.'

'Luckily you were with me.'

Oliver's eyes shone black in the firelight. 'You know, you don't have to face everything alone anymore. Not if you don't want to.' He gently cupped her face in his hands and kissed her on the lips. 'I'm right here for you as long as you need me.'

'I think I do need you,' she whispered.

They kissed again and held each other close, as they talked late into the night.

Chapter 19

Marcus pulled the pump towards him, slowly levelling the glass with a pint of creamy-topped ale for one of his regulars. He wasn't in the habit of doing table service, but he made an exception for Tom, an elderly regular who always came in around twelve o'clock. He placed the glass in front of Tom, who was reading the local paper.

'What's new in Lostmor?' asked Marcus.

'Oh, you know, the usual. It says here the council are planning roadworks along Thornbush Way.'

Marcus smiled and went back to tidying the bar. He liked living where he worked; he was used to that. There was rarely any trouble; it wasn't that kind of place or town, for that matter. Apart from weekends, when the locals ventured out, February was quiet, with just a few diehards like Tom for company.

The Black Dog inn was Tudor-fronted, squashed between an Italian restaurant and a gift shop overlooking the harbour. Over time, once humble fishermen's cottages had become restaurants, cafes and pubs crowded together in ancient, cobbled streets. Only a handful of fishermen still operated out of Lostmor, but people had learnt to diversify, just like other Cornish coastal towns. In the summer, Tresor Bay was lined with motorboats and larger vessels that offered boat trips and deep-sea fishing experiences. Now, there were mainly smaller boats hunkered down under canvas, their 'For hire' signs stored away.

Marcus glanced out the window at the dramatic rock formations almost enveloping the bay, as if to protect everything within. Meanwhile, Horace sloped into the bar, wagging his way over to Tom's table.

'Good day to you,' the old man said, one hand on his pint, the other rubbing behind the dog's velvety ear. 'Didn't you say you were going away this weekend, Marcus?'

'Yep. I'm visiting a lady who lives in Norfolk. But I'm not sure what to do about Horace.'

'Can't he go with you?'

'He would be miserable. It's a six-hour drive, maybe longer if there are delays. That's why I'm going overnight.'

'Can't you take the train?'

'He doesn't like trains; the motion upsets him. Anyway, there are too many changes. It might take even longer.'

'Can't he stay here, then?' Tom asked.

'Well, the staff aren't here twenty-four seven.'

'I'd have you, Horace, but there's not much space in my apartment, and the landlord says no pets.'

The dog grunted and slumped to the floor, resigned to his predicament.

'You know, there's an advert in the paper here for some fancy kennel opening.'

'A kennel? I don't know.' All the same, Marcus wandered over to take a look.

'There.' Tom pointed. *Fern Retreat. Open seven days a week. A home from home for your dog.*

'Oh, it's not far, then – just up on the coastal road.'

The bell above the door pinged as a young family shuffled in from the cold.

Marcus greeted them with a smile and returned to the bar. 'Looks chilly out there. What can I get you?'

The following morning, Marcus set off to find Fern Retreat. He wasn't keen on the idea. He had visions of a long line of cold kennels awaiting them, filled with frustrated dogs barking a crescendo whenever someone approached. Susie, a student who worked part-time behind the bar, had agreed to look after Horace but had since let him down. He was running out of options.

'We're just going to take a look, okay?'

Horace looked glumly across at him from the front seat of the truck. Marcus turned into a lane and saw a dark green sign with 'Fern Retreat: a home from home for dogs' painted in swirling gold letters. It swung from a frame mounted on a post, giving it a quirky semblance of a pub sign. He clipped a lead onto Horace's collar (not that he would have strayed, but just in case other dogs were loose). A young springer spaniel came happily bounding towards them.

'Hello!' A lady waved from where she was painting a wooden gate which led to a row of new, empty kennels.

Marcus walked over to her, and she rose to greet him.

'Hi,' she smiled, 'I'm Julia. How can I help?'

'I'm Marcus, and this is Horace. You look busy. I take it you're not open yet?'

'The grand opening is in two weeks, but I'm happy to show

you around. Are you thinking of booking Horace in for a stay?'
She momentarily dropped to one knee and stroked him. 'Is he
okay with other dogs? If not, I'll put Bella inside.'

'No need, he's fine.'

Horace stood wagging while the eager-to-play spaniel
danced around him.

'I saw your advert in the paper, but I didn't notice the
opening date.'

'What dates were you thinking of?'

'Just one night – this coming Saturday. Someone was
supposed to have him, but they've let me down.'

'Oh, I see. That's a nuisance.'

'Never mind, my mistake.'

'I'm sorry you've had a wasted journey. Have you come far?'

'No, not at all. I'm in Lostmor. I take it you live here at Fern
Retreat? Are you from these parts?'

'I grew up in West Hill but moved to South Devon with my
family years ago. I'd been thinking for a while about opening
up my own kennel in this area. So, when this place came up, I
jumped at it. It's such a lovely spot, don't you think?'

He noticed she had flecks of white paint on her face. A few
long strands of hair had broken loose from her ponytail, and
her cheeks were flushed red from the exertion of painting.

'It's a great spot, all right, and you seem to have a lot of
space for the dogs.'

Julia beamed. 'Do you want to take a quick look around
anyway, whilst you're here?'

'Sure, why not.'

She showed Marcus the kennels, which were spacious, with
separate enclosed sleeping areas.

'I've just had heaters installed in the sleeping quarters, and they even have piped classical music. It's meant to have a calming effect!'

'Maybe Horace wouldn't have minded that so much. Would you, boy? We live in a pub, so he's used to a bit of background music.'

'Oh, really?'

'The Black Dog inn. It's in Tresor Bay. Do you know it?'

'I remember seeing it but haven't been there. To be honest I haven't been anywhere lately! I've been so busy trying to get this place ready in time for opening.'

Adjacent to the kennels was a brand-new wooden hut with a small reception area for customers. On one wall were various framed diplomas in canine care and welfare achieved by Julia, and an official Dog Kennel licence.

'The place looks really great,' he smiled.

'Thanks. I was just about to exercise Bella in the paddock. As Horace is obviously fine with other dogs, do you want to let him have a run around with her for a few minutes?'

'Sure. He could do with letting off some steam.'

They watched their dogs happily bounding around together in the enclosed area.

'Well, it looks like we're redundant,' she laughed. 'I've been thinking, but it's up to you of course – I could have Horace this Saturday, if you really are stuck? As it's only one night, he could stay in the house with Bella and me.'

'That's really very generous of you, considering we've just met. Are you sure?'

'Of course. They obviously get on, so why not.'

At Julia's invitation, Marcus poked his head around the

kitchen door, where a red-brick inglenook housed a big old Aga.

'This is where Bella sleeps. She knows the warmest spot.'

Although Marcus was thankful for Julia's offer, he was still a little nervous about leaving Horace.

'Um, Horace is not used to being parted from me. Are you sure you're okay with this? Having him in your house?'

Julia sensed his uncertainty. 'Well, I used to foster dogs before I moved here so I have experience of caring for dogs at home.'

He nodded. 'Sorry, I don't mean to be ungrateful. You are really helping me out...'

'I understand completely. He's your family. I can show you my credentials if it would put you at ease?'

'No need. I'm sure he'll be in safe hands.'

'Why don't you tell me a bit about Horace? What's his daily routine?'

So the two of them talked and Julia soon allayed any concerns Marcus had.

'Thanks so much for this. He really won't be any trouble,' he said when leaving. 'Should I pay you now or later?'

'When you pick him up is fine.' She handed him a leaflet. 'These are the rates and opening times.'

'Do you have many other bookings?'

'Four so far, and Horace makes five,' she grinned. 'I'm hoping word will get around.'

'If you like, I can hand out some of your leaflets to my customers,' he offered. 'And I get local storeowners coming in, so I could ask them to take some too.'

'That's really kind. Thank you.'

Armed with a pile of leaflets, he retrieved a reluctant Horace from the paddock and bade Julia goodbye. He wasn't looking forward to his trip, but at least he knew his dog was in safe hands.

99

Chapter 20

Lily watched through the kitchen window as Oliver's Land Rover bumped down the track. Since their evening at the farm, they had become more than friends, which excited and worried her equally. He had shaken her quietly ordered world, opening her eyes to new possibilities. Amidst all the disruption of the past few weeks, had she found someone special?

She watched him walk towards the cottage, Flynn trailing behind, and realised she was sad to leave tomorrow. Not long ago, she couldn't wait to return home; she missed spending time at The Blue and painting in her studio. But now her mother was gone, what else was waiting for her in Bristol?

'Here, I picked up a few things for supper,' he said, placing the bag on the kitchen counter and kissing her gently.

'That was thoughtful.' She peered inside. 'Ooh, is that seabass?'

'Yep, fresh from the fish market this morning.'

'And champagne!'

'I'm spoiling you as it's your last day in Lostmor. After our walk, I thought we could have a nice fish supper.'

'That sounds wonderful,' she said, unpacking the food and putting it in the fridge for later.

'You'd better wrap up warm; it will be cold up on the cliffs.'

'I'm prepared,' she smiled, pulling on a heavy coat and grabbing a scarf and gloves.

Flynn wagged his tail hopefully but he still had two weeks to go before his cast was removed and today's walk was a little too challenging for him.

'Sorry fella,' Oliver knelt down and gave him one of his favourite chewy treats. The dog eagerly took the bribe and settled on the rug to devour it.

Lily had been to Penny Cove before when she was much younger. It was a small, secluded, crescent-shaped beach and Oliver was keen to show her a place called Brea Point.

Once they had parked, they walked a few hundred yards to the bay and climbed the steep cliffside steps leading to the coastal path.

Despite the cold, it was worth the effort. From the top, the clear day offered spectacular views. They walked for about an hour, following the path as it wound around the headland.

'There's Brea Point. Over there,' said Oliver.

As they drew nearer, Lily saw a hollow in the rocks in front of a grassy outcrop.

'Wow!' she gasped. 'You can see the whole of Tresor Bay from here.'

'Plus,' he smiled, stepping into the hollow and offering her a hand down, 'there's somewhere to sit out of the wind.'

Perched together on a convenient large slab of stone, Lily nodded at the rocks planted in a circle in the grass before them. 'What are those?'

'They're known as the Stone Sisters. Legend has it they were turned to stone for dancing on a Sunday.'

'That's harsh!'

'Good for tourism though, eh?'

She liked how deep laughter lines formed at the corner of his eyes when he smiled, his face heavily tanned from years of outdoor work. She leaned closer to Oliver, and he put his arm around her.

'I haven't been up here for a while – not since last summer. Lostmor has a tall ships' race most years; I come up to watch the parade of sails. So far, no one else has had the same idea. Most people head for the harbour.'

'Your secret's out now though isn't it?' she teased.

'Well, I guess I'll have to trust you,' he said, giving her a squeeze.

For a while, they watched silently as a blood-orange sun inched towards the horizon until the blazing sky gradually dulled.

'I'm going to miss having all this on my doorstep.'

'I'm going to miss you,' he said.

On the drive home, she thought about how much her life had changed since arriving for what was supposed to be a two-night stay.

Returning to Lostmor stirred up memories of her beloved Alice that left her feeling sad and confused. Yet she was strangely drawn to this windswept corner of Cornwall, where within seconds, lush moorland could transform into a ghostly, mist-covered landscape and calm waters become brawling surf.

Later, at Kleger Cottage, Oliver added more logs to the fire, and Lily laid the table. They cooked supper together: she prepared the vegetables while he perfectly grilled the fish. Outside, the wind was picking up, rattling the windows and whistling around the cottage's ancient walls. But they were oblivious to it as Oliver poured the champagne.

The dinner conversation came easily. Lily told him about her plans to reopen The Blue and catch up with potential clients. 'That's if I have any customers left,' she joked. 'How about you? Don't farmers have to get up at the crack of dawn?'

'Sometimes. It just depends. It's the dairy farmers who have the early starts. Mostly, I'm up around six.'

'Even so, it must be hard in the winter when the mornings are cold and dark.'

'I guess I'm used to it.'

As they finished their meal, he refilled their glasses. 'To us.'

She touched her glass to his. 'To new beginnings,' she added, meeting his eyes with a steady gaze.

Unexpectedly, the front door flew open, making her jump and Flynn to look up from where he was sleeping in front of the hearth. 'Oh! I can't have shut it properly.'

The force of the sea gale hit Oliver as he closed the door and slid the bolt across. 'This place may have panoramic views, but it's wide open to the elements. I expect you'll be glad to get back to your nice warm apartment,' he said, collecting plates and taking them to the kitchen.

'Actually, I've grown quite fond of this cottage, though I do miss my studio.'

'Where's that painting you were working on?' he asked, looking around.

'I'll show you,' she grinned, briefly disappearing into the bedroom before coming back with the completed seascape. 'I hope you like it.' 'Wow. It's stunning. I mean, the colours are so dramatic.'

'I want you to have it. You've been so good to me these past weeks; it's my way of saying thank you.'

Oliver carefully placed the canvas down and drew her to him. 'I love it. And I will think of you every time I look at it.'

He leaned down and kissed her on the lips. 'I wish you weren't leaving.'

'I'll be back next weekend!'

He laughed. 'I know.'

'You know, you could stay here tonight,' she whispered, wrapping her arms around his neck.

In the early morning, a storm moved in, and black clouds raced across the sky. Thunder boomed and crashed above the little cottage on the cliffside. But, safely within its thick stone walls, they made sweet, tender love. Rolling together under the sheets, they caressed each other with their hands, lips, and tongues. He wanted her so badly that his whole body ached in anticipation.

She smoothed her hands down the tensing muscles in his back and drew him slowly into her yielding to his rhythmic thrusting. He whispered something inaudible as his grip on her tightened and they soared together before falling, exhausted, into each other's arms.

That night, as they lay silently listening to the storm recede, it felt as if no one else in the universe existed.

Chapter 21

Marcus had been on the road for over five hours, only briefly stopping to grab a sandwich. Earlier, he dropped Horace off at Fern Retreat before setting off for Norfolk. Today he was meeting Maggie King. Maggie King was one of only two people to witness Rose's death. The second being Maggie's granddaughter, Ellie, who was then seven.

A few weeks earlier, with the help of Steve, an ex-army colleague now working as a private investigator, Marcus acquired Maggie's landline and home address. He then called her and explained that it was recently the second anniversary of his daughter's death. He hoped talking to her in person might help give him some closure. Although hesitant at first, she sympathised that no one had yet been brought to justice and agreed to meet.

Of course, the police had interviewed her and her granddaughter, Ellie, immediately after the collision, so there was no reason to think he would learn anything new. But he was tired – tired of waiting for the police to do something.

Last year, the *Crimewatch* programme had uncovered a few leads, all of which were dead ends. Her killer was still out there, and it was eating away at him like a canker.

Upon reaching Norfolk, Marcus checked in to a local guest house and a short time later, sat patiently waiting in Maggie's small sitting room, while she made them tea. Knick-knacks collected over a lifetime were dotted around the room; family photos smiling cheerily back at him. Sitting opposite him, looking uneasy, was Amanda, whom Maggie introduced as her daughter, Ellie's mother. He hadn't expected her to be there but was glad of the opportunity to talk to her too.

'Is that Ellie?' Marcus asked, nodding at a framed school photo of a beaming little girl missing her front teeth.

'Yes. She was eight then; she's nearly ten now.' Amanda's smile faded when she remembered that this man, a stranger to them, had recently lost his own daughter.

Maggie came back with the tea. Amanda helped with the tray while her mother slowly sat in a tall, upright chair.

'I am sorry to disturb you both like this,' he said, looking at them in turn.

'I understand, Mr Cole,' Maggie replied. 'What happened that day never really left me, and I am so sorry for your terrible loss.'

She was thin and frail-looking, unlike the photo on the windowsill of her with Ellie in which her granddaughter looked to be five or six. They were standing on a palm tree-lined promenade in the sunshine, looking relaxed and tanned. She was barely recognisable as the woman before him now.

'Thank you, Mrs King.'

'Please, call me Maggie.'

Marcus smiled.

'What is it you think my mother can help you with?' Amanda interjected.

'I'll try to make this as quick as possible. I realise you've already told the police what you remember, but I wondered,

Maggie, if you could tell me anything more about the man, the biker? I know this is a little unorthodox me being here but he's still out there…Rose's killer.'

He stared at the red-patterned carpet, trying not to show the wave of grief which had just hit him so hard. He rarely spoke of Rose to anyone; the last time (other than the police) had been at her funeral.

'What is it you want to know, Mr Cole?' Amanda probed.

He took a shaky breath. 'I was hoping Maggie could tell me what she remembers of that day. I can't change what happened, but I can try and find the man responsible. I have waited two years, for the police to find him and bringing him to justice is the only thing that keeps me going.

'The motorbike he rode that day was stolen, and they no longer have any leads. A few times they've given me fresh hope, some new snippet of information, but nothing has ever come of it. They say the investigation is ongoing, but the more time passes, the less communication I receive from them. My calls either go unanswered, or I'm met with the same old thing: "We're doing everything we can. You'll be the first to know…"'

'I'm truly sorry for your loss,' sympathised Amanda. 'But what makes you think you can find this man when the police can't? Especially after all this time.'

'That's why I'm here, to see if there is anything – no matter how small – that your mother or daughter may have remembered since that day.'

'I wish I had,' said Maggie, 'but I don't remember much after the first few moments of impact. The force of the crash fractured my spine and I was in and out of consciousness. Ellie described him as best she could to the police, but he wore a helmet, so she never saw his face.'

'I understand; the police explained that to me.' Marcus turned to Amanda. 'How is your daughter? It must have been a terrifying experience. Has she managed to put it behind her?'

'She's better now but it took time for her to get over it. Anyone would have been traumatised, let alone a child. Afterwards, I think shock set in. She struggled to settle at night – had bad dreams. But we've encouraged her to talk openly about it, and I'm relieved to say she is more her old self now.' Marcus smiled. 'That's good to hear, Maggie. I hope you don't mind me asking, but were you staying with Amanda and Ellie at the time? Norfolk is a long way from Cornwall.'

'Yes. Amanda moved from here to West Hill when she married. Her husband, Peter, is often away on business, and she invited me to stay for a few weeks. It was supposed to be a change of scenery for me. And as Amanda had just started working at a local jeweller's, I was helping out with Ellie too. I was dropping her off at school that morning. It was just pure bad luck we were on that stretch of road.' Her voice trembled. 'I don't know what else to say to you.' She regarded him with pink-rimmed, rheumy eyes. 'If I could somehow go back and change what happened, I would. It would have been better if I had died rather than your daughter. But that bike came from nowhere; it flew around the bend, and I could do nothing to avoid hitting it.'

'Oh, Mum, you mustn't talk like that,' said Amanda. 'None of this is your fault. You and Ellie were victims. You could have been killed too. The only one to blame is the cold-hearted man who cruelly took Mr Cole's daughter.'

'I'm sorry, I didn't mean to upset you, Maggie. Perhaps I'd

better go.'

'No, really, I'm all right.' She straightened in her chair and dabbed at her eyes with a tissue. 'But I can't tell you anything to help you find him. Have you discovered anything more about this man?'

'I've spoken to Rose's best friend, Lisa. She repeated what she had told the police, which was shortly before the accident, Rose had confided in her about her new mystery boyfriend. She didn't tell her his name but did mention that he was older and that she was flattered that a man was interested in her. He was exciting and much more fun to be with than the usual boys she hung out with. Rose also told her that he had family in Lostmor. That's all I have to go on.

'The police investigated – went door to door. There was an appeal on local TV too, all to no avail.'

'Lostmor? Isn't that where you've come from today?' Amanda asked.

A young girl suddenly appeared in the doorway. 'Mum, I've finished my homework.' She looked shyly at Marcus, then to Amanda, wondering who the stranger was. Granny didn't have many visitors.

'Well done, Ellie. This is Mr Cole, he's... Well, he's come to visit Granny, just like us.'

'Hello, Mr Cole,' said Ellie, balancing awkwardly on the arm of her mother's chair.

'Hello, Ellie. Nice to meet you.' Though he had hoped she might be here, now faced with such a young girl, it didn't seem appropriate to start quizzing her about the accident.

Amanda sighed. She put an arm around Ellie and hugged her. 'Mr Cole is just trying to learn more about the motorbike accident,' she explained. 'About the man riding the bike.'

'You mean Helmet Man. Are you the police?'

'No, Ellie, but you could say I'm trying to help the police. I knew the girl who died that day; I cared for her very much. So, if you can remember anything about the biker – Helmet Man...' Marcus spoke softly, not wanting to upset her. 'Even something that may seem unimportant might be useful.'

'It's up to you, Ellie,' said her mother. 'You don't have to talk about it if you don't want to.'

Ellie was perceptive for her age; she wondered if this was the dead girl's daddy.

'I don't mind,' she shrugged, 'but it's the same as I told the police.'

'I understand,' said Marcus. 'I know he kept his helmet on, but did you see him up close?'

'He came to the car window. He had a black helmet and leather jacket. He hurt himself. He was bleeding from his leg, his left one. His jeans were red from the blood.'

'It must have been very scary indeed,' he sympathised.

'You were so brave that day, you really were,' her grandmother added. 'And you looked after me until help came, too.'

'It was awful. After the man left, we had to wait a long time.'

'I'm so sorry you and your gran had to go through that. So, the biker just walked off? Did he leave straight away?'

'He looked at us in the car, then he walked up the road a bit. He was limping. Then he saw the girl fall. He came back; saw she was dead. Then he staggered into the woods. I never saw him after that. He wanted to get away.'

Marcus knew from the police that Rose had died instantly. For the millionth time, he tried not to visualise it.

'When he was up close, did he say anything to you?' he asked.

'No.'

'Could you see the colour of his skin? Maybe you saw his hands or his neck? Did he have any tattoos or scars?'

'No, he had gloves on. I told the police that, too.'

'Okay. Thanks for talking to me, Ellie. You have been really helpful.'

'Well, I'd better get going.' He rose to leave. He was disappointed but not surprised. He hadn't learnt anything new, but was glad to have met Maggie and Ellie. They were connected for all the wrong reasons, but on some level, he found it a relief to have finally spoken about Rose.

Since the funeral, he and Rebecca had not seen each other or even spoken on the phone. Why would she want to? She probably blamed him. Maybe their daughter wouldn't have rebelled or taken so many risks if he'd been around more.

'Is your mother okay?' he asked Amanda as she showed him to the front door.

'Not really, but she's a tough lady. She's suffered from chronic back pain ever since the crash.'

'Does she live here alone?'

'Yes. Ellie and I are just visiting for a few days. We lost Dad five years ago. Before the accident, Mum was beginning to get her life back on track. That's partly why I invited her to West Hill. She was helping me with Ellie, but it was supposed to be fun. I thought the trip would be good for her. The three of us had planned to go shopping, take Ellie to the zoo...'

He nodded. 'I am sorry for upsetting her. I don't like to ask, but would you mind taking this just in case Ellie should remember anything else?' He offered Amanda a business card with the Black Dog inn contact details.

Amanda considered him for a moment. 'Okay, sure. I can't imagine she will, but I know how I would feel if anyone hurt my daughter. I don't blame you for wanting to find this man, but when you said to my mother on the phone you were looking for closure, we thought you just wanted to talk. Is it closure you want, Mr Cole, or is it revenge? Suppose you get your wish and you do find him. What then?'

'If I find out who he is, or where he is, I'll tell the police; let them deal with him,' he lied.

As he walked away, she eyed him suspiciously. She noticed he limped slightly but still looked like he could handle himself. She hoped he knew what he was doing.

Chapter 22

Lily smiled at her fickleness. Initially keen to return to her painting, now she was in Bristol she couldn't wait to return to Lostmor and see Oliver again.

A steady stream of people visited The Blue all week, some browsing but quite a few purchasing. She had been working on a new commission: a painting of the Christmas Steps, a famous historical street in Bristol. From her easel in the rear of the shop, she smiled back at a well-dressed lady who had come in a few minutes earlier. For once, she was glad when the customer headed for the door. It was nearly closing time, and she was eager to get home and pack.

No sooner had she let herself into her apartment when her mobile rang.

'Hi, how were things at The Blue today?' Oliver asked.

'Busy. Things are going well. How about you? What have you been up to?'

'Spreading slurry ready for sowing wheat when the last frosts are over.'

'Wow, and here's me just wafting a paintbrush about!'

He laughed. 'You have a talent. Farming is just work; anyone can learn to do it.'

'I'm not so sure about that. You must be pretty disciplined.'

'It can be a struggle when it's pitch-black outside and

blowing a gale, but most of the time I love it. I feel cooped up if I'm inside too long. What time are you coming tomorrow? I can't wait to see you.'

'Um, I'm opening the shop in the morning, so maybe around four, depending on the traffic.'

'Okay. Well, I'll leave the key on the shelf inside the porch. Something's come up – I have to go into St Oswald to meet my mother's solicitor,' he explained. 'Sorry, he only rang yesterday. It's just some signatures he needs with regard to ownership of the farm. I should be back by 6:30 p.m. at the latest.'

'Not to worry. Don't rush. Flynn will keep me company.'

Lily's journey the following day was long and frustrating, with frequent queuing due to roadworks. She finally arrived at Bligh Farm close to 5:00 p.m., welcomed by an excited Flynn. Together, they wandered around the yard for a while. A pale winter sun sank towards the horizon, and the acrid smell of freshly spread fertiliser lay heavy in the air, carried across open fields by a low wind. She shivered and turned back towards the house.

By 7:00 p.m., Lily fed a hungry-looking Flynn with dog food she found in the cupboard. By 8:30, she was worried; he should have been back hours ago. She had tried his mobile umpteen times, but it was switched off. What if he had crashed? It was so dark this time of year, and the A roads were mostly unlit. She lit a fire and sat on the couch, picking at some leftover chilli she had found in the fridge. All she could do was wait and keep trying his phone.

After another hour of worrying and willing her phone to ring, Lily called the hospital in St Oswald, who confirmed that no one of his name or description had been admitted that day. She searched for contact details in an address book on the kitchen dresser, but no one was listed as a solicitor, and she didn't know the person's name. She tried Janet Morgan several times, knowing she would help if she could, but there was no reply. As a last resort, she called the local police station. They were helpful, taking down as much information as she could give them, but stressed they would not pursue any lines of enquiry until he'd been missing for twenty-four hours. She thanked them and agreed to call back tomorrow. It wasn't much consolation, but at least she'd done what she could.

Eventually, she fell asleep on the couch. She awoke just before dawn, shivering from the cold. Flynn, who was curled up beside her, jumped down, head tilted, wondering what this new game of someone sleeping on his bed was. Lily squinted in the half-light. There were no missed calls on her phone. She knew she would have heard the landline but checked the machine anyway.

Visions of Oliver lying unseen in a ditch filled her head. She told herself she was being melodramatic. He had probably broken down miles from anywhere, his mobile out of charge. He would walk through the door any second now, and all would be well. She stood in the kitchen, sipping a mug of hot tea, wondering what to do next when she heard a car pull up. She rushed to the door and flung it open.

'Oliver! Thank God.'

Chapter 23

Marcus checked out of his accommodation early the next morning. The journey home was quicker, but still took over five hours. Not that he minded. Since moving to Lostmor, it felt like he had spent more hours behind the wheel than he had sleeping; hours spent tailing anyone suspicious, especially bikers. He would track their movements and investigate their backgrounds. He knew he was clutching at straws, but he had to try.

At the Black Dog, he listened to customers but never talked at length about himself. He kept things vague if anyone asked where he had lived or worked before. His stock answer was that he had managed a bar in Bristol, then moved south after his divorce. People generally believed what they were told without question. He knew he needed to stay anonymous. And he definitely didn't want people to know he was Rose's father.

After she died, it was Rebecca who had received the most media attention – another thing he felt bad about. He was abroad and refused to speak to the few reporters who had managed to track him down.

When Marcus first arrived in Lostmor, he also spent hours walking the coastal paths, having only recently acquired Horace, who was young and full of energy. What started as a necessity became a welcome distraction from the sadness he felt so acutely. He often awoke with an all-encompassing wave of despair, so crushing it seemed to pin him to the bed. But gradually, their walks shook off this fog of grief. Horace nudged him to get up daily, shaking him out of despondency. Together, they walked their way through a very difficult time in his life.

Having returned to the pub from Norfolk, Marcus checked in with the bar staff. Business was slow. He took a quick shower before deciding to walk to Fern Retreat to collect Horace. He needed to stretch his legs after such a long drive. At the far end of the bay, he climbed the steep track leading to the coastal path beyond. His head cleared when he reached the top, and he felt a new lightness of heart.

He watched the sea rolling in fast onto the rocks below, where spiralling lengths of froth flicked up spray. Today, the wind was up; overhead, scores of gulls pitched and turned weightlessly on the updraught. He turned up his collar against the cold and walked for a couple of miles, before cutting across pastureland that eventually met the road. As he walked through the gate to Fern Retreat, he could hear Horace barking and found him in the paddock, chasing after a ball, hotly pursued by Bella. Julia was wrapped up in a puffer jacket, bobble hat and gloves, hurling the ball repeatedly at an impressive overarm distance.

'Hi, there!' he called out to her.

Horace immediately dropped the ball and came bounding over.

'Hello! I didn't hear your car,' she called in return.

'No, I'm on foot today,' he smiled, kneeling to hug Horace. 'Hello, big fella!' Horace stuck his head into Marcus's side. 'I thought Horace would enjoy the walk back.'

'It's a nice day for it,' Julia agreed, 'if a little brisk!' She threw the ball for Bella one last time before they retreated to the warmth of the house.

Inside, Marcus paid for Horace's stay. 'Did he behave himself?'

'He's been no trouble at all. I feel bad charging you; I've enjoyed having him around.'

'You're going to have to be more businesslike than that if you want to make any money!'

She laughed, pulling off her hat and unravelling the long woolly scarf from around her neck. 'You're right. I'll try to be more assertive at the open day.'

'Ah, yes, of course. Have you got any more customers?'

'A few people have dropped by and booked their dogs in, and I've had enquiries over the phone. So, things are looking up. I think your distribution of my leaflets must have helped.'

'They might have seen your ad in the *Lostmor Gazette*. Either way, I'm glad things are working out.'

'If my future clientele are as well-behaved as Horace, my job will be easy,' said Julia. 'And as he was my first guest, he's welcome to stay in the house if ever you need to drop him off again. He is very affectionate, isn't he?'

'I think the word is needy!' laughed Marcus. 'But that is a very generous offer, thank you.'

Horace softly woofed at them both, his tail swishing on the kitchen slabs in agreement.

'To be honest, it was probably a one-off trip. But if you need any extra help getting ready for the open day, I'm pretty handy.'

She hesitated and looked like she was trying to gauge whether she should accept.

'No strings.' He raised his hands in submission.

'That is an offer I just can't turn down!' She smiled. 'What are you like at fixing fences?'

Chapter 24

'I was so worried about you.' Lily hugged Oliver close, but he slowly removed her arms from around his neck and walked past her into the kitchen.

'Are you hurt? What happened?'

'No, it's nothing like that.' He sat down heavily, for once ignoring Flynn's excited bids for attention. 'I'm sorry. I turned my phone off. I had some news... Some very bad news. I've been sitting in my car for most of the night trying to get my head straight.'

She looked into troubled eyes. He looked exhausted. 'Why? Whatever's wrong?'

He sighed. 'What I'm about to tell you changes things for us forever.'

'I don't understand. Oliver, you're scaring me. Surely, whatever it is, we can work it out. I'm here for you, just as you said you were for me. Remember?'

'Of course, and I meant it. But this is different; things are different now. You'd better sit down.'

Slowly, she sat.

'You know I went to see Mr Reece yesterday?'

'Your mother's solicitor?'

He nodded.

'I tried to find a number for him but I didn't know his

name. Weren't you signing papers?'

'I was... I did. But he also gave me this.' He placed a large envelope on the table. 'Apparently, my mother instructed him to wait six months after her passing before handing this to me. Now I've seen its contents, I think I know why: she was waiting until after the funeral to lessen the blow.'

Lily stared at the envelope and then at Oliver, who looked lost. 'What does it say?'

'I don't think I have the words. Maybe you should just read it.' He pulled out two smaller envelopes from inside and passed her the one with his name handwritten on the front. 'This is the letter my mother left.'

My dearest Oliver,

This is not an easy letter to write, but I need to tell you something I should have told you long ago.

When I was young, I did something impulsive that I bitterly regretted. I betrayed your father with another man, and what happened changed everything. You see, I fell pregnant. The man in question never knew about you, and I never saw him again.

George, who loved you as his own, couldn't have children. When he was a young man, he contracted measles and became very ill. He survived a terrible infection, but it left him sterile. I told him it didn't matter to me and that I loved him all the same. And I meant it. I guess I was a foolish young girl impressed by an older man's attention.

I must have taken leave of my senses to have risked everything that way. But the one thing I know to be true is that from the second you were born, you were George's and mine; you were our *son, and the most precious and cherished of gifts. We loved you with all our hearts, and I know how proud he would have been to see his hardworking boy grow into such an honourable man.*

When you were still very young, we talked about whether we should tell you the truth one day. Rightly or wrongly, we decided against it. We just wanted to give you the best start in life, and I hope that in your heart, you can find it within you to forgive me, just as George forgave me my betrayal even though I hurt him deeply.

When he was taken so early from us, you were still a boy. I did not have it in me to break your heart a second time. Only a few years later, I learnt that your birth father had also died prematurely. With them both gone, it seemed easier to say nothing.

Knowing that I will soon die has made me reflect upon my own blessed life. George and I were content together, but when you came along, you made us even happier; you completed our family.

I am sorry for lying to you, son, and for not having the courage to tell you who your birth father was. You have the right to know.

Your loving mother

Lily looked perplexed. 'I am truly sorry, Oliver. This must be a terrible shock for you. But I don't understand what this has to do with us.'

He pulled his birth certificate from the second envelope,

placing it flat on the table. 'Here,' he said, almost in a whisper, pointing to his birth father's name. For a moment, Lily said nothing, staring at her own father's name in disbelief. She looked anxiously at him.

'But how can this be? It can't be real!'

'It is. Why wouldn't it be? Mother hid this certificate from me. She lied. She told me it was lost long ago, and I had no reason to doubt her.' He saw the fear in her eyes.

'Lily, I want more than anything for this to be somehow wrong. I can hardly believe that your father is also mine, but I don't see how my mother could be mistaken. She knew George could not have children.'

A chill ran through her, and she sat motionless. 'You're right, this does change everything,' she said sadly. 'We're half brother and sister.'

'I'm so sorry,' he said, equally distraught. 'I've been running this through my head all night. Mother knew Vincent had died, so she must have heard what happened to him. She may have known that you and your mother moved away. She had no reason to think we would ever meet, let alone... *be together*.'

Lily looked at him in dismay. Had she not felt so heartbroken, she would have laughed out loud at the sheer irony. She had finally found someone special, someone she wanted to be with, only to find out they were related. Worse than that, they had spent the night together. She felt ashamed and devastated. Yesterday morning, she couldn't wait to see him and was looking forward to their weekend together. Now, because of a single piece of paper, everything was ruined.

Oliver looked on helplessly as she gathered up her things. 'Can't you stay awhile and talk? I know things can never be the same between us, but that doesn't stop me from caring about you. And that night we spent together... Christ, I don't know... It didn't feel wrong.'

Lily couldn't trust herself to speak. Grabbing her bag, she smiled weakly, tears falling before she reached the door.

Chapter 25

Douglas flicked the pull tab off another beer. 'I don't want to live anywhere else. Why do we have to leave?'

He and his brother sat in front of a dwindling fire in armchairs that sagged and bowed with age. The living room was sparse, devoid of furniture, apart from an old chest of drawers littered with empty beer cans and dirty plates. Douglas's older brother, Luke, leaned forward and carefully placed more logs in the hearth. He was tired of having no money.

'Unless we sell this place, Doug, we only have a few hundred left. That's it.' That wasn't entirely true, but it was close enough.

'But we've always lived here. Where would we even go?'

'Not sure. St Oswald or Bristol? Somewhere there's more work.'

Since his brother had managed to blow his job at Bligh Farm, and their contract with Eastgate Skips had ended, they were skint again. But Luke was confident that if he could get his hands on some real money, he could turn things around, buy them a decent home.

'I know we grew up here, but it's still a shithole. The place isn't worth much but selling it would give us enough for a deposit on something better. We can start again.'

Douglas stared at the flames. It was a cold evening, and

an icy chill rapidly crept through Blackthorn Cottage. The broken-down bungalow was exposed to the elements on three sides, with a dense thicket of conifers behind and an adjacent breeze block garage overlooking disused fields. The only access was via a long, narrow track.

'Maybe we don't have to leave,' he suggested, suddenly animated by an idea slowly forming. 'What if I've found a way to make us both some easy money?'

Luke regarded him with sharp, suspicious eyes. It wasn't the first time his younger brother had devised a get-rich-quick scheme. They invariably led to nothing but trouble. Not that he was any saint himself.

His late father once told him he was the only one in the family with any brains. He encouraged him to study hard and make something of himself. Luke had enjoyed school at first. Learning to read came easily; he devoured storybooks from a young age. But once he reached high school, he lost patience. He found classes extremely dull. The teachers were often incompetent, and his fellow students were immature boys, mock fighting and bragging about who scored the most goals or made the best tackle.

The girls weren't much better, giggling and pulling up their skirts whenever some kid they fancied passed by. Except for one girl, he remembered with a wistful smile – she had been special. She had the most amazing poker-straight blonde hair which fell to her waist, and mesmerising blue eyes. They were in the same year and met in the library over a mutual love of books. Each day after lessons ended, they talked for hours in earnest, debating such titles as the *Lord of the Flies* and *The Outsiders*. He liked to challenge people's perceptions of what constituted 'normal' – of what was considered right and wrong. She had listened to his theories and opinions and taken him seriously. Until that dickhead Josh had come along, with his perfect white teeth and stupid flicked-back hair. Her visits to the library became less frequent, but she was adamant she still wanted to be his friend. Unfortunately, it wasn't mutual, and he told her as much. He was so mad at her that he wanted to set the whole fucking school alight, send all those petty conformists to hell in one glorious blaze. But instead, he started to skip classes. By the age of fifteen, he stopped attending altogether.

The school, and eventually social services, wrote letters to his father, most of which he managed to intercept. (Thankfully there was no phone line at home.) Once, someone from social services came to the house – at least he assumed it was them. The woman looked official, and no one else ever called. Fortunately for him, his father was out, so he and Doug played a game, hiding in their bedroom until the nosy woman had given up and gone away. It was their secret, one of many he had easily coerced his younger brother into. When Luke turned sixteen, no one bothered him anymore.

Ever since 'the bitch' had walked out on the family, Luke refused to refer to his mother in any other way. After she left, their father did his best, but it was all too much for him in the end. His enduring memory of the old man was of him sitting by the fireplace, drinking whisky and chain-smoking. It was hard watching him like that, constantly coughing and wheezing. When he could no longer get out of the chair unaided, Luke took matters into his own hands. He barely felt any resistance when he smothered his father with a pillow.

He told Douglas it was a blessing, him slipping away in his sleep like that. His brother was more upset than he expected; his drinking and visits to the bookies escalated. Eventually, Luke took control of the few thousand pounds they had left. The last of his father's savings was unimaginatively stashed under his mattress. He taped half to the bottom of a drawer in his bedroom and buried the rest behind the house in the thicket. Doug had protested for a while but eventually gave up trying to find it. It was how things had always been between them: Douglas fucked up, and Luke sorted it out.

Now, he watched his drunken brother with curiosity. He was shorter and heavyset, with a broad forehead and slabs of chest and shoulder muscle. It didn't seem fair; he ate and drank whatever he liked and never worked out. Luke was more like his mother, of slight build with jet-black hair and a pale complexion. He hated his noodle arms and envied his brother's bulging biceps. Not for the first time, he suspected Douglas was the result of one of 'the bitch's' frequent dalliances. What did it matter? All they had now was each other.

'Luke! Are you listening to me?' he slurred. 'That massive house we went to the other day.'

'Penwyth House? What about it?'

'Well, the place was being cleared out. It doesn't look like anyone was living there. We should take a look. There could still be valuables inside.'

'Hmm, it's risky. We don't know for sure it's empty.'

'We could check it out though, right? Keep watch, see who comes in and out.'

Luke pondered the idea. 'Maybe. But what about that guy you saw?'

'Oliver Bligh? What about him?'

'What was he doing there?'

Douglas shrugged. 'Dunno. Does it matter?'

'You told me he recognised you. That means he could connect you to that place. And by default, me too.'

'He's just a farmer. Probably doing some work on the estate.'

Luke sighed. 'I'll think about it some more tomorrow. That's enough beer for tonight, okay? If we do this, you need to get sober.'

Douglas threw his empty beer can at the log basket, complying with his brother's wishes.

Above their home, the last of the day's light drained from the sky, and the woodland sheathed the cottage in shadow, while in the canopy of trees, roosting crows struck up a cacophony of noise, their black avian eyes alert and watchful.

Chapter 26

Lily drove towards the motorway, feeling weary and downright miserable. It was hard to comprehend what had just happened. One thing was certain: it was over between her and Oliver.

From what she knew of Megan, she and her father seemed an unlikely union; they would not have moved in the same circles. But she remembered how he behaved around women, always flirting and laughing too loud, leaning in just that bit too close.

On one occasion, when their house was filled with people, Lily had heard voices when passing her father's study. She'd pushed the door open slightly and saw him fawning over a younger woman. They were kissing and giggling like teenagers. She had quietly backed out and walked away.

Her father was no saint – a poor father and an even lousier husband. The more she discovered about him, the more disappointed she felt.

She approached the slip road, the contours of the landscape opening out onto more level plains, when she was struck by something: she didn't want to leave. At the last moment, she changed lanes and drove back the way she'd come, heading for Penwyth House.

She had told Joe she would drop by at the weekend and explain what was happening at the house over the coming weeks. With all her heart, she wished it could have been with Oliver by her side, but it didn't mean she had to give up everything else. She resolved not to think about him; to bury what had happened. She was good at doing that, after all.

A short time later, she was driving through the orchard of her newly acquired estate (another fact she still found hard to fathom). For the first time, she noticed the recently pruned apple trees standing dark and naked. Suddenly, she was startled by the appearance of a pure white peacock which had dropped from the branches of one of the trees. She watched in disbelief as it ruffled its feathers before crossing the road in front of her car. Despite her low mood, the curious sight made her smile. It had to be Joe's. She recalled how much he loved birds and caring for her mother's aviary.

She decided to park at Penwyth House and walk to Joe's. It would give her time to gather her thoughts. A sharp coastal wind buffeted her as she stepped onto the drive. In the unseen distance, angry fists of water smashed against the rocks. Buttoning up her coat, she walked through the woods to Edhen Cottage. There was no reply, so she decided to walk to the clearing where the old glasshouses were. As she passed under the trees, what took her by surprise was the noise – the twittering and chirping of what sounded like hundreds of birds.

In front of her, side by side, were the two Victorian structures with impressive, arched roofs. As girls, she and Alice had spent many hours in both, either sitting amongst the flowers or kitchen produce, the air filled with the earthy smell of tomatoes and herbs.

Most of the glass panes were gone. Instead, heavy netting

had been erected and attached at various framework points. She approached open-mouthed, in awe of the spectacle before her. Joe was sitting inside the glasshouse to her left. He was facing away from her trying to fix part of the netting. She slid the door open and then quietly shut it behind her (not that he would have heard her above all the commotion).

Small pots filled both sides of a narrow wooden walkway, containing all manner of evergreens and tropical plants. Grass and a few young trees had grown up through its base. Dispersed amongst all of this were orchids, covering shelves and makeshift tables. Dozens of varieties, laden with exotically shaped petals or elegant tubers, formed a rainbow of colours adorning the green.

Above her, she saw bird tables attached at varying heights to the frame and perches that ran the length of the roof. Finches, canaries and even parakeets were perched in groups or darting and swooping amongst the vegetation. The air around her was alive with birds.

Since seeing the framed photo of her mother at Edhen Cottage, she knew Joe had written the notes hidden in her book. She wanted to ask him about it but could not find the words. Now, being here in this beautiful place full of vibrant life and colour, she knew it was built on love; it was an ode to her mother. She felt overwhelmed that he had remained so dedicated to a woman he had not seen for over twenty years.

'Lily!' he called, beckoning her over. There was a small crow perched on the table next to him. 'Oh, don't mind Roy, he's harmless. I fixed his wing six months ago, but he flies a bit crookedly, so he mostly hangs around here now.'

She hugged Joe tightly as he stood to greet her.

'Well, that's a nice welcome,' he smiled.

'Joe, this place is unbelievable. It's so beautiful! How long has it been like this?'

'A long time, but it happened slowly.'

She noticed more netting was hung between the two glasshouses, forming a tunnel. 'May I?' She gestured towards the makeshift walkway.

'Yes,' he beamed, 'I'll show you.'

They walked through the second glasshouse, also filled with lush greenery and orchids, replacing the herbs and vegetables of her childhood. In this one, Joe had built a miniature waterfall that trickled down a purpose-built rockery into a large, raised pond.

'Shall we sit?' he suggested, fetching a blanket from a nearby chest and placing it on a bench near the water.

He grinned as a finch landed briefly on his shoulder before skimming across the pond. Now she understood why he was rarely at home. The estate no doubt kept him busy, but she imagined he also spent much of his time in this secret and magical place.

They sat side by side, watching the birds on the water for a while. Then Joe started to talk.

'It must have been so hard for you back then – you so young, losing Alice and your father like that. I grieved for your family, for your loss. When you and Elizabeth left, I didn't know what to do next. It was like there was this gaping hole left behind. Luckily, Timothy asked me to stay on. To be honest, I had nowhere else to go.

'For years, I hoped you and your mother might return one day. In the meantime, I looked after the estate as I always had.

Now that I'm in my sixties, I've had to slow down a bit and let some of the less important jobs go.

'Your mother's old aviary became too small as the number of birds increased, partly through their breeding. I also collected a few lame ones along the way, and others just flew in! So, I moved them here. The plants and orchids I nurtured, and they seemed to have grown along with the birds. I grew herbs in here for a while, but with no one here but me, they went to waste. Plus, I was running out of space for my birds, so I opened this one up for them too. As you can see,' he smiled, 'it is something of a passion.'

'What I see is a little corner of paradise. It truly is lovely here.' Lily watched two yellow finches dozing high up on a perch. 'I'm guessing the white peacock I saw in the orchard is yours, too?'

'Ah, that's Percy. In the orchard, you say? He shouldn't have roamed that far; it's too near the road. I'll try to round him up later. He came from breeding a pair I took on years ago. I've other birds that still fly in and out; injured ones mostly I've helped that can't quite seem to cut the apron strings!'

Lily smiled. He was full of surprises.

'The orchids remind me of Mother. I think she loved them nearly as much as her birds.'

'Aye, she did,' he replied.

'Joe,' she said softly, 'I found the notes you sent her. They were in her bedroom, hidden in one of my old storybooks.'

He looked stunned. 'Notes? *My* notes? I didn't know she kept them.' He looked away from her and gazed across the pond. 'I'm sorry, Lily. I never meant to cause you or anyone any upset. It just happened... I loved her, and I would have done anything for her. Anything.'

Lily squeezed his hand reassuringly. 'It's okay.'

He sighed. 'Elizabeth told me she and your father were once happy and in love. I don't know how much you remember from your childhood, but things changed. As his drinking got worse, he spent more time away from her and your home.

'It was about then that she decided to keep birds. She explained it was something she had always wanted to do. So, I built her an aviary, and we learnt how to care for its residents together. We laughed a lot and enjoyed each other's company. I fell in love with her, it's as simple as that, and she loved me for a while, too. I truly believe she did.'

'Go on,' said Lily softly. 'Please.'

Joe paused and looked at her. 'What memories do you have of your father?'

'Things have faded as I've got older, but I do remember his drinking. He would get angry and shout a lot at Mother; us too if we didn't make ourselves scarce. Sometimes he disappeared for days on end. I used to feel relieved when he wasn't around.' Lily fell quiet for a moment, thinking. 'They used to laugh together sometimes, but I think things were pretty bad between them towards the end.

'In the summer months, it was easier for me and Alice. I would take her away from the house, and we'd spend whole days playing in the woods or the gardens.'

Joe nodded. 'So, it won't come as too much of a shock if I tell you how much your father's drinking spiralled out of control.

'One day, Elizabeth came to find me; she was distraught. Your father had come home drunk, out of his mind. He taunted her and told her he could have any woman he liked. She screamed at him to leave her alone and said she didn't care what he did anymore. He grew angry and struck her across the face. Her eye was bruised for days. I think that was why she ended our affair – his violent outbursts were escalating, and she was afraid of what he might do to me if he ever found out about us. I told her I didn't care. I begged her to leave him. I wanted to tell him that we were in love. But she begged me not to. Anyway...' He sighed and shook his head slightly before continuing.

'That was that – we stopped seeing each other. She tried hard to make their marriage work, and he never knew of our affair.

'I think things were okay for a while – she even persuaded him to stop drinking – but it didn't last. By the time Alice came along, he had gone back to his old ways, staying out late and coming home drunk. It broke my heart to see her unhappy and not be with her, but I stayed, just in case she needed me.' He lowered his head, visibly upset. 'In the end, I failed her.'

'What do you mean, Joe?'

'I don't know what happened on the roof that night, Lily, but maybe if I had been stronger, tried harder to get her to leave him...'

'It's not your fault. My father broke her heart.' She spoke gently, not wishing to upset him further. 'I now understand how difficult things were for her, and I'm glad she found some fleeting happiness with you.'

They sat quietly, watching the birds on the water, both lost in their thoughts. For a short time, she felt cocooned in Joe's sanctuary, protected from the wind by the tropical plants and trees.

She awoke with a start, not to the sound of birds calling (they were mostly roosting) but by a loud rattling sound. For a moment, she was confused as to where she was. The wind had picked up and tugged at the netting like a spiteful child. She peered upwards, noticing lots of holes and tears in the fabric for the first time. She was slumped against a cushion Joe must have fetched. Her neck was stiff from dozing at an awkward angle, and a dull pain pulsed in her forehead.

'You okay?' he asked from somewhere behind her.

'Yes.' She twisted round to see him reaching from a ladder, trying to attach some newly patched netting to the frame. 'Sorry! I can't believe I fell asleep like that!'

'No problem. You must be tired.' He smiled down at her.

'How long was I asleep?'

'About an hour. I was going to wake you soon. It looks like there's rain coming. It might be best if we head off.'

Lily shivered. She was tired after her restless night on Oliver's couch. After his disturbing news, it would have been easier to hightail it back to Bristol, her heart heavy knowing they couldn't be together. But if she hadn't come to see Joe, she may never have seen his beautiful aviary or learned of his true feelings for her mother.

She wondered what other secrets hid behind Penwyth's solid, unyielding walls...

Chapter 27

Julia wasn't sure if anyone would show up at first.

She and Marcus had spent hours hanging bunting the day before, which now flapped wildly in a bracing sea breeze. Two recently acquired stone Labradors, affectionately named Bert and Ernie after the *Sesame Street* characters, sat on either side of the front gate. Above the hut's door hung a welcome banner, and inside, a large tea urn bubbled and churned.

Julia's leaflets stated a 10:30 start for Fern Retreat's much anticipated opening day.

'Don't worry,' Marcus said reassuringly, 'it's only 10:40.'

Sure enough, five minutes later, several cars crawled up the drive. Parents unloaded warmly dressed children, and dogs bounced on leads, barking excitedly.

Julia and Marcus welcomed the gathering crowd with hot drinks, squash and homemade cookies. By lunchtime, a dozen cars were squeezed into the gravelled parking area, and the urn was on its second refill. People wandered along the wooden walkway running the length of the empty kennels, which were decorated with more bunting.

Julia explained how each unit had a comfy bed, toys, and piped music, and that the private sleeping areas to the rear of each kennel were heated and housed an additional bed. Marcus's job was to show people the paddock, and grateful parents watched as their dogs and children ran around and played. By late afternoon, most people had drifted away, and Julia was counting the number of provisional bookings she had taken.

'Hello, you two!' she said to Marcus, who had just returned with Horace from his last tour of the exercise area.

'I thought that went well,' he commented. 'And Horace loved all the attention, didn't you, boy?'

Horace grumbled an acknowledgement of his name, but his eyes remained on the now empty tray of cookies he'd spotted. There was always hope...

'It did, didn't it? I've got fifteen bookings so far,' she said closing her appointment book.

'Well done. That's a good result.'

'I'm relieved. Thanks for all your help,' she said giving him a hug. A surprised Marcus wrapped his arms around her in response. She drew back smiling, the two of them standing close together.

'Honestly, I don't think I would have got everything sorted here without you. And the amount of people who turned up today – you must have given out a lot of leaflets.'

'A fair amount. I left some on the bar, too.' He gazed at her fondly. 'Julia, I really enjoyed today.'

'Me too. It was fun watching the kids throwing balls and their dogs tearing around.'

'Yes, but that's not what I meant. I meant I've really enjoyed your company. I've looked forward to coming to Fern Retreat every day.' He laughed. 'I've been making excuses to my staff at the pub for being late or for swapping shifts.'

'Oh. I hope I haven't made things difficult.'

'No... not at all. I guess what I'm trying to say, rather clumsily, is that I really like you.'

'Well, thank you... I like you too. I've kind of got used to having you around this past week.'

He had never met anyone like her before. She was bubbly and easy-going, yet she wasn't afraid to take risks. It was gutsy of her to start up a business alone.

And he couldn't help noticing how her ponytail swished when she walked, and the dimples that appeared high up on her cheeks every time she smiled or laughed, which was often.

This time, he moved towards her and placed his hands gently on her shoulders. 'In that case, how about you come to the Black Dog tonight for a few drinks? We could celebrate your opening day success.'

'Okay,' she agreed.

Every time he looked at her, he was captivated by her eyes, which were the most dazzling blue colour. Impulsively, he leant in and kissed her briefly on the mouth. She looked surprised but didn't back away.

'Sorry,' he said. 'I got carried away.'

'Maybe a little. But that's okay,' she smiled. 'So... tonight. Would you say that our celebration is kind of a date too?'

Marcus grinned. 'I hope so.'

Later that evening at the Black Dog inn, a few couples enjoying a quiet drink gradually became livelier as locals gathered at the bar.

'I'll be with you next,' Marcus told a customer while

pulling a draught beer. He nodded and accepted the money being proffered. 'A bit busier than I thought,' he commented to Julia, perched on a stool at the end.

'So I see! Don't mind me. I'm enjoying being out for the evening.'

He returned to her a few minutes later. 'Things should die down soon. The younger clientele usually head off to Revellers' nightclub around now.'

Sure enough, by 10:00 p.m. the pub suddenly became quieter. Marcus and Julia moved to a small table by the window. She gazed across the harbour, where strings of multicoloured bulbs hung between the streetlights. Above, a brilliant full moon illuminated the sky, transforming the bay's black water into sparkling shards of light. 'I'd forgotten how pretty the bay is,' she smiled.

'This place certainly grows on you,' he agreed.

Marcus realised it was the first time he had felt truly attracted to someone in a long time – not just physically but emotionally. He cared about her. But Julia was not part of the plan. There were still nights when he was back on the edge of that precipice. He had come to Lostmor to find Rose's killer and was determined to do so. Only now, he felt conflicted.

Over the past few weeks, each time he took the coastal path to Fern Retreat, with Horace bouncing alongside him, he felt his spirit lift. More often than not, Julia would be outside, waving enthusiastically when he appeared over the brow of the hill. After years of solitude, he was surprised how easily he had fallen into step with someone else

'You okay, Marcus?' She had been chatting excitedly about what her first week running Fern Retreat might be like when she noticed how distracted he looked.

'Marcus!' Andy shouted across the bar, interrupting Julia. 'There's someone on the phone asking for you.'

Marcus couldn't think of a single person. 'Who?'

'Amanda. Maggie's daughter?'

That was the moment the shutters went down; when everything good that had happened to him since coming to Lostmor slipped away.

Chapter 28

Late afternoon, under a blackening sky, Lily drove out of Penwyth Estate, her thoughts reeling after her conversation with Joe. She had learnt so much more about the dear man. He had always been kind to her and Alice and was the only person she still knew from childhood. She understood now that he was still deeply in love with her mother. Theirs was not a hasty affair quickly forgotten, a joyless escape for a woman trapped in an unhappy marriage. They had risked everything for over a year. Ultimately, she had sacrificed their love, choosing her husband in order to protect Joe. But Joe had lost her.

Just as I have lost Oliver, she thought sadly.

Without her noticing, a low fog had crept over the cliffs, flowing like volcanic lava across the landscape, smothering everything in its path. Lily flicked on her fog lights and tried to focus on the road ahead. She was still tired and couldn't face the long drive back to Bristol. A hotel would do for the night.

Then her car began to lose power. She checked the petrol gauge: the tank was still half full. Try as she might to accelerate, the car slowed to a stop. 'No, no, no. Not now, please!' She tried the ignition several times, but the engine was completely dead. She peered through the mizzled windscreen. The dwindling light and eerie mist had created a strange wilderness. She had no choice: either she called someone (though she wasn't sure who) or made her way on foot to Lostmor, which was still a few miles away.

Then to her relief she saw headlights in her rear-view mirror intensifying as the vehicle drew closer. Momentarily it struck her how vulnerable she was alone on a deserted road, but she couldn't pass up the opportunity for help. She flicked her hazard lights on and jumped out, waving at the vague human outline visible through the windscreen. The station wagon slowly pulled in behind hers. A figure turned to check something on the back seat before climbing out.

Lily could see it was a woman, and as she drew nearer realised it was Dr Morgan from the veterinary practice.

'Hello again!' said Lily with relief.

'Ah! You're the lady who brought Flynn in!'

'That's right. Thank you so much for stopping.'

'Has your car broken down?'

'Yes, it's given up the ghost I'm afraid.'

'Oh dear. Would you like a lift? You're staying at Kleger Cottage, aren't you?'

'I was but not anymore. If it's not too much trouble, do you think you could drop me off in Lostmor?'

'Of course. Good job I found you. The weather is awful, and it's getting dark.'

Luckily, Lily had managed to steer her car to the roadside before completely losing power, so vehicles had enough room to pass.

She grabbed her overnight bag and gratefully climbed into Dr Morgan's car. 'Thanks again. I've no idea what the problem is. It just died on me. I'll have to call someone in the morning and get it towed away.'

'Yes, I'm afraid it's too late to sort it out now. Where in Lostmor would you like me to drop you?'

'Tresor Bay? I should be able to book a hotel for the night. I was supposed to drive home to Bristol earlier, but something happened, and time got away from me.'

'It sounds as if you've had a bit of a day.' She glanced at Lily. 'Look,' she added, 'if you haven't booked anything, I own a small holiday let. It's an old stable that I had converted, and it is empty. You're welcome to stay there for the night.'

'Well... that is kind. But I don't want to inconvenience you any more than I already have.'

'It's no bother. It's next door to my cottage and it's only two minutes away from here. But if you prefer a hotel, I'm happy to drop you off somewhere else.'

Lily was exhausted and Dr Morgan's offer was tempting. 'Well, if you're sure? I'll pay you whatever the nightly rate is, of course.'

'I'll just charge you the minimum as it's out of season. I'll find you the number for Taskers later. That's the local garage. You can call them in the morning.'

Just then, Lily heard a rustling from behind and, to her surprise, turned to see a large white peacock settled on the back seat.

'Ah, yes. I forgot he was there. I picked him up not long before I found you. The damned silly thing was in the middle of the road barely visible in the fog; I nearly hit him. He seems quite tame, though. What a strange evening! Picking up two passengers on my way home!'

'My goodness. This must be Percy!'

'You mean to say you're acquainted?'

'I only met him today. He belongs to a friend of mine, Joe
– Joe Newman. He must have roamed from Penwyth House.'

'Not sure I've heard of the place.'

'It's a few miles back the way you came.'

'Perhaps you can explain to me where it is later so I can
return him?

'Here we are, then.' She turned down a lane and parked in
front of a small cottage. The headlights illuminated a pretty
front garden with an iron rose trellis over the gate.

'Are you sure this is okay?'

'No trouble at all. That's The Old Stable,' she said nodding
at the building next door. 'I'll just get the key.'

A few moments later, she returned, carrying a basket with
a carton of milk, bread, a packet of Cornish cookies, jam and a
pat of butter. Having unlocked the door to the holiday let, she
flicked the light on and placed the basket on the kitchen unit.

Dr Morgan looked at the basket. 'This is what I usually
supply for guests, and you'll find tea and coffee in the
cupboard.'

Lily followed her through to a quaint *en suite* bedroom.

'You'll have to make the bed up. There's fresh bed linen in
the wardrobe, and toiletries in the bathroom.'

'Thank you again for this,' Lily smiled.

'My pleasure. Now I'd better go and settle my other guest
in the shed for the evening. I'll pop round in the morning at
around eight with the garage number,' she explained, handing
Lily the door key.

When the doctor had left, having not eaten since breakfast,
Lily made herself some tea and toast before quickly making the
bed.

She had not yet had time to process the events of the past twenty-four hours, and as she crawled under the duvet, all she wanted was sleep. For once, she fell into a deep, dreamless slumber.

147

Chapter 29

'Hello, is that Marcus? Marcus Cole?'

'Yes.'

'Hello, it's Amanda. Ellie's mother.'

'Yes, of course.' He could hardly hear her above the sounds of *Sweet Child O' Mine*. 'Sorry, can you hold on?' he half-shouted. 'It's noisy here. I'm in the bar.' He glanced over at Julia, mouthed 'sorry', then went upstairs to take the call. 'Hello? Can you hear me now?' Amanda asked.

'Yes. How are you and your family?' he asked, pushing Horace and Bella along the couch so he could sit.

'We're fine, thanks. I know this is out of the blue, but you did ask me to call if Ellie or Mum remembered anything about the day of the accident.'

'Yes, of course. What is it?'

'I've found something in Ellie's room that may, or may not, help you. I was moving the furniture in there because we're redecorating. She's getting too old for fairy-themed wallpaper.'

'I see.'

'Anyway, I found a little silver trinket – a dragon's head – behind her chest of drawers. I asked her what it was because I hadn't seen it before. At first, she seemed unsure, but then she remembered and looked worried. She told me she found it on the road that day... where the accident took place.'

She hesitated.

'Please, go on.'

'After the collision, when the biker had gone, and she couldn't wake Mum up, she got out of the car. She ran up and down the road, hoping someone would come. She remembers tripping and falling, and that was when she saw something shiny among the leaves. So, she picked it up and put it in her pocket. When someone finally arrived, she was back in the car, clinging to her grandmother, and had forgotten what she had found. Ellie thinks she may have put it on top of her chest of drawers later that day. Somehow, it must have got knocked off and fallen down the back. She then forgot all about it. I realise it may have nothing to do with the accident, but I thought it wouldn't harm for me to take it in to work.'

'Work?' Marcus probed.

'I work in a jeweller's.'

'Oh yes, sorry, I remember now.'

'I asked the manager if he had seen anything like it before and luckily, he recognised what it was. When he was younger, he had worked in a collectables' shop that sold accessories for bikers. He says he's pretty sure it's part of a wallet chain.'

'A wallet chain? What's that?'

'That's what I said. Apparently, the chain attaches to a person's belt, and the other end fastens to a wallet kept in a jeans pocket. He said often the chain is just hooked onto a belt and worn as a fashion accessory. He thinks the head is a link in a chain of other heads. As I said, it may be nothing.'

'I'm not sure, but I would like to see it.'

'You can have it. It's of no use to us.'

'Well, I appreciate you thinking of me.' Marcus paused for

a moment. 'I take it you haven't mentioned this to the police yet?'

'No,' replied Amanda. 'I was in two minds, but... Well, I'm not sure why I've contacted you instead; it just felt like the right thing to do.'

Amanda agreed that Marcus could come straight over to collect the trinket. So, a short time later, he parked outside her house in West Hill and rang the doorbell. Amanda invited him in, explaining that Ellie was on a sleepover and that her husband was out for the evening. He wondered how her husband felt about his wife handing the dragon's head over to him rather than the police. Either way, it was her decision.

'Here,' Amanda said handing the chain link over to him.

He studied it with interest. Maybe he could trace where the chain had been purchased, but it was a long shot (it would have been bought at least two years ago and there were a lot of antiques and bric-a-brac shops in town). And that's if it was even bought locally.

'Thanks.' He stuffed the trinket inside his jacket pocket and turned to leave.

'Marcus?' He turned back around. 'It's frightening to think that Ellie and my mother could have been killed that day. I want you to know that whether that dragon head helps you or not... whatever happens. Your secret is safe with me. If anyone ever asks after you. I will say you came to visit me and my mother once at her home seeking some sort of closure. That's all. Okay?'

Marcus held her gaze for a moment and nodded his understanding. He guessed that her husband probably knew no more about him dropping by tonight then he did about the link in his pocket.

His mind raced as he drove back to Lostmor. He felt terrible running out on Julia after speaking to Amanda. Unsurprisingly, she had looked bewildered when he dashed for the door, Marcus promising to explain to her as soon as he returned.

His thoughts were interrupted by the sight of a large, white transit van parked near Oliver Bligh's farm. Its lights were off, but the road was iridescent, bathed in moonlight. He glimpsed the face of the man in the driver's seat as he drove past. He looked heavyset, with short, thick hair. A couple of things struck Marcus: firstly, he recognised the man and, secondly, why was he parked there?

'Fuck it,' Douglas muttered under his breath. He hadn't noticed the truck's headlights in his rear-view mirror or heard it approaching until it was almost upon him. Luke was down by the side of the van, screened from the road and busy watching the farm through a gap in the hedge.

'Luke! Get back in here.'

Luke got back into the van, sliding the side door quietly shut. 'What's up?'

'I think the landlord from the Black Dog just passed us. He was staring at me.'

'We're not breaking any laws, are we? Anyway, it looks like Bligh's settled in for the night. We may as well get going.'

The brothers had also been watching Penwyth House. So far, Luke had only seen one person leave the estate – last weekend, a woman in a red Ford Fiesta. Whoever she was, he hadn't seen her since, and she had a face you remembered.

After she drove off, he had waited a good hour before approaching on foot. It was dark, and he kept to the drive for as long as he dared. Then, he crept closer, using the woodland as cover, until he saw the ominous outline of the mansion house. There were no lights on, or cars parked out front. This was his third visit. Each time, the place looked deserted. He was convinced no one was living there. Last time, he had walked right up to the front door and peered through the window, but he couldn't see a thing, even using a torch. He had been tempted to smash the glass, but then what? If there were valuables inside, he might need the van, which was parked on the road. Having walked around the side of the house and discovered a good place to break in through a basement door, he had left.

Now, Douglas started the engine and drove off, only flicking his lights on when they were past the farm. Luke still didn't know Oliver Bligh's connection to Penwyth House but was beginning to think he was just there on business, as his brother had suggested, maybe doing some work on the estate.

While Luke had been staking out the farm and Penwyth House, Douglas had stayed at home, rebuilding the old man's Triumph. The motorbike had been in pieces in the garage for years. Douglas was always good at mechanics, so Luke had encouraged him to have a go at rebuilding it. This had not only kept him sober but out of his hair too, until yesterday, when Douglas had reached a hiatus, waiting for a new bike part to arrive.

Ahead, Marcus was driving back to the Black Dog inn

when, on impulse, he parked along the high street. It was the only road into Lostmor, so it was possible the van might pass him unless it had turned off. Still, it was worth a shot.

His patience was rewarded when it drove past a few minutes later. Marcus followed, making sure he kept his distance. The van drove out of town using the coastal road. He slowed a little in case Douglas caught sight of his headlights. When its rear lights disappeared down a single-track lane, Marcus pulled in. Being unsure if it led to a dwelling or was just a dead end, he decided not to follow in case he gave himself away. For now, he swung the truck around and headed back to town.

Douglas had looked decidedly suspicious parked outside Bligh Farm. Whatever he was up to, he intended to find out.

Chapter 30

'Good morning. Did you sleep okay?' asked Dr Morgan when Lily opened the door to her the following morning. 'Very well, thank you.'

The doctor breezed into the kitchen, promptly followed by a large ginger cat.

'Who's this then?' Lily asked.

'Oh, that's Red, he thinks he's a dog, bless him. Follows me everywhere.'

'Aw. He's lovely.' She bent to stroke him as he wound himself around her legs.

'He's good company. I have another at home asleep,' she smiled. 'Here's the number for Taskers, the garage I mentioned. I don't think they open until nine.'

'Thank you. I'll give them a call. Hopefully, they can get it towed away for me. I found a taxi number on the fridge. I'll get them to drop me down to the garage later.'

'Well, don't feel you have to rush off. Taskers is the only garage in Lostmor and they can be busy. You're welcome to hang around here until you know the verdict. Fingers crossed it's nothing too serious.'

'Oh, I hope not.'

'Worst comes to the worst, you can stay another night,' she suggested. 'Up to you, of course.'

'That is generous, but I feel like I've already imposed enough.'

'Not at all,' she smiled, sympathetically. 'I like to see this place being used. Usually, it only gets booked up in the summer months. As it stands, I've got no one booked in until Easter!'

'Well, if you're sure? I'll have to see what the garage says. If there is a delay, it would be easier than trying to find a hotel.'

'Great. I have to open up the surgery for nine, but I'll be back sometime after lunch.'

'I should pay you now for last night in case my car is roadworthy sooner than we think.'

'Why not wait until you know if you're staying? Here's my mobile number.' Dr Morgan gave Lily her business card. 'If your car is fixed this morning, just give me a call. You can always leave me a cheque. If not, we can settle up tomorrow.'

'That's very trusting of you.'

'I like to think I'm a good judge of character,' she smiled. 'Good luck! Let me know how you get on. Come along, Red!'

Lily called Taskers at 9:00 a.m. The owner said they would tow her car away at 10:00 and let her know the problem as soon as possible. At 1:00 p.m., having not heard from them, she gave them a call. The owner apologised. Unfortunately, a previous job was taking longer than expected. They hadn't had a chance to look at hers yet but would call her back with their progress by 3:00. Lily texted Dr Morgan to explain.

Now she had time on her hands, it wasn't so easy to put Oliver out of her mind. She thought back to yesterday morning and the conversation that had changed everything between them. She longed to call him – to hear his voice again. But what would she say? What could she say?

A short time later, there was a knock at the door.

'Hello!' Dr Morgan smiled. 'Gosh, that was a busy morning at the practice! Sorry, I didn't check my messages until I was leaving work. Have you heard yet?'

Just then Lily's mobile rang. It was Taskers. After a brief conversation, she hung up.

'It won't be ready until tomorrow. Apparently, it was a faulty alternator that drained the battery. They replaced that and got it going but then realised one of my front tyres had a slow puncture. They don't have the right one in stock, but have ordered one in.'

'Just think, if you hadn't broken down, you could have had a blowout on the motorway.'

'I know. That doesn't bear thinking about!'

'Well... as you're stuck here a little longer, why don't you come round for supper in a bit? You can't live on bread and cookies for the rest of your stay.'

Lily looked surprised. 'It's too kind. I can make do with toast, honestly.'

'It's only chicken pasta from the fridge. It's no bother and to be honest, it would be nice to have some company for a change – the cats aren't big on conversation!'

'All right, thanks, that would be nice. I feel I'm doing nothing but thanking you, Dr Morgan.'

'Please call me Janet, everyone does.'

'Janet,' she smiled. 'I'm Lily, by the way.'

That evening, Lily gazed around the charming kitchen. Unlike The Old Stable, which had been renovated in quite a modern style, Janet's home was similar to Kleger Cottage – traditional Cornish stone with slate-tiled floors and low-beamed ceilings.

'Please, take a seat. Make yourself at home. I'm just warming the food. Would you like tea, coffee, or perhaps a glass of wine? I have some Chardonnay.'

'Wine would be great.'

A tortoise-shell cat lay flat out next to Red in front of a recently lit wood-burning stove. Lily carefully stepped over them.

'That's Admiral,' Janet smiled, placing a casserole dish on the table. Lily's stomach rumbled; she hadn't eaten much in the past twenty-four hours.

'Someone left them outside the surgery, must be two years ago. They stole my heart the moment I set eyes on them. I've no idea where they came from but they're very affectionate.'

'Well, they certainly seem at home. Oh, that reminds me – how's Percy? Is he okay?'

Janet joined her at the table and poured them both some wine. 'Our feathered friend is tucking into some grain as we speak. He seems quite content in the shed for now. I'll drop him home tomorrow. Where did you say he came from?'

'Penwyth House. It's on an old estate about three miles back the way we came. Joe Newman, the man I mentioned, is the groundsman there. He lives at Edhen Cottage. But I can return Percy once I've got my car back. It's the least I can do.'

'Oh, I'd forgotten about that old place. Isn't that where

there was a terrible accident years ago?'

'That's right.'

'I didn't realise there was anyone living there.' She passed Lily the serving spoon so she could help herself.

'This is delicious,' Lily commented, changing the subject.

'I'm glad you like it. I always end up making way too much, so you're doing me a favour,' she said, spooning some into her own bowl. 'What is it you do, Lily? Is your work in Bristol?'

'I run an art gallery there. I had planned on reopening it yesterday, but I guess a few more days won't make any difference. I'm just not used to having so much time off.'

'I see, how interesting. So, you're an artist?'

'Yes, I'm lucky. I get to do what I love for a living. It doesn't feel like work.'

'How wonderful to have such talent. I've always wished I could draw, but I'm utterly useless! What sort of thing do you paint?'

'Landscapes and seascapes are my passion. Give me a blazing sunrise or a raging storm at sea and I'm at my happiest.'

'Well, there should be plenty of inspiration for that around here.'

'Lostmor is beautiful. Kleger Cottage has panoramic views of the coast. Whilst staying there, I would stand outside looking out to sea and visualise painting it.'

'Perhaps next time you're here, you'll have time to enjoy the scenery a bit more. There are amazing walks all around here. I take it you had to close the gallery while you dealt with your late mother's affairs?'

'Yes. It's going to take me a while to finish sorting out the house, though. I think I'll be making a few more trips back to

Lostmor.'

'Is your mother's house in town?'

Lily took a long sip of the crisp wine. There wasn't much point in lying. 'No, actually her home – our home – was Penwyth House.'

'Oh! Where Percy lives?'

'I was born there, but no one has lived at the house for a long time – not for years. Mother and I moved to Bristol when I was still a child. I'm only here now because of an unknown will she left with a local solicitor.'

'How mysterious. But weren't you here, anyway, clearing your mother's house out?'

Lily drained her glass. 'No. The reading of the will came first. The matter of the house came later.' The food and wine had relaxed her, and she found herself opening up to Janet.

'This will sound unbelievable, but until I read the contents of the will, I thought Penwyth was sold long ago. I was just a child when we left. That's why I rented Kleger Cottage. I thought I was just here for a quick meeting then leaving again. It was a total shock to me that I had inherited my childhood home.'

Janet looked stunned. She put her knife and fork together and sat forward, resting her chin in her hands. 'Goodness! You really have had a lot to deal with, haven't you?'

She nodded. 'I didn't know that my mother arranged for Joe to stay on and look after the grounds, either. I came across Percy when meeting with him yesterday. And then I discovered that he keeps birds. Lots of them! Housed in a giant aviary on the estate.'

Janet was intrigued by her guest's story. 'So, your friend is an aviculturist.'

'Apparently so.' Lily smiled, gratefully accepting a top-up of wine.

'How about you, Janet? Have you always lived in Lostmor?'

'Not always but I've been here a long time, nearly thirty years. I moved here for work and fell in love with the place. Now, I think I'm just about accepted as a local,' she joked. 'Especially amongst the farming community. My time is very much split between the surgery and visiting the surrounding farms. Luckily there is another surgery in West Hill, and we often cover for each other.'

They chatted amiably for a while. Janet was a charming host. She regaled funny stories about some of the stranger animal encounters she'd had over the years; Lily explained how much renovation work Penwyth House needed and her plans to sell it. But Oliver was never far from her thoughts. She imagined him sat in front of the fire at his farm and wondered if he was thinking about her, too.

'Are you all right?' Janet asked as Lily yawned.

'I'm sorry. I think all this food and wine has made me sleepy.'

'I've been talking too much, I expect.'

'Not at all. I've enjoyed myself.' She stifled another yawn. 'Oh, dear. I may have to excuse myself. Thank you, though, for a lovely evening. Will I see you in the morning before I leave?'

'I'll pop round about eight again, before I go to work.'

Lily soon fell into an exhausted sleep, but in the early hours of the morning she awoke, unsure for a moment where she was. She had been dreaming and was drenched in sweat.

Once more she had seen her younger self, a frightened child, standing in the open doorway leading to the roof. She hesitated, not knowing what to do. Her father was holding his arms out to Alice as she ran towards him through the rain. Lily heard her mother calling to her from the house. She ran back down the steep stairs as fast as she could, but as her foot reached the bottom step, it felt like an invisible force was holding her there. Again, a strange, pinched face appeared, almost like a warning, telling her to stop.

She awoke with arms flailing, trying to protect herself, but from what she did not know.

Chapter 31

It was nearly 11:00 p.m. and the bar staff were calling last orders. As Marcus was still not home, Julia decided to take the dogs for a short walk along the seafront and then leave. Earlier, she had heard Andy say it was someone called Amanda, Maggie's daughter, on the phone, so that must be who he'd gone to see. But why in such a hurry?

When they first met at Fern Retreat, Julia was instantly attracted to Marcus. At thirty-nine, he was seven years older than her, but they had hit it off immediately. She liked the deep timbre of his voice and his wry humour. When he returned to pick up Horace, she willingly accepted his offer of help.

And she had let him kiss her. Since then, things had moved quite fast between them, but it felt right, and she had shrugged off any concerns. In the past, she had been too cautious; trying to fit in with her ex-boyfriend Alex's idea of what was best for them. Alex tried to talk her out of setting up kennels. He was keen for them to marry and start a family which she hadn't felt ready for. Not surprisingly, things hadn't worked out. After that, she was determined to follow her heart.

Buying Fern Retreat and following her dream was exciting and meeting Marcus seemed like the cherry on top.

But what did she really know about him? He didn't like talking about himself. When she asked him about his family, he told her he was divorced with no children. He had lost both parents years ago and he was an only child. In other words, he was alone.

Now, as Julia turned around and slowly walked the dogs back to the inn, she hoped he would be waiting for her, with a perfectly reasonable explanation for his sudden departure.

She was relieved to see his truck in the car park and quickly took the stairs to his apartment. 'Hi,' she said, as Horace clambered up beside Marcus on the couch.

'Hi. Thanks for walking the dogs.'

She sat down next to him. 'You okay?'

He nodded.

'So, what's going on?'

'I'm sorry I disappeared.'

'What happened? I was just about to leave.'

'I can explain. Do you have time for a nightcap?'

'Okay.'

Marcus returned with two whiskies. 'I haven't been honest with you. But only because I didn't want to burden you. We haven't known each other that long... And it's hard for me to talk about my past.' He paused, trying to find the words.

'Marcus, what is it?'

'A long time ago, I was married, just as I said. But I didn't tell you about our daughter, Rose.'

She was puzzled. 'You said you didn't have children.'

He took a large swig of his drink before speaking in a lowered voice. 'I don't anymore. She died in a road collision two years ago.'

She took his hand. 'Oh, I'm so sorry.'

'She was on the back of a motorbike. It hit a car head-on.

The accident happened not far from here, in West Hill. I was stationed in Croatia then. I hadn't seen her for over six months. The bike she and her so-called boyfriend were on was stolen. He fled the scene, and the police never traced him. To this day, I don't know who he is.'

'How terrible,' she whispered. *No wonder he sometimes seems distant. He is a father grieving his daughter.*

'He left Rose lying dead in the road and a seriously injured woman alone in the car with her young granddaughter.'

'Did the woman recover?'

'Maggie? Yes, although her daughter, Amanda, told me she still suffers from chronic back pain.'

'What about the girl? Was she hurt?'

'Ellie? No.'

Julia hugged him. She was at a loss as to what to say. 'So, the phone call earlier – I heard someone mention Amanda. Was it Maggie's daughter calling you?'

'That's right. Ellie's mum.' He paused.

She squeezed his hand and studied his face, looking for answers. 'You can trust me.'

'I know.'

'Then please, don't shut me out.'

So, Marcus told her how he discharged himself from the military because he could not cope with losing Rose.

Like the police, he knew her boyfriend had family in Lostmor. When they failed to track him down, he decided to take matters into his own hands.

'So, is that why you moved here?'

'When I left the army, I was a mess – drinking too much. It may sound macabre, choosing to live in the place where she was killed, but in some ways, it helped; it made me feel closer to her. But the real reason I came here was to find the man responsible for her death.

'I didn't have much to go on, and my own efforts were proving fruitless, so I reached out to Maggie. A resourceful ex-colleague of mine helped track her down. She lives in Norfolk and was only visiting West Hill at the time of the accident, staying with her daughter Amanda and her family. I explained who I was over the phone and she agreed that I could visit her at her home. That was the reason I brought Horace to Fern Retreat that day. Norfolk's a long drive, plus it wasn't appropriate to turn up with a dog in tow.

'I hadn't expected to meet Amanda that day, but when I arrived at Maggie's, she was there with Ellie.'

'I see,' she said, trying to take it all in. 'So, tonight Amanda was calling you from West Hill?'

'Because of this,' he said, placing the silver dragon's head on the coffee table. 'When we first met, I asked if she would contact me if Maggie or Ellie remembered anything that might help me find this man.'

'What did they think about you looking for him?'

'Amanda was wary of me at first but I think she understood – she could have lost Ellie and her mother that day. I didn't expect to hear from them, but then she found this behind some drawers in Ellie's room. When she asked where she got it, Ellie said she found it that day on the roadside. She got out of the car and was wandering around looking for help. It was a little used route; it was over half an hour before anyone came across them.'

'Poor Ellie.'

'I know. A terrible thing for her to have gone through.'

'So, what about this?' asked Julia, picking up the dragon's head. 'Why is it important?'

'I don't know that it is yet. Amanda took it to the jeweller where she works and asked the manager if he'd ever seen one like it. Luckily, he knew it was part of a wallet chain, apparently something bikers sometimes wear. That's why she rang me, and why I ran out on you like that. I'm sorry, I shouldn't have, but the chance to finally get my hands on something tangible...'

'It's okay.' She still had questions, but they could wait.

His eyes shone darkly in the low lamplight. 'Julia, we've only known each other a short time, but I care about you. I thought maybe there was a chance for us. But now... I understand if you want to walk away.

'I'm glad you told me about Rose. And it doesn't change how I feel about you. I care, too. But, Marcus, looking for this man can only lead to trouble. Can't you give that dragon's head to the police? They may have resources that can help.'

'Maybe, but so do I.'

'All right, let's suppose you do find this person. Then what will you do?'

'Oh, I *will* find him, no matter how long it takes. And when I do, I'm going to kill him.'

PART III

Chapter 32

At The Old Stable, Lily finally retrieved her car the following morning from Taskers (courtesy of Janet dropping her into Lostmor). Having folded down the back seats, they gently manoeuvred Percy into the back. Janet watched in amusement as Lily drove away, the bird's tiny head staring passively back at her through the rear window.

At Penwyth Estate, Lily stopped close to the woods and lifted Percy out, who seemed none the worse for his little adventure.

She intended to turn around and head straight back to Bristol but found herself drawn to the house. She stepped back, hands on hips, staring up at the roof. Chimney stacks and spires of varying heights protruded like a giant pumpkin mouth of jagged teeth. *Now is as good a time as any*, she thought. Impulsively, she grabbed the house keys from the glove box.

A few moments later she was inside, gazing at the resplendent staircase. Since cleaning the area as best she could, the worst of the cobwebs were gone, and the newly polished stairs dazzled in the light streaming through the dome. Lily walked slowly up the stairs, turning left where it divided in the middle. She lightly trailed a hand along the cool banister. Today, no familiar wind whistled through the chimneys nor rattled the windows. The house was silent, as if it had been waiting all these years for her return, for this moment.

Suddenly, a familiar feeling of foreboding came over her and her heart quickened.

She heard voices below, raised voices...

June 1971

From where she sat on the staircase, Lily saw her father standing in the hallway. He had slammed the front door a little too hard.

'Shh, Vincent, you'll wake the girls,' her mother hissed at him as he sloped into the parlour room.

Lily crept downstairs and hid behind the open door.

'Did you even remember it was Alice's birthday today?' Sited on either side of an ornate marble fireplace, her mother sat on one of two burgundy velvet couches.

'Of course I did. I got waylaid, that's all,' he slurred.

'Oh please, spare me the thinly-veiled excuses.'

Through the gap, Lily watched her father lurch to the dresser and pour himself a whisky. Her mother regarded him with disdain. She no longer looked afraid of him. Now, her eyes were filled with hate.

'Do you know how many times Alice asked where you were?'

He didn't answer.

'She's going to work it out soon, now she's getting older, just what a drunk her father is. Just like Lily has.'

Lily shrank back a bit, convinced they must know she was there.

Her father ignored her mother's outburst and asked if Alice enjoyed her party.

'Yes, no thanks to you. But at bedtime, she cried because you had promised to be there. I had to read her stories to console her until she finally fell asleep.'

'I told you, I was waylaid. It was business.'

'Don't make me laugh, Vincent. I can't remember the last time you did a day's work!'

'Don't push me or you'll regret it.'

'Regret. Now that is a word I understand. Aren't you wondering why I'm still up? Why I've waited for you?'

'Do tell,' he sighed.

'I want a divorce,' she said quickly.

Vincent paused a moment, then swung unsteadily round to face her. She could see a vein pulsing in his temple.

'Don't be ridiculous. Have you gone mad?'

'I can assure you I'm perfectly sane. I have never been more serious. I will be seeing my solicitor in the morning. I was hoping that we could be grownups about this, for the children's sake. Either way, I'm leaving you. Or, more accurately, you'll be the one who's leaving. After all, I do own Penwyth Estate.'

Behind the door, Lily gasped and shrunk back against the wall. She couldn't believe it.

'Listen here, you little bitch,' he snarled, 'you are not throwing me out of my own home.'

Lily dared to peer through the doorway once more. He was sitting opposite her now, leaning forward, drunken eyes bulging. He grabbed her mother roughly by the arms.

'I am your husband, and if you insist on doing this, I will fight for my share. I'm entitled to half.'

'No court in the land would grant you anything,' she mocked. 'What have you ever contributed? Not to mention your infidelities. Most of the town knows. I imagine it would be fairly easy to prove.'

Her father's eyes narrowed. 'I'll take the children.'

Her mother looked shocked, and her bravado quickly fell away. She must have expected him to fly into a rage, attack her, even. But not this. This was far worse.

'Why? What interest have you ever shown in them?'

'They're my flesh and blood.'

'You can't just take them. I won't allow it. The law won't allow it!'

'The law!' he scorned, pulling her closer still. She tried to push him away, but he was angry. He suddenly let go, pushing her back against the couch.

'Go ahead! Divorce me. See what happens.' He spat the words at her. 'Lily and Alice are mine. If I have to leave this house, you can be sure I'll be back for them. You won't know when. Maybe at night when you're asleep or at work one afternoon. You can't be with them all the time.' His lip curled in an ugly sneer as he rose to refill his glass.

The colour drained from her mother's face. He knew he had worried her.

'Maybe I'll take them abroad, start again, somewhere far from here where you'll never find them. You think it's just talk? Try me.' He smirked, raising his glass to her.

She composed herself and sat up straight. 'Actually, Vincent, they're not strictly speaking yours. At least, not both of them.'

'What do you mean?' He swayed, regarding her suspiciously.

'You're not the only one who strayed from this joke of a marriage.'

'You're lying. I would have known,' he retaliated.

She laughed out loud. 'How would you? You were never here, and when you were, you were too drunk to realise what was going on right under your nose.'

He paused, trying to think his way out of the chemical fog shrouding his brain. 'You're telling me ... what, that Alice is not mine? That you slept with someone? That you're a dirty little whore!'

Lily's hand went to her mouth.

'Not Alice, Lily,' she replied, unfazed by his insult. 'It's true, Vincent. But unlike you, I didn't sleep with just anybody.' She spoke calmly. 'I had an affair. He made me happy, and I loved him.'

His face turned red with fury. 'Who is he?'

'It doesn't matter. It was over a long time ago. I ended it because he wanted me to leave you. How I wish I'd been brave enough. When I realised I was carrying his baby, I was so happy. But I was young and scared of what you might do. So, I made out she was yours. I shared your bed for the first time in months; I lied to you about my dates. You lost so many days to drinking, your memory was fuzzy.' She gave a small, humourless laugh. 'I even convinced myself for a while.'

'But her birth certificate.'

'I lied.'

He drained his glass and threw it at the fireplace. The sound of the glass smashing propelled Lily to move. She strode up the stairs as fast as she could and stood breathless behind her bedroom door, her heart pounding. She heard her father's angry voice then heavy footsteps on the landing.

Chapter 33
January 1995

'Lily? Is that you?' called Joe. He could just make her out through the shafts of light on the stairs. She was ashen and sat clinging to the baluster.

'I saw your car, and the door was open. What's happened? Are you all right?' He quickly went to her, mindful that it was the first time in over twenty years he had stepped foot inside Penwyth House.

'Joe,' she whispered, visibly shaken. 'I'm okay, really. I just felt lightheaded.'

'Why don't you come back to mine for a few minutes?' he said, helping her to her feet. 'Here, take my arm.'

They walked slowly to Edhen Cottage, where he made her a large mug of hot, sweet tea while she rested on the couch.

'Are you sick? Shall I call a doctor?' he asked, looking anxious.

'No, I'll be fine. I was just... unnerved.'

'Unnerved by what?'

'Sometimes,' she admitted, 'I have nightmares about the night Father and Alice died. I can never quite piece things together. A moment ago, I had a flashback. But this was different. It felt much more real. Usually, I recall standing on the roof of the house, watching my father. There's a storm. And Alice is there, running towards him. Mother calls my name, and I turn to go. But there's always this strange man blocking my way.'

Joe looked bewildered. They had never spoken of that evening, and it upset him to see her so traumatised. 'Lily,' he said quietly, 'it was only me and your family there that evening. There was no other man. You were just a little girl who witnessed something terrible. It's understandable you've had nightmares. Maybe it's time for you to let it go.'

'I don't know, Joe. I don't think so. Since coming home, I've learned so much about my family, and you.' She smiled at him affectionately. 'I want to know the rest; *need* to know the rest.

'In the house just then, it felt like I was watching a film. I saw my parents arguing like I did that evening. I must have blocked out what happened, but being here is helping me to remember.'

'What were your parents fighting about?'

'Before I tell you, can I ask you something?'

'Anything. I have nothing to hide. Not anymore.'

She gazed into his kind, emerald-green eyes. 'Are you my father?'

'It's possible. The truth is, I don't know. By the time I discovered Elizabeth was pregnant, we were already apart and barely speaking. There was one day, we found ourselves alone, and she could no longer hide her bump. I asked her if the baby was mine. She denied it, said that you were Vincent's.' He paused. 'It feels wrong to be talking this way about your family.'

'Please, Joe, tell me what you know.'

He sighed and sat back in the armchair. 'We met often for

the year or so that we were together. It wasn't that difficult because Vincent was not around much. But for some reason, he was at home all the time for about three weeks that summer. So, Elizabeth and I agreed to stop seeing each other for a while; she didn't want to risk being caught. It wasn't until much later, when I asked her about the baby, that she told me what happened back then.

'In a drunken rage one night, he kicked in her bedroom door and forced himself upon her. She had tried to fight him off but couldn't. She said she never told me for fear of what I might do. But that was how she knew who the father was because she and I were not together during that time. I'm sorry, this is not an easy thing to explain.'

'It's okay. Go on.'

'Well, I believed her. But years later, after the accident – Joe's mouth twitched slightly – 'and you and Elizabeth had gone, I had a lot of time to think.' He swallowed. 'I always wondered about you.'

'I don't quite know what to say.' She gazed at him through a sheen of tears. 'I'm beginning to understand how terrible this must have been for you. You lost everything, and I've hardly given you a thought all these years.'

'You didn't know. How could you?'

Lily wiped her eyes and tried to gather her thoughts. 'You asked me what my parents argued about that evening. I remember I was on the stairs and saw Father come in. It was late, and he was drunk. Unusually, Mother was still up. I watched him go into the parlour and heard raised voices. I crept down, hid behind the open door and listened. She was angry with him for missing Alice's birthday. I'd never heard her speak to him that way before, with such disdain. But I was even more shocked when she asked him for a divorce.

'Things got out of hand. She told him he had to leave Penwyth House. He retaliated, saying that if she made him go, he would come back for Alice and me when she least expected it. He taunted her, saying he would take us far away and she would never see us again.' She paused, trying to recall her mother's words. 'That was when she told him about your affair. She said it was over long ago but that she had been in love and had had his child, and I was that child.'

Lily reached for Joe's hand. 'I think she finally told him the truth, and only lied to protect you and her family. Who knows? Maybe she would have been honest with you too if events hadn't taken such a terrible turn.'

'Thank you,' he whispered, his bottom lip quivering. 'Thank you for sharing that with me.' His eyes filled with tears. 'I never forgot about any of you. I often wondered where you were and what you and Elizabeth might be doing. Seeing you again and having you home has made me a happy man. But if I *am* your father that is more than I ever dared dream of.'

Chapter 34

Later that day, at her Bristol apartment, Lily played back her answerphone messages. As expected, none were from Oliver. Her surveyor had called informing her that he was still working on the report for Penwyth Estate and would forward it to her as soon as possible A few clients had left enquires about submissions, and there was a message from Janet:

'Hello, Lily! I hope you managed to drop Percy off okay. Don't forget to give me a call if you ever need a place to stay when you're in Lostmor. Best of luck with everything. Bye.'

She smiled; it was nice to hear a friendly voice. She also had three messages on her mobile from a slightly worried Timothy, reminding her she had missed their weekend appointment. He had attained copies of the deeds for Penwyth House showing the estate's layout and borders, and they were supposed to discuss the parcel of land she was bequeathing Joe. After her unsettling experience at Penwyth, she had completely forgotten.

The following day, Lily returned the missed calls and apologised to Timothy. They rescheduled for next Saturday, and he cheerfully agreed to her offer of buying him a drink afterwards at the Black Dog inn.

Over the next week, Lily spent long hours at The Blue catching up on her commissioned work, but she was preoccupied with what she had learnt from Joe. She desperately wanted to tell Oliver but what if she was wrong? Megan had no reason to falsify her son's birth certificate or to make up such a thing. But at the back of her mind was a nagging doubt. What if her mother wasn't sure who her father was? She could have told Vincent he wasn't her father in the heat of the moment or because that's what she wanted to believe.

In her small studio at the gallery, she distracted herself by working on a large, commissioned landscape. Losing herself in the task, she blended thick, bold strokes of green and gold, adding rolling sun-drenched hills. At the forefront, she used her palette knife to edge in autumnal trees and build up their leafy texture. The scene was taken from a holiday photograph, a cherished memory, shortly to become a piece of art and a wedding anniversary present for her client's wife.

At closing time, lights flickered on in the shopfronts opposite. Outside, a steady queue of cars crawled towards the brow of the hill, and people hurried past, eager to get home. It was early March and still light, but tall buildings blocked out large segments of daylight, and the street looked grey and dreary. Returning to her apartment, the answer machine remained stubbornly dormant. She felt deflated. Something had shifted: her perception of what mattered; things that previously seemed important, she no longer cared about. Her apartment and gallery were just rented spaces. Her mother's passing made her realise there was nothing to keep her in Bristol anymore. Her neglected friends were all gone, and she had pushed other people away. Until she had met Oliver.

Now, even if their relationship was doomed, she knew she couldn't return to her old way of life. Her brief time at

Penwyth House had given her a sense of belonging. And even though her recent recollection had shaken her, it also revealed much about her family.

She stared at the grand Georgian buildings on the opposite side of the leafy street and wished she was back in Lostmor, spending time with Joe or visiting Janet again at her quaint little cottage. Even her regular business meetings with Timothy were always a pleasure. She realised that Lostmor was no longer just about settling her mother's affairs – she felt drawn to the place and to the people she'd met.

Over the past few weeks, she and Joe had grown close, and even if she and Oliver were not reconciled, she so wanted to believe that this dear man was her father. Any feelings she had for Vincent had drifted away over time. All she had left were vague memories of him drunk, angry, or both. She sighed and drew the curtains on the now amber-lit street.

That evening, she called Janet to let her know about Percy's safe return. She mentioned she would be back on Saturday and agreed to pop round for tea in the morning before her meeting with Timothy.

Whatever her future now held, she knew it would no longer be in Bristol because her heart was still in Lostmor.

Chapter 35

Julia had been put in an impossible situation since Marcus revealed the truth about his daughter and his desire to avenge her death. She couldn't begin to imagine what it was like to lose a child or what that did to a person. But she was afraid he was on an endless search that would only cause him more pain. And what if he did find him?

Marcus wasn't your average guy. He was Major Marcus Cole, a decorated officer, who had seen armed combat on numerous occasions. Unlike most, he had killed before. She had tried to dissuade him. Surely, he didn't want to go to prison for murder. But he refused to listen, so that was that. She told him she couldn't be with him anymore.

He tried to persuade her to stay, but she had to walk away.

She threw herself into her busy new role at Fern Retreat and, as agreed, Marcus kept his distance. But a few weeks later, after another evening spent alone and missing him, she impulsively picked up the phone and dialled his number. Half an hour later, he was on her doorstep.

'I'm so happy to see you,' she said, hugging him tightly.

'Me too,' he whispered in her ear.

They talked late into the night. She was keen to tell him how things were going at the kennels, and he listened with interest. They laughed a lot and enjoyed each other's company and, for once, didn't speak of Rose.

After that evening, they spent more and more time together. Their brief separation brought them closer.

Late one night, as they sat by the fire enjoying a glass of wine, he told her about his family. He spoke of the good times they had shared but also of his regrets at his long absences from their lives.

'Do you still want to find the man responsible for the accident?' she tentatively asked.

'Yes,' he said, with finality.

Julia knew then that she had to decide. If she stayed with him, one day she might have to face some very serious consequences. Or she walked away now, this time for ever.

She had decided to stay.

'I don't want to lose you again,' he whispered, after the first time they made love. 'You have changed my life. You have given me hope.' He held her close and stroked her long blonde hair. She had kissed him softly on the lips.

Now, she lay listening to his slow, rhythmic breathing. She lightly ran her hand down the hard contours of his back and felt the numerous scars across his torso. He didn't like to talk about his time in the military, but his body told its own story. She understood that he had seen and experienced things he would rather forget.

A few nights later, she noticed him missing from her bed. From the window, she saw him leaning on the paddock gate in the moonlight. She ventured outside to join him and gently touched his arm. He swung around so fast he made her jump. The moment was fleeting, but she saw a glint of something behind those steely grey eyes that looked like rage. She wanted to ask what was wrong, but suddenly, she was afraid of the answer. Then his expression had softened.

'I'm sorry,' he smiled. 'I couldn't sleep. Come on, it's cold; let's go back inside.'

Chapter 36

'Hello! Come in, come in!' Janet took Lily's coat and scarf and showed her into the lounge, returning shortly with tea for them both.

'Believe it or not,' she said, gently sliding the cats along the couch so she could sit, 'these two do sometimes venture out during the day!'

Lily laughed. 'They seem low maintenance at least.'

'True. I used to own a springer spaniel called Bailey. We'd go walking on the moors every day. I still miss him. But work's busier than ever. I don't have the time to commit to another dog. Maybe one day, when I retire. How about you? Do you have any pets at home?'

'Not now. When we first moved to Bristol, Mother bought me this beautiful pure white kitten. He was such a minute ball of fluff that I named him Tiny. Little did we know he would grow into the most enormous tom!'

They chatted amiably, Lily relaying her busy week at The Blue. She had just finished her client's painting in time for their anniversary. Janet cheerfully recounted her attempts to trim the trotters of a big old, lop-eared pig called Gloria at nearby Willow Farm.

'Oh, and I bumped into Oliver Bligh earlier outside the Spar...'

'Oh? Is he well?'

'I'm not sure. I mentioned that I'd bumped into you when your car broke down and that you'd ended up staying at The Old Stable for a few nights. He looked at me strangely then rushed off without another word. Something was off with him.' She leant forward. 'You can tell me to sod off if you like, but did you two have further words or something?'

'Well, as you've brought the subject up, yes.' Lily paused. 'I was quite close to Oliver for a while.'

'Really?'

Lily explained how Oliver had dropped by Kleger Cottage to apologise for being rude to her at the farm and then cheekily asked her out for a drink.

Janet's face brightened. 'Like a date?'

'I suppose it was. And despite our rocky start, I found myself warming to him. Then he offered to help me with the removals at Penwyth House, which turned into several weeks of seeing each other most days and well... We quickly became more than just friends.'

Janet could tell from Lily's troubled expression that there was a 'but' coming.

'Things were going well,' she sighed. 'But something unexpected happened that changed everything...'

'Goodness. What?'

'His mother left him a letter. She asked her solicitor not to pass it to him until six months after her death. He presumes because the contents were upsetting, she thought it best to wait until her funeral was over and things had settled down.'

Janet looked concerned.

'What I'm about to tell you, can I ask that this remains just between us?' Lily asked.

'Of course. You have my word.'

'It's just that this is deeply personal, and Oliver doesn't know I'm confiding in you.

'The letter his mother left for him was a confession. In it, she said that George was not his real father.'

'What? Are you sure?'

'Yes. I've seen the letter and Oliver's birth certificate, which backs it up. He'd never seen the certificate before because she told him it was lost, and he had no reason to think otherwise.'

'So, if George wasn't his father, who was?'

'Vincent Sanders.'

'Sanders?' She looked puzzled. 'That's your surname, isn't it?'

'Vincent was my father.'

'Oh, my god!'

'I know how improbable this sounds, but I'm afraid it's true. Oliver and I have different mothers but the same father.'

'So, you're saying Megan had an affair?'

She nodded. 'We don't know the exact circumstances. In her letter, she said it was just the one time. When she fell pregnant, she knew it couldn't be George's. He had contracted measles as a young man and suffered a serious infection that left him sterile. Did Megan ever talk to you about any of this?'

Janet was astounded. 'No, no, she didn't. I mean, we were good friends, but she never spoke of it. And there's no chance Megan could have been wrong?'

'I wish she was, but how? Why would she lie? She carried the secret for so long, it seems that knowing her time was short she wanted to come clean, get it off her chest.'

'I suppose… And what were the chances that you and Oliver would ever meet?'

Lily met Janet's gaze. 'I know. I've been trying to come to terms with it. I was in shock when he told me; we both were. I just walked out on him and haven't seen him since.

'That was the same day my car broke down. I left Bligh Farm that morning.' She so rarely spoke about personal matters that talking about Oliver upset her and her eyes filled with tears. 'And since then,' she sniffed, 'I have uncovered even more secrets about my own family…'

'Oh, Lily, have you been dealing with all of this on your own?'

'Trying to.'

Janet fetched her some tissues. 'Well, you don't have to anymore,' she reassured her. 'Now, why don't you tell me everything?'

So, Lily did. She told her about losing Alice and Vincent in such tragic circumstances and the nightmares she'd experienced ever since; of her growing friendship with Joe and his eventual confession to having an affair with her mother and the resultant pregnancy.

'So, what you're saying is that it's possible Joe is your birth father, not Vincent?'

'Yes.'

'Have you asked Joe?'

'I did. At the time he thought he might be, but my mother denied it. He thinks that's why she broke it off between them. She was frightened of Vincent and of what he might do if he found out about their affair, let alone a baby.'

'And if Joe is your father, and Megan and Vincent are

Oliver's birth parents—'

'It means Oliver and I are not related after all. But he doesn't know about Joe yet. I'm going to ask Joe if he would be prepared to do a DNA paternity test.'

'Do you think he will?'

'I think so. I'm going to drop in at Edhen Cottage after I've met with Timothy.

'Sorry for getting upset like that, Janet. I've been bottling it all up for so long.'

Janet leant across the coffee table and took Lily's hand. 'I'm glad you confided in me. I know we haven't known each other long, but I hope you consider me a friend and someone you can trust.'

'I do,' she smiled gratefully. 'I want to believe Joe is my real father. Yet it was Vincent who brought me up for the first nine years of my life. So I feel guilty.'

'You mustn't feel that way. You need to know the truth. Everything you've discovered about your family – goodness, it's a lot to process. And then getting involved with someone you like, only to find that your families are entangled by all these secrets.

'From what you've just told me, Vincent was never there for you growing up. When he was, he treated you badly; he treated his whole family badly.' Janet looked thoughtfully at Lily and smiled. 'You have to grab what happiness you can in this life. Tell me, how does Joe feel about the fact that he may be your father?'

'Overwhelmed, I think, but he wants to know the truth as much as I do. It's funny, but even though we hadn't seen each other since I was a child, the moment we met again, I felt there was a bond between us. And this may be wishful thinking, but I think we look similar. We both have green eyes and the same high cheekbones.'

Janet smiled kindly at her. 'Well, I really hope everything works out for you. And remember, whatever the paternity test shows, it won't change the special relationship that the two of you share.'

Later that day, Lily and Timothy entered the Black Dog inn, accompanied by a sharp gust of wind.

Marcus looked up from his paper and folded it in two. 'Hello,' he smiled. 'What can I get you?'

Lily paid for the drinks while Timothy found a table tucked away in a booth. Their meeting at his office had been lengthy. First, she had signed the deeds, giving Joe ownership of his beloved Edhen Cottage and the small acreage they had agreed upon. She just needed Joe to co-sign to make him the new owner. Next, they waded through the surveyor's report for Penwyth and its many highlighted issues. Unsurprisingly the entire roof needed replacing; the west wing was structurally much worse than the east wing, and the interior required major restoration work.

The pub was a welcome interlude after reading endless pages of finite details, but she was secretly itching to get away. She was impatient to see Joe. Not just to hand over the deeds for his home but to ask him to consider taking a paternity test.

'Thanks for the beer,' Timothy said, raising his glass slightly.

She touched it with her soda and lime. She needed a clear

head.

'Sorry for missing our appointment last week. I really appreciate your help in deciphering that report, and with everything else, too. When I first returned, I had no idea the scale of work Penwyth House needed.' She laughed at her naivety. 'What an idiot! It's clearly a massive undertaking.'

'You weren't to know,' he sympathised. 'I imagine all of this has been a very steep learning curve. Have you considered your options? You could get the roof repaired to stop any further deterioration and sell it as it is. It's worth a lot less in its current state, but Lord knows how much it would cost to renovate the place, or how long it would take.'

'I could... but what if I were to go ahead and renovate the entire building? Do you think you could help me find someone to project manage it? Someone who could be on site full-time?'

'If you're sure that's what you want, I'd be happy to help. I know the local estate agents who will doubtless have contacts in the building industry.'

'Okay, thanks,' she smiled. 'I have some family matters to sort out first, but I'll get back to you soon. I really don't know what I would do without you.'

'I'm just doing my job.' He leaned forward slightly and put his hand on her arm. 'How are you? I mean, it must have been difficult coming back to Lostmor and finding out Penwyth was never sold. I hope being here hasn't been too daunting.'

'It has at times. But I've also learnt a lot about my family, and made new friends, which I was not expecting. Revisiting Penwyth House has admittedly stirred up some demons. But I'm okay. In fact, I'm happy to be here.'

<h1 style="text-align:center">Chapter 37</h1>

Joe sat on his porch thinking about his recent conversation with Lily. Having signed the deeds, he could hardly believe that he actually owned Edhen Cottage. And he hadn't hesitated about taking a paternity test. He wanted more than anything to believe that she was his daughter. The doctor told them the results would be quick. They only had to wait a day or two, but he was impatient to hear.

To distract himself, he decided to do his evening round of the house and gardens. It was a routine started as a young man, back when the Sanders' family were reassured by his daily patrol. He knew the estate was too large for him alone to protect and there had been intrusions over the years. He had found remnants of fires and empty beer cans strewn around in woodland closer to the road. A few times, some of the ground-floor windows at Penwyth House had been smashed; once or twice other signs of forced entry. Although he'd never caught anyone in the act, he presumed it was kids. After making the usual statement to the police, they would advise him to speak with the absent owner about increasing security. He merely nodded in agreement, knowing that was not possible.

Even Timothy Walker had no knowledge of Elizabeth's and Lily's whereabouts. Now he no longer reported any trespassers. He just repaired the damage as best he could and cleared up the mess.

Joe loaded two cartridges into the barrel of his shotgun and snapped it shut. He left the door to his home slightly ajar on his way out. No intruders had ever discovered Edhen Cottage or his aviary. They were buried deep in the woods, and not easy to reach unless you knew of their existence.

He set off towards the gardens, knowing that nowadays the only person reassured by his evening stroll was himself, and that was just fine. Because all he was thinking about was Lily and how fortunate he was to have her back in his life.

That same evening, at Blackthorn Cottage, Douglas was busy in the garage while Luke cleared out the amassed junk from the back of their van, adding it to the pile of scrap on what once functioned as a front lawn. He slipped two sets of gloves and a torch into the glove compartment and shoved a crowbar in the side pocket of the driver's door.

'When you're done in the garage, we need to chat, Doug.'

'All right, I'm just finishing up. What's for tea?'

'Takeout. It's in the kitchen.' Douglas ate quickly, devouring his food. Luke, on the other hand, ate slowly and deliberately, savouring each mouthful. For once he resisted the urge to comment on his younger brother's eating habits.

'How are you getting on fixing Dad's old bike?'

'Good. The carburettor needed a clean, but I can't do much more till I get those parts.'

'Do you think you can get it back on the road?'

'Probably,' he mumbled, shovelling a large chunk of pie

into his mouth.

'We could sell it if you do. You know how strapped we are.'

'Yeah, I know, but I wanna have a go on it first; take it out a few times.' He wiped his mouth with the back of his hand. 'What's happening about Penwyth House?'

'Funny you should ask. I think it's time we paid it a little visit,' Luke smiled.

'Really? When?'

'How about tonight?'

A few hours later, dressed in dark clothing, the brothers jumped in the van and drove to Penwyth Estate.

'So, you haven't seen anyone at the house?'

'Nope. Well, only once,' Luke replied. 'I saw a woman in a red car drive out of the place about a week ago, but nobody since. I've gone on foot to the house three times now, and each time it's been dead – no lights, no noise, no cars.'

'Do you know who she was?'

Luke shrugged. 'Nope. She was pretty hot, though,' he sneered.

Douglas snorted and play-punched him in the arm. 'Well, I wouldn't mind if she was there, then!'

As they wound their way through the estate's orchard, Luke switched to sidelights, then pulled over before reaching a large bend in the road. Any further, and they would be visible from the house. 'Okay, grab the gloves and the torch,' he whispered, pulling the crowbar out of the side door pocket. 'And don't slam the door.'

They stayed under cover of the trees, picking their way along the road's edge. Ahead, the house looked to be in total darkness. 'Think we're in luck,' Luke said as they drew closer.

'There's no one here. Once we're inside, if there's stuff worth taking, I'll run back and get the van.'

Douglas was staring at the jagged rooftop, its various appendages vaguely silhouetted in the pale moonlight. 'Christ, this place is creepy.'

'Never mind that, come on. There are steps around the side, leading to the basement.'

Using the crowbar and his considerable strength, Douglas easily jimmied the door to the kitchen. He threw the crowbar noisily aside and ran his hands through his hair, his thick lips stretched into a broad grin. 'Now what?'

Luke could see he was worked up. 'Don't make so much noise. I know the place looks empty, but we need to stay quiet just in case.'

They made their way through the downstairs rooms, checking for anything worth taking, but the place was stripped bare. Floorboards creaked, and the torch threw strange eerie shapes across the walls. Luke shone it upwards, where the corridor met the main hallway.

'Woah!' he whispered, catching sight of the giant French, crystal chandelier centrepiece. 'This place must have really been something once.'

Their footsteps echoed in the vast reception as they looked around for anything of value, but again there was nothing.

'Over there!' Douglas exclaimed, a little louder than Luke would have liked. Sure enough, something covered in canvas was leaning against the wall.

'Who are you?' someone called out from the darkness of the corridor behind them.

Luke jumped. He swung round and shone his torch in the

direction of the voice. Joe moved closer and into the beam of light.

He pointed the shotgun at waist level towards the two men, eyeing them defiantly. 'I said, who are you? You shouldn't be 'ere, you're trespassing.' He moved closer again; fifteen feet away now.

Luke was standing close to Douglas. He whispered in his ear, 'Follow my lead.'

'Hey, sorry, please don't shoot!' he called out, raising his hands and nudging Douglas to do the same. He wasn't about to be intimidated by an old man. The gun probably wasn't even loaded. Luke suddenly hurled the torch without warning, throwing the room into darkness. As Joe ducked, Douglas took his cue. He lunged at him, easily tackling him to the ground, which forced the barrel of the gun upwards just as Joe pulled the trigger. Two rounds of pellets shattered the arched window to the left of the door, sending shards of glass flying, the noise reverberating around the vaulted space.

Douglas used his bulk to pin Joe down. Sitting astride him, he punched him hard. Joe reached for his assailant's throat, but he was no match for the younger man. Douglas raised a meaty fist to hit him again, but Luke beat him to it, smashing him in the face with the butt of the shotgun. Joe clawed at Douglas's clothing, struggling not to lose consciousness, but Luke jabbed him again with the gun.

Douglas slid off Joe's limp body, as casually as if he'd just got out of bed, and walked over to the covered paintings. 'Look!' he said, grabbing the discarded torch. He threw the canvas to one side. 'Told you! Paintings! There must be five or six. They've got to be worth something.'

Luke gazed at Joe's bloody face. 'Shit, he was pretty badass for an old man.' He joined his brother. The artwork didn't look like much to him. 'If these were worth anything, they wouldn't be left lying around.'

'I suppose so,' said Douglas, deflated. 'Maybe we should check upstairs?'

'Hmm, no we should probably go now.' Luke took the torch and knelt over Joe, curious to see what damage they had inflicted. He pressed his finger into Joe's right eye, causing more blood to pool in the socket. A slow smile appeared on his face, proud of his handiwork.

Douglas reluctantly left the paintings and picked up the discarded shotgun. He then knelt, reaching into Joe's jacket pockets to reveal a handful of unspent cartridges.

'Well done' – Luke jumped up – 'now we have a gun.'

Chapter 38

In Bristol, Lily flipped the sign on The Blue's front door to closed, locked up and hurried home. Late afternoon, she had received a call regarding the paternity test. As Joe had no phone, she had promised to let him know in person as soon as she could.

The following morning, she drove to Lostmor. She made good time on the motorway and was only a short distance from Penwyth Estate when she decided to pull over on the side of the coastal road for a moment (she was thirsty and needed to stretch her legs). Leaning against the car, sipping from a water bottle, she was admiring the stunning view of the moors when she heard another vehicle approaching.

It was the familiar sight of Oliver's battered old Land Rover. He slowly pulled up behind her car and got out. As he walked towards her, smiling, she couldn't hold back any longer. She ran to him and hugged him tight.

'Well, hello yourself! What are you doing here?'

'I've just driven from Bristol and stopped for a drink. Oliver, I've got so much to tell you.'

'You have?'

'Yes! I was on my way to see Joe. I have some important news for him. Then I was going to come and see you.'

He looked puzzled. She had left so abruptly that he thought

he might never see her again.

'Um, has something happened?'

She couldn't stop smiling. 'I was going to explain everything later. But...' she hesitated. 'Now that you're here in front of me, I don't think I can wait! Do you think we could go to the farm? Joe doesn't know I'm on my way to him, so it won't make any difference if I turn up later. I know he'll understand.'

'Understand what?'

'You may need to sit down for this!'

Five minutes later, Lily stood in Oliver's kitchen while Flynn, who had finally had his cast removed, wove excitedly around her feet.

'Whatever this is about, it's great to see you,' he said, pulling out a kitchen chair for her.

'You too, and I'm sorry to keep you guessing.'

She looked as beautiful as ever. 'I've missed you,' he said, looking at her fondly. He pulled up another chair and sat beside her. 'I knew you were in Lostmor a few weeks ago – I bumped into Janet in town.'

'Yes, she told me. She's been so kind. My car broke down on the coastal road, and by some miracle, she came along and rescued me. She even let me stay at her holiday let while my car was in the garage.'

'She's a good egg, all right. You must still be busy with Penwyth House. But I take it that's not why you're here.' His dark eyes regarded her carefully.

'I've got something to tell you about my family's past that will sound just as unbelievable as the contents of your mother's letter.'

Oliver leant in close. All his attempts to forget about her

melted away. He couldn't contemplate her as his half-sister, only as the woman he still adored. He wanted to sweep her up and hold her; instead, he touched her arm reassuringly. 'Go on.'

'I'm sorry I ran away like that.'

'Don't apologise. My mother's letter was a terrible shock for both of us.'

She nodded. 'When I left you, I was going to drive home to Bristol and never return. But I remembered I was supposed to call in on Joe. So, I went to Penwyth instead. That was when I discovered his aviary.'

'Aviary? Where?'

'It's hidden away on the estate. I came across it by accident when I was looking for him. Do you recall the glasshouses I told you about?'

'Yes. You and Alice used to play in them as children.'

'Well years ago, he converted them into an aviary after Mother and I left. He told me how the two of them had learnt about keeping birds. Left alone, Joe started rehoming the birds from her old aviary, but over time, he filled the glasshouses with orchids and all sorts of plants. He's turned the whole thing into the most beautiful oasis.'

'Wow. He really is full of surprises, isn't he?'

'There's more.'

He moved closer to her. 'What is it, Lily?'

'Joe was more than Penwyth's loyal groundsman. He was in love with my mother. They had an affair.'

'Are you sure? How do you know?'

'Because he admitted it. I found some notes hidden in a book in the house, not long after I returned. They were brief and unsigned, arranging to meet with her at the agreed places. They were obviously from a lover. I already suspected they were from Joe when I saw he had a photo of her at Edhen Cottage, and then when I stumbled across the glasshouses full of birds and orchids, both of which she loved, it confirmed my suspicions. I knew it was for her; he built it all for her.'

'What a story. Did she love him?'

'Very much. Joe and I have become close over the past few weeks. At first, he was reluctant to talk about her in case he upset me. But once he understood how important it was to me, he spoke openly about their time together.'

'So, if they truly loved each other, what happened? Why didn't she leave Vincent? From what you've told me, it wasn't a happy marriage.'

'She wanted to, but she couldn't find the courage. She was afraid of Vincent and what he would do if he found out about Joe, especially after she fell pregnant...'

Oliver gasped. 'Are you saying that *you* were the baby?'

She nodded. 'My mother and Joe secretly met for over a year, but when she realised she was pregnant, she broke off the affair. She lied, Oliver. She told Joe Vincent was the father.'

'But how do you know all this?'

'From talking to Joe. And because we've since done a paternity test. Oliver, his and my DNA are a match. Joe Newman is my birth father. That is what I was on my way to tell him.'

'This is wonderful news! Is it certain? There's no chance the test could be wrong?'

'It's something like 99.999%. Is that good enough for you?' she smiled.

'I can't believe that you have found all this out since we last met. It's a lot to take in.'

Lily leant forward and kissed him lightly on the cheek. 'So, you and me – different mothers, different fathers.'

'Wait a minute,' he said, shaking his head. 'That means that Alice was your half-sister, and mine too...'

'Yes.'

He was at a loss for words. He gently touched her neck with his hand. 'I wish things had been different for you, Lily; I wish things had been easier. It seems we have both lost a sister, yet sadly I never even knew she existed. You have had to deal with her death ever since, and Vincent's too.'

She looked into his gentle eyes. She had missed him so much. 'I had a strange flashback when I was last at Penwyth House. I remembered an argument between my mother and Vincent. It was the same night he and Alice died. I was eavesdropping and heard everything. She told him in the end, told him she had had an affair and that I wasn't his daughter. It all came back to me, Oliver, so clearly.

'I'm still not sure how Vincent and Alice died. But I'm hopeful that it will come back to me one day. Either way, I can't change the past. But if you still want me, maybe we can change the future – *our* future.'

Chapter 39

Early evening, Marcus parked his truck out of sight just inside a farm field's open gate. Since watching Douglas's van disappear down the lane he was now sat alongside, he had spoken with Steve who on investigating further confirmed that there was a dwelling called Blackthorn Cottage (originally owned by a Mr Frederick Holt, now deceased) at the end of the lane.

Frederick Holt had two sons Douglas and Luke who still resided at the cottage. Background checks on the brothers were disappointing. Luke was clean. Douglas had two arrests for being drunk and disorderly. Nothing else apart from a shoplifting offence as a kid and a three-year-old speeding ticket. Even so, Marcus's gut was telling him to look a bit closer at these guys.

Armed with a torch, he cut across the field and found his way through a gap in the hedgerow onto the lane. He trod carefully as it dwindled into a narrow track. Ahead, he could just make out the cottage. It was little more than a shack but with a large garage to the side. Both buildings were overshadowed by a dense patch of woodland behind.

He approached cautiously, but there were no vehicles in sight and the house was in darkness. He could see it wouldn't take much effort to break in but decided to check out the garage first. Its door was an up and over. He tugged on the handle and it creaked open. He pulled it up just enough to slide inside and take a look.

Judging by the amount of stuff dumped out the front, he had expected to see the place in disarray. He was wrong. One self-lined wall was filled with neatly arranged boxes and tins; large cardboard boxes were stacked against another wall. To his left was a motorbike with some parts laid out on newspaper, and next to it was what looked like an old chest. His stomach turned over – someone living here owned a bike. *Let's not get carried away*, he thought, *lots of men own bikes*.

He turned his attention to the chest. Inside was a faded old tweed suit jacket with patched pockets that smelt of cedarwood. The label said, Dunn & Co: he was pretty sure they went out of business years ago. This stuff probably belonged to the brothers' old man. For all he knew the bike could be his too.

He was about to check the house when something caught his eye: a domed shape sticking up from one of the boxes. He pulled it out – a motorbike helmet – along with leather boots and gloves. There were some smaller items at the bottom. He tipped them out on the floor to take a closer look. His heart missed a beat. Next to a large belt buckle in the shape of a skull and a broken strap from the helmet, was a silver chain of dragon heads glinting in the torchlight.

One of the links was missing.

Just then, he heard a vehicle approaching. He shoved the wallet chain in his pocket and hastily stuffed the rest of the items back in the box. He switched off the torch and waited. Through the crack in the door, he saw the headlights dim. He heard a van door slam shut, and then a second one.

More than likely it was the brothers. Marcus listened to the murmur of low voices, followed by the sound of keys jingling. Another door slammed as they went inside the house. Having found the wallet chain, part of him wanted to confront them both there and then. It was a big coincidence to find the same dragon head links in their garage, but he didn't know for sure yet who owned the chain or the biker gear. If one of them was his man, he could wait a few more days.

He slid through the gap and quietly pushed the door shut. Then he slipped past the van and hurried back to his truck.

Back at the Black Dog inn, he made his excuses to the bar staff and went upstairs. All thoughts of Julia were gone. Horace eyed him warily. He recognised that look.

Chapter 40

'I should go,' Lily said.

'I know,' Oliver smiled. They had been talking for hours about their families and the strange twist of fate that had brought them together again. Now they sat quietly by the fire, and it was easy to imagine they had never parted.

'You could stay here tonight and see Joe in the morning,' he suggested.

Lily felt her resolve weakening. Soon, she would share her news with Joe, and they would be united as father and daughter. But the man she adored, the man she thought she'd lost, was so close. She wanted to touch him, to be with him.

Oliver turned to face her. In the firelight, her eyes looked multifaceted, like shimmering green and gold mosaics. She was here, within his reach. Without another word, they fell into each other's arms, naturally and completely, and didn't let go as they moved into the bedroom.

This time, it was not just desire he felt but a profound sense of affection. They peeled off each other's clothes and fell into bed. He kissed her slender neck, running his hands over every curve and hollow of her body. And, when her fingers lightly stroked his aching, work-weary muscles, every nerve ending in his body came alive. They made love, slowly and tenderly until finally, when their exhausted bodies collapsed onto the sheets, they clung together in the darkness, neither wanting to let go.

It was barely light when Lily stirred.

Sensing she was awake, Oliver rolled over to face her.

'Good morning,' he smiled sleepily, gently brushing a wisp of hair from her face. He kissed her slowly on the lips before sliding out from under the sheets and drawing back the heavy chintz curtains. 'Do you fancy a stroll?'

Lily stretched and sat up in bed. 'Now?' She eyed him curiously.

'Come on, it's a surprise!' he said, tugging at the bedsheet.

'Luckily for you, I'm a morning person.' Right now, she couldn't have felt any happier.

Soon, they were walking across the fields behind the farm. When they reached the cliff's edge she could taste the brine in the cool sea air.

'Here.' On the wooden bench in front of them, he laid the small blanket he'd slung over his shoulder. 'I thought we could watch the sunrise together.'

'What a lovely idea.' She sat and gazed at the horizon and ran her fingers over the smooth, thick slab of oak upon which she sat. 'How did this get here?'

'I made it about a million years ago when I was a teenager. It was a surprise for my mother's birthday – so she could sit here and read, or just look out to sea.'

'And did she?'

'Yes. I think she used to come here to feel closer to my dad. He loved the sea. He always dreamt of buying a small boat, nothing fancy, just something with an outboard motor so he could go fishing. But he was always too busy with the farm, he never did get around to it.'

Lily squeezed his hand. 'It must have been a terrible time for you both, him dying so suddenly.'

'It was at first. I was just a boy, and I missed him a lot. I missed hanging out with him on the farm and the sound of his booming laughter which used to fill our home.' He sighed. 'When he died, I think Mum and I kept each other going. It made us closer. She was a strong woman. She threw herself into keeping the farm afloat, and I helped as much as possible. When I was about fourteen, she sat me down and asked me what I wanted to do when I left school. I was baffled because it never occurred to me to do anything else but work on the farm. She wanted me to have the choice, but it was an easy decision for me.'

For a while, they sat huddled together on the bench he had lovingly crafted all those years ago, both lost in their thoughts. Dawn emerged, a pink and golden canopy, the stars gently nudged out by daylight.

She nestled into him. 'I wish you and I could stay in this moment forever.'

'Me too, my love,' he whispered, and they watched in contented silence as pale rays of light cascaded into the calm waters below.

Back at the cottage, Lily perched on a kitchen stool, sipping tea.

'I can see why you put the bench in that spot. I've never seen such a beautiful sunrise.'

'Well, consider the bench officially yours. I know Mum

would approve,' he smiled, passing her a slice of freshly buttered toast.

'I hope you don't mind but I told Janet about us.'

He looked surprised. 'Why?'

'I suppose because she's been so good to me, and I needed someone to confide in.'

'OK. I'm glad you had someone to talk to about all this.'

'I was so upset about your mother's letter; I didn't consider what it meant for you. Finding out Vincent was your real father must have been a shock.'

'It was at first. But Dad was always there for me; he was a good parent. Mum too. I think they kept the truth from me because they thought it was the right thing to do.'

'Do you think it was?'

'Maybe. It would have been hard to take after losing him so young, certainly. Perhaps when I was older? But I can see how, as more time passed, it was easier for her to say nothing.

'What about you? How do you feel knowing Vincent's not your father?'

'Honestly? Ours was a very different relationship to the one you shared with George. I remember being scared of him when he was drunk. He would lose his temper and shout at Mother a lot. I learnt to make myself scarce when he was like that and to take Alice with me.

'After the accident, Mother rarely spoke about him, but once, she told me he used to be a decent person. She said he was charming and made her laugh all the time. It was after he tragically lost his brother, David, in a car accident that he started drinking more heavily. I was too young to remember him but Mother said he and Vincent were very close. They were in business together too, buying and selling antiques. Apparently, after David's death, Vincent lost interest and the business soon folded. That was when his drinking spiralled even more.'

She reached out and took Oliver's hand. 'I want to be with you,' she smiled. 'So, finding that piece of paper, proving he wasn't my father when I thought I'd lost you for good, I felt nothing but relief.'

The irony of how events had played out was not lost on either of them.

'It feels a bit like we are pawns being moved in some indulgent chess game of the gods!' she said.

Oliver couldn't help but laugh at her analogy. 'Like in *Jason and the Argonauts*, you mean?'

'Yes! Monsters and all,' she said wryly.

'You know, I couldn't stop thinking about you,' he said, kissing her tenderly on the lips. 'I've worked sunrise to sundown to distract myself, but still the time dragged endlessly.

'Whether by God's hand or otherwise, we've been given another chance. And I won't lose you a second time.'

Chapter 41

Lily took a quick shower, then headed for Penwyth Estate. She felt buoyed as she hummed along to Tasmin Archer's *Sleeping Satellite* on the car radio. She was looking forward to telling Joe what she had discovered.

As the house came into view, she felt nervous, but in a good way. She knew he would be pleased, but it might still be a shock to learn he had a daughter after all these years.

She was about to drive on to Edhen Cottage when she noticed a lone seagull stood defiantly in the middle of the drive. Normally, a bird would move at the close approach of a car but this one stood fast. Perplexed she tooted the horn but it still didn't budge. She was about to drive around it when she glanced up at the façade of Penwyth House and saw one of the large stained-glass windows was broken. Lily switched the engine off and grabbed the house keys from her bag. She gingerly made her way through the glass fragments towards the door. It was probably kids trespassing, breaking the window as a dare. Joe had mentioned that it had happened a few times, always at night.

Incredibly, the emboldened seagull jumped towards her and gave an agitated, guttural sound as she drew nearer. She shouted and waved her arms at it, but it held fast. Lily swallowed, then slowly knelt in front of the bird. *This is crazy,* she thought, *gulls don't behave this way.* Then she remembered the gull on her first morning at Kleger Cottage, its cold beady eyes regarding her with disdain. She knew it was the same creature.

Suddenly it dipped its head, as if bowing, and stretched its wings before hopping a few feet away, allowing her access.

Finally, she unlocked the door... and looked in horror at the scene confronting her. Joe lay motionless, his face covered in blood.

'Joe?!' She leant over him and gently shook his arm. His face was a bloody mess, his blackened eyes so swollen she doubted he could have opened them even if he was conscious. She pulled off her scarf and gently placed it under his head, then took off her coat and laid it on top of him. He was icy cold to the touch.

She felt panic welling up inside her and shouted for help. Of course, no one could hear her except the gull, parading up and down outside. She looked down at Joe's ruined face. She had no idea how long he'd laid there or what other injuries he had. Pulling out her phone, she dialled 999. Then she called Oliver.

A few hours later, Oliver found her in the St Oswald Hospital waiting room. She rose to greet him, and he hugged her tight.

'Are you okay?' he asked with concern. She looked pale and drawn, the opposite of the smiling face of earlier, waving and promising to ring him later.

'I'm okay. It's Joe I'm worried about. I've been waiting for hours and still haven't seen him.'

'Do you think it was a break-in?'

'The window was broken.'

'Do you think he disturbed an intruder?'

'It looks that way. When I found him, he was unconscious. He felt so cold, and his face was all bloody and swollen.' She wiped her eyes, which were brimming with tears. 'If only I'd gone to him sooner.'

He placed a reassuring arm around her. 'Hey,' he said gently. 'This is not your fault. Have you spoken to a doctor yet?'

'Yes. A Dr Lake told me he's regained consciousness. He's concussed and has a broken nose and possibly a fractured jaw. And he has three cracked ribs. I couldn't tell them how long he was lying there, but he's apparently dehydrated and suffering from hypothermia.'

'Well, he's awake. That's good news, isn't it?'

'Yes, but it's such a nasty business. How could anyone do such a thing?'

Oliver hugged her. 'I wish I knew.'

Just then, Dr Lake walked into the waiting room. She spoke calmly, explaining that Joe's scan had shown a fractured right cheekbone, as they suspected. Worst still, she thought he might lose the sight in his right eye; it was so severely damaged.

'It must have been a shock for you to find him that way, Miss Sanders. He's taken quite a beating from someone. It's too soon to say how much of his sight he will regain, but given time and a lot of rest, there's no reason he shouldn't recover fully from his other injuries.' She smiled reassuringly at Lily. 'He seems a pretty tough character. He was trying to get out of bed, so we've given him a mild sedative. You can go ahead and see him but just for a few minutes.'

Lily was stunned; Joe was unrecognisable. His head was

covered in bandages, his chest and arms attached to bleeping monitors, and there were wires and tubes everywhere. He couldn't speak, but when she softly said his name, he raised his hand, seeking contact.

Lily whispered to him that everything would be fine and that he mustn't worry about anything. Before being politely ushered out by a nurse, she promised to look after his aviary for as long as needed. He squeezed her hand, and she was surprised at his firm grip. Dr Lake was right: Joe, her father, was pretty damn tough.

Chapter 42

Lily left Oliver's contact details with the hospital, so it was no surprise when the police arrived at Bligh Farm the following day.

'Miss Sanders?'

'Yes.'

'I'm Sergeant Weeks. I'm here regarding the assault on Mr Newman at Penwyth House.'

'Do come in. This is my partner, Oliver Bligh.'

'Pleased to meet you both,' he said, nodding at Oliver. They all sat and, having turned down the offer of tea, the sergeant pulled out his notepad while Lily did her best to explain the chain of events.

'So, you are the current owner of Penwyth House?'

'Yes. I inherited the place. My mother recently passed.'

'I'm sorry to hear that.'

'Thank you.'

If he was aware of her childhood home's tragic history, he kept it to himself.

'So, I take it you're not residing at the house and that's why you gave the hospital Mr Bligh's address?'

'Correct. I have an apartment in Bristol, but I've been staying in Lostmor on and off while I clear out Penwyth House. The only person who lives on the estate is Mr Newman. He's the groundsman. He's been at Edhen Cottage since he was a young man. Mother took him on back in the 1950s.'

'The hospital gave me a few details about the circumstances in which you found Mr Newman. Do you know if anything had been taken from the house?'

The house was recently emptied; there's nothing of value inside apart from a few old paintings left stacked near the entrance. It's been stripped bare, ready to be sold.'

'Can you take me through what happened when you arrived at Penwyth Estate yesterday? What time did you get there?'

'Late morning, around eleven.' She pictured the seagull so determined to block her way. 'Um, I was on the estate driving to Joe's cottage when I noticed a front window was broken at Penwyth House. I let myself in and Joe was... lying there in a pool of blood. It was awful and he doesn't even have a phone, so he couldn't call for help.'

'It's fortunate you came across him when you did, Miss Sanders. We haven't been able to talk to him yet because of the severity of his injuries. But it would be helpful to carry out some investigations at Penwyth House today, if possible.'

That afternoon Lily met with Sergeant Weeks, a constable, and a forensics officer at the estate. They established that the intruder (or intruders) gained entry via the basement. Fingerprints were taken from the basement door and some of the internal doors downstairs. She was advised that unless there was a precise match with someone already on their database, it was impossible to eliminate the prints of everyone who had recently been in and out of the house.

Forensics took blood samples from the hallway and bagged

up shell casings and shotgun pellets found lodged in the front door and on the drive. Lily hadn't noticed the gun shells before but remembered Joe used to own a shotgun. There was no obvious sign of a weapon, but the constable did find half a box of cartridges at Edhen Cottage.

Before Sergeant Weeks and his men finally packed up and left, he assured her they would do their utmost to apprehend whoever was responsible.

'We hope to gain a clearer picture from Mr Newman when he is well enough to talk, but it certainly looks as if he surprised whoever broke into the house and a struggle ensued. Forensics may give us more information regarding fingerprints, and the blood samples taken from the house may tell us whether another party other than the victim has been injured.

'It's fortunate that Mr Newman wasn't shot in all the confusion, but we are taking the assault very seriously. Let's hope he can provide us with some clues as to who did this to him.' He smiled sympathetically. 'We will do our very best to find his attacker.'

'Thank you, Sergeant Weeks.'

Despite his assurances, it seemed to her they didn't have much to go on.

Two days later, Lily and Oliver arranged to meet Janet at Penwyth House. A cacophony of noise greeted them as they walked from under the canopy of trees into the clearing that housed the aviary. Even though Lily had described it to them, they both stared in disbelief.

'My god, these glasshouses must be twenty feet high and what, fifty feet long?' marvelled Oliver.

Just as Lily had been overwhelmed, so were they. Janet explored the various nooks and crannies, noting as many species as possible. She saw mainly parakeets, finches and canaries, but was sure she spotted a couple of quails underneath the bowed branches of an apple tree. There were also many common or garden birds – sparrows, blackbirds, tits and chaffinches – that presumably found a way in through the gaps in the netting. Meanwhile, from his residential bird table at the centre of everything, Roy the crow observed all.

'Have you seen Percy?' Janet asked, as the three of them later sat watching birds skim across Joe's pond.

'Who's Percy?' asked Oliver.

Both ladies laughed.

'I can't believe I haven't told you about the peacock!' said Lily. 'Oh, and that's not all. I don't think I've told either of you about the seagull!'

This time, Oliver and Janet exchanged glances.

'Think Johnathon Livingston. You know, the book. This bird is not your run-of-the-mill gull. He must be Joe's. I've seen him twice. The first time was at Kleger Cottage, the second time when I found Joe injured. He was on the drive. I swear it was trying to stop my car.' Lily noted their bemused faces.

'Honestly, I am not kidding!'

'Okay,' Janet appeased. 'Some birds can get very used to being around humans, so I can see how Joe may have rescued an injured gull, and like Roy, it sticks around or visits now and then. But how do you know it's the same gull you saw at Kleger Cottage? I mean, surely it could have been any gull?'

'I know it sounds crazy, but I'm certain it was the same bird. Both times, it came right up to me and looked me straight in the eye. Have you ever known any wild bird behave that way?'

Janet shook her head.

'And Percy the peacock – is he another of Joe's rescues?' Oliver asked.

'No, he came from a breeding pair Joe already owned. I bumped into Percy in the apple orchard and mentioned it to him. He was concerned that the bird was roaming too much. Then, unbelievably, Janet found him sitting on the same stretch of road where my car broke down. She rescued us both that night!'

Oliver looked incredulously from Janet to Lily. 'Life isn't dull with you two around!'

Janet grinned. 'Joe's the interesting one, creating all of this singlehandedly. I hope I get to meet him when he's better.'

Oliver squeezed Lily's hand. 'That makes two of us. Now then, in the meantime, Janet, how on earth do we look after this little lot?' He nodded at two cute little green parakeets huddled on a perch on the other side of the pond.

For a couple of days, Lily had fed the birds using a bag of pellets left in the glasshouses, but she wasn't sure what else they needed. So, Janet went through what food she thought they should leave out daily and roughly how much. Between them, they needed to clean all the perches and tables weekly to prevent disease, as well as watering Joe's little patch of paradise.

Lily had no idea how he had managed to take care of the place and still tend to the estate's garden and grounds.

Even after discharge, it was doubtful he would be fit enough to look after his beloved aviary for quite some time.

But she was confident that with help, she could take care of things. Her main concern now was her father's recovery.

Chapter 43

Following Joe's facial surgery, the police finally interviewed him. With the help of a nurse and a pen and paper, he told them about his daily rounds of the house and gardens, a routine he had continued for over forty years.

He explained as best he could that during his evening round, he walked around the side of the house and noticed the door to the basement had been forced open. He had crept through the door and heard voices. He had followed the sound of the intruders, eventually confronting them in the hallway. There were two men, maybe in their early thirties. Joe had his shotgun with him, and when he challenged them, one of the men lunged at him, accidentally setting off the gun. No one was injured by the blast, but his attacker then punched him in the face. He couldn't remember much after that. (A doctor had already given the police details of his injuries.)

Sergeant Weeks pointed out that his gun was missing. Joe mentioned he had also been carrying spare cartridges in his jacket pocket. A nurse confirmed that none were found when he was admitted. He wasn't sure he could identify the intruders but thought one had longish hair and the other, the one who attacked him, was heavy-set.

When Lily arrived at the hospital a few hours later, Joe struggled to speak. 'How are birds?' he mumbled.

She understood and assured him they were being fed and watered daily, and that she had friends helping, one of whom was a vet. She explained that getting hold of fruit was easy enough, but the pellets were running low. He pointed to the pen and pad by his bedside. Lily held the pad while he wrote a few words. He scribbled that there were more supplies stored in the old stables.

She nodded and smiled at him. Obviously talking was painful and laborious for him, but his eyes looked a little less raw.

On her way out, she spoke to the nurse, who explained that he was regularly offered painkillers but didn't always accept them. She added that since his intravenous fluids ceased, he was constantly trying to get out of bed unassisted. Lily sympathised though secretly took heart from his determination to get better. Her father was a fighter.

It seemed ironic to resume her daily routine of driving to the estate again, but instead of dealing with the house, she was tending to the aviary.

She arranged for a carpenter to fix the basement door and met with a glazier who boarded up the broken front window until he could return to fix it properly. Most afternoons, she drove to the hospital to see Joe, while Oliver helped feed the birds in between working in the fields.

A week later, Janet dropped by at the farm after visiting the aviary.

'Feeding and cleaning them out is straightforward enough,' Lily explained, 'but if one became injured, I wouldn't know what to do.'

'Well, that's what I'm here for! And when are you going to

show me the actual house? You know I'm dying to see it!'

A short time later, Janet's jaw dropped when she entered the vast reception and gazed at the majestic staircase and breathtaking glass dome above.

She and Lily were wandering through the gallery when Janet's mobile rang. Stanley, an elderly boxer dog, had collapsed at home, and its owners were driving him to Lostmor surgery. So, with Janet's grand tour cut short, Lily locked up and left.

Pulling away in her Ford Fiesta, she watched the spires and chimneys slowly recede in her rear-view mirror and reflected on her odd love/hate relationship with Penwyth House.

'You look thoughtful,' said Oliver, sinking onto the old leather couch next to Lily.

Flynn, who was enjoying an ear rub, reluctantly jumped down.

'I guess I am.' She smiled.

He looked at her quizzically. 'What is it?'

'On my last trip home to Bristol, the place just didn't feel the same.'

'What do you mean?'

'My apartment doesn't feel like home anymore – not since Mother passed.' She turned to face him. 'It seems like everyone and everything I care about is in Lostmor.'

'And?'

'Well... how would you feel about me moving closer?'

'Really? I'd be over the moon, of course!'

'I could find a flat nearby. I don't want you to feel

bamboozled into anything.'

'You can bamboozle me whenever you like,' he joked. 'But seriously, I want you to know that you are always welcome here.

'Thank you. That means a lot to me.'

'What about your apartment? Will you give that up too?'

'It still has six months on the lease. But if I do move, obviously I will have to close The Blue.'

'So, you're serious about this?'

'I think so. Everything that has happened has made me reconsider what really matters.'

'Which is?'

'You... and Joe of course.' She leaned in and kissed him gently on the lips.

'Lily, it broke my heart when I thought I'd lost you. Having you back in my life means the world to me. I hope you know that.'

She kissed him again, entwining her fingers around his. 'I feel the same way about you. And the day I found Joe so badly hurt, I thought he would die. It made me realise how much he matters to me too. I nearly lost him, and I haven't even told him he's my father yet.'

He squeezed her hand. 'You will. The doctor said he's recovering well.'

'Yes, he's getting there.'

'What about your art? You could open something similar here, couldn't you?'

'I am contemplating it. I'm going to do a bit of research first, make sure it's a viable business before I rush into anything. I'm hopeful, though. And we're surrounded by beautiful scenery so I've plenty of inspiration.'

'I'm not sure how many galleries there are in town but tourists flock here in the summer months.'

'Running The Blue taught me to appeal to a broad customer base. I do sell some higher-end art, but I also produce less expensive pieces and prints. Plus there's my commissioned work of course.'

'Well, I think it's a great idea, and if there's anything I can do to help, just ask.

'What about Penwyth House? Will you put it on the market soon?'

She hesitated. 'Not just yet. This is going to sound crazy, but I'm thinking about renovating it. I've been mulling over the idea for a while.'

'Wow, you really have been reconsidering things.'

'So, do you think I'm mad to take it on?'

'No, of course not. It would be incredible to restore such a unique place, and you have the resources. But it is a massive undertaking. Would you have time to manage that and run an art gallery?'

'Probably not. I could find someone to project manage the house for me, someone who can oversee the day-to-day running and help me find a reliable workforce. That way, I wouldn't have to be so hands-on. Timothy's got various contacts and has offered to help with that.'

'It sounds like you've made up your mind. I have every faith in you but be prepared to be on call twenty-four-seven. Even with a good project manager, your phone will probably never stop ringing. Are you sure about this?'

'I know it won't be easy, but yes, I am.'

'What changed your mind about selling?'

'It's hard to explain – a feeling that I need to set things right; to move on from the past and breathe new life into the place.'

Oliver hugged her. 'Lily Sanders, you never fail to surprise me.'

Flynn came trotting up and barked.

'I think someone wants to go out,' he said, getting to his feet. 'Do you fancy a walk? It's a lovely evening.'

'Why not? Maybe we can sit on your mother's bench on the way back and watch the sunset.'

'*Your* bench.' He smiled.

Hand in hand, they strolled along the edge of the fields, which Oliver had recently ploughed, then walked along the clifftops. Flynn darted this way and that, excitedly chasing every fresh scent.

'If I'm going to move to Lostmor, I'll have to return to Bristol for a day or two and start putting things in motion. In the meantime, I'll take a look around Tresor Bay, get a feel for the place and see what galleries, if any, already exist. I'm sorry to ask again, but is there any chance you could help feed the birds until I'm back? I can rope Janet in too.'

'I've got crops to sow soon but luckily I have some hired help in at the moment. I'll liaise with Janet. I'm sure we can make it work for a few days.'

'Thanks.'

'And I'll keep an eye on the house while I'm at it. You should think about getting some security in place.'

'You're right. I'd better start with a new entrance gate. Then I'll look at installing an alarm system.'

'Have you heard any more from Sergeant Weeks?'

'Not yet.'

'Did Joe get a look at the men who attacked him?'

'Not really, it was too dark.'

They walked the rest of the way in silence and reached the bench just as orange sunlight filtered through pink-tinged clouds hanging low over the water. There, they sat watching guillemots skim the frothy crests of waves before flying home, silhouetted against the fiery sky.

Chapter 44

In Bristol, Lily hung a 'closed for business' sign in the window of The Blue and packed as much of her artwork as she could into crates.

Having explored the Tresor Bay area, she was confident she could run a successful business there if she could find the right premises. She had come across three galleries, all of which focused mainly on local landscapes and seascapes. On visiting one premise, the owner was more than happy to talk about her time working there (unsolicited by Lily who was merely looking around). She explained how her business had grown over fifteen years and how, despite it being out of season, she was busier than ever. The second was located near the first, close to the seafront at the more popular end of the bay for tourists. She discovered it was also leased long-term, over ten years. Both were well-presented, unlike the third which was set slightly further back and away from the main shopping area. The latter's artwork was locally produced and of a high standard, but in her mind over-priced, and the shop front and general presentation was tired and in need of an update. It also had limited opening hours that could perfectly suit the owner's needs or suggest a lack of business.

The following day, with the help of a hired man with a van, they moved office equipment and most of her artwork and materials to a local storage facility in Lostmor. It took two days to complete the transfer; on the third morning, she packed some of her personal belongings and clothes, ready to return to Lostmor. She left a message for Mr Carne from Lostmor Antiques regarding the recent auction of her family's possessions, before locking up and leaving her apartment. Although it was not yet for good, symbolically, it felt that way.

No more looking back, she thought. And no more hiding away, never reaching out to anyone. She had opened her heart to someone special and, in doing so, was beginning to see herself in a whole new light.

She understood how fortunate she was to have inherited Penwyth Estate and the money left in trust by her mother. And she couldn't wait to spend time exploring Lostmor; to capture on canvas the raw beauty of its rolling moors, tumultuous seas and chameleonic skies.

A few hours later, she dialled Oliver's mobile.

'Hi, Lily,' he answered. 'How are things? Are you still coming home today?'

'Yes! And I'm very close.'

'How close?'

'Outside!' she said, hanging up.

Oliver opened the door.

'Surprise!' she grinned.

He welcomed her with open arms while Flynn leapt about, weaving excitedly between her suitcases.

'I missed you,' he said, gently kissing her.

'It's only been a few days!'

'I know, I'm a hopelessly besotted fool,' he joked, helping her with her luggage. 'So, how did it go at The Blue?'

'Fine. It needs a proper clean before I return the keys, but nearly everything is in storage or at the apartment.'

'Talking of keys, I got this cut for you,' he said, producing a front door key from his pocket. She looked at him with surprise. 'As far as I'm concerned you can move in right now. But I don't want to rush you. At least have these until you find your own place.'

'This is very generous of you.' She wrapped her arms around his neck and kissed him.

'You are more than welcome,' he smiled.

While she showered and unpacked a few things, Oliver lit a fire and cooked lamb cutlets, mash and peas for supper. Afterwards, they snuggled on the couch and watched the flames dance.

'How are things at the aviary?' she asked.

'Good. Joe's eclectic bunch of birds seem to be thriving. Janet fed them yesterday, and I went earlier today.'

'Great. I'll give her a ring in the morning to thank her. Any news from Sergeant Weeks?'

'No, he's not called here, but he might have paid Joe another visit.'

'I was going to see him tonight, but I don't think I can face any more driving.'

'It's getting late. Why not go tomorrow? Maybe I can come with you, if you think he wouldn't mind another visitor.'

'That's a good idea. I don't think he'd mind at all. I spoke to the ward nurse earlier. She said he's doing well. He sits out of bed most of the day and walks with help. His right eye is still blurry, but his left eye is fine. He's still in pain from his ribs, but that's to be expected. He's asking to go home, but they won't discharge him until he can manage independently. I didn't say anything to the nurse, but his house is the least concern: I'm more worried about him climbing up ladders or chopping firewood.'

'Well, at least he doesn't need to take care of the estate anymore.'

'No, just as well. Timothy's drawn up the paperwork signing the cottage and surrounding land over to him. I can arrange for a landscaping company to come in and start managing the estate.'

Lily's mobile rang. 'Oh hi, Timothy! How are you?'

'I'm fine, my dear. I wondered how you were, and how Joe's recovery is going.'

'I'm fine thanks, and Joe is doing well. He's keen to go home but he's not quite ready yet.'

'I'm so glad he's okay after such a nasty attack. Lily, I think you should consider tightening the security at the estate.'

'I know. You're right. It's long overdue.'

'I have the number of a reputable company if you would like it?'

Lily gratefully copied the number down before telling him of her plans to open up a gallery in Lostmor and giving him Bligh Farm as her address for the foreseeable future.

Before he hung up, he thought he should mention what he'd just read in last week's *Lostmor Gazette*.

'I see,' she replied. 'And does the article also mention my family's history?'

Oliver could tell from her face that Timothy's reply was not what she wanted to hear. After the phone call ended, Lily told him how apparently, after the police had given a quote to the press about the break-in and assault on Joe, an overzealous reporter had linked the incident with the Sanders' tragic past, suggesting that the house was cursed.

The following day, Joe gave Lily and Oliver a pained smile from his chair as they entered the hospital room.

'You look so much better!' She embraced him lightly so as not to hurt his ribs.

'I hope you don't mind, but I have brought someone to meet you. This is my boyfriend, Oliver Bligh. He's been helping me to look after your aviary.'

'It's nice to meet you. And thank you, Oliver, for helping Lily,' Joe said.

'My pleasure. It's an amazing place.'

Joe's face was still severely bruised, but the swelling had gone down. He looked from Lily to Oliver with a twinkle in his eye. 'A handsome couple you two make!'

Oliver smiled and held her hand. They talked to Joe about his aviary for a while, reassuring him his birds were okay. When she told him of her plans to move to Lostmor and open a gallery in the bay, he was delighted.

'That's wonderful news. Things are looking up!'

Just then, a porter appeared to take him for a scan, so they said their goodbyes.

As they were leaving the hospital, Oliver turned to Lily.

'You haven't told him, have you?'

'Not yet. I want to, but when I first saw him in the hospital, he was so poorly and in so much pain. It wasn't the right time.'

He gently placed his hands on her shoulders. 'And now? Lily, Joe is a lovely man, and you saw how thrilled he was about you moving here. Imagine how happy he'll be when he finds out you're his daughter. He will love you just as much as I do.'

Lily gazed at him. 'You love me?'

'Yes, I love you, Lily Sanders. Every time I see you, you leave me breathless. I know it's only been a few months since we met, but I have never felt this way about anyone. Admittedly, I hadn't planned on saying any of that in a hospital car park!'

Lily looked into his mahogany-coloured eyes, which radiated warmth and humour.

'I love you too, Oliver Bligh.'

Chapter 45

In Tresor Bay, Lily walked along the narrow, cobbled back street until she reached the Seaward Lets Agency.

'How nice to see you again, Miss Sanders.' Adam rose and shook her hand. 'Please, take a seat. You said on the phone that it's a shop premise that you are interested in renting?'

'That's right, I am hoping to open up an art gallery.'

'That sounds exciting. Well, we do have one on our books. It was formerly home to an antique shop called Hidden Treasures and it includes accommodation on the floor above. Is that something you might be interested in?'

'Well, yes, I think so. Where exactly is the premise?'

'It's situated at the busier end of the bay and has been run by a married couple for the past twelve years.'

'That's a long time. Do you know why they are leaving?'

'Retiring, I believe.'

'Well, it sounds promising.'

'Would you like to take a look? It's only a short walk away.'

The location was perfect. The end-of-terrace property had a separate entrance at the side leading to a living space above. Once inside, Adam pulled up the window blinds, allowing the light to stream in.

The room was narrow but three times the depth of The Blue – perfect for her needs. Downstairs had recently been painted white, giving it a fresh, clean feel. At the rear was a door leading into a small kitchen, attached to which was a storage room. The room was large enough to use as a studio.

While the ground floor was functional and fine for her needs, upstairs was unexpected. Adam had shown her a few photos at the agency, but she was still pleasantly surprised. The floors throughout were varnished oak, with funky, multi-coloured knotted rugs on top. A small kitchen with chunky oak units and worktops was at the far end; a rectangular island with stools created a division between the dining area and the lounge, which had an inviting turquoise couch and armchairs. Three other doors led off the landing. The first was a small, spotlessly clean bathroom with floor-to-ceiling tiles, followed by two more bedrooms. One was no more than a box room, but the second was much larger, with a king-sized bed and double-aspect windows overlooking quaint cobbled streets. A small ironwork chandelier, floor-length purple velvet curtains and a matching two-seater couch gave the room a boutique feel.

'Oh, and there's central heating throughout,' he continued. 'Do you think you might be interested, Miss Sanders?'

Despite Oliver's tempting offer for her to move in to the farm, whilst she was occupied with the opening of her gallery, she could see the advantage of being able to stay at her place of work, at least for now.

'Yes,' she replied. 'I think I am.'

Back at the agency, Lily signed a six-month contract, paid the deposit, and arranged to pick up the keys in a few days' time.

Perhaps she was being a little impulsive, but the truth was

she loved the apartment, and the shop space was ideal.

She was about to drive to Penwyth House to help Oliver at the aviary when her mobile rang.

'Hello. It's Mr Carne of Lostmor Antiques. I've just heard your answer phone message, Miss Sanders. Apologies it's taken me a while to get back to you.'

'No problem. I'm sorry I missed the auction. I had some things to sort out in Bristol but I'm back in Lostmor now. How did it go?'

'Very well. Most items were sold, and I think you'll be pleased with the final amount raised. You're welcome to drop by whenever it's convenient for you.'

Well, as I'm in town, I could meet with you now, if you have time?'

'Perfect. Also, one of my men recovered a photo album concealed in a desk. We think it came from one of the bedrooms.'

'Goodness. I thought I'd checked everywhere for my family's belongings.'

'It's unlikely you would have found this. It was concealed behind the draw itself. We only came across it because we routinely inspect things before they go to auction.'

'Well, I don't have many photos of my family, so this is very exciting. Thank you.'

Lily texted Oliver and arranged to meet him an hour later, then walked the short distance to Lostmor Antiques.

At the rear of the shop, Mr Carne's office was barely visible behind a row of large wardrobes. She circumnavigated an aisle created from a collection of chairs before spotting him at his desk pushing buttons on a calculator.

She gratefully accepted tea while they discussed the auction. Free entry to the event and reasonable reserve prices had paid off. (The room was apparently packed to breaking point.) From the impressive sum of nearly £28,000 profit, he deducted his fee, the rest being divided equally between Lostmor Community Centre and the local hospice.

'Oh, and here's the album I mentioned.'

Lily thanked him for everything, then drove to Penwyth Estate and parked on the drive to wait for Oliver. With trembling hands, she unwrapped the album that Mr Carne had carefully packed inside a box.

Enclosed were potentially lots of photos of her family, including Alice, whose face she could now barely remember.

The edge of a large black-and-white photo was sticking out the inside cover sleeve. She recognised the subjects as her maternal grandparents, Alfred and Jeanie. Jeanie sported a short hairstyle, as was popular in the 1920s, arranged in smooth, sculpted waves. She wore a simple string of pearls and a light-coloured sleeveless flapper dress. Alfie looked tall and was clean-shaven with slicked-back hair and a tweed suit. She smiled and slipped it back in.

Each page held two photos secured by paper corner mounts. Some were black and white, the more recent in colour. There were no dates, but some of the house itself looked to be taken shortly after her mother moved onto the estate in the early 1950s. There was no driveway, and the gardens were unkempt and overgrown. Joe had certainly transformed the landscape since working there.

She realised how hard her mother must also have worked to restore the place. Now, here she was, about to do the same.

There were photos of her mother's wedding at Penwyth House. She gazed at an image of her standing with Vincent before the oak door, its arch adorned with hundreds of peach and white roses. She looked stunning in a long veil and slim-fitting white gown with a delicate lace bodice that revealed her shoulders. Her hair was loosely swept up and entwined with gypsophila.

Images followed of the couple making their vows. Guests filled rows of tastefully embellished chairs on an immaculate lawn. She recognised a couple of faces from the group shots: Margaret, the house cook, wore a large floppy hat and long flowing skirt, and there was a much younger Timothy, possibly in his mid-twenties. He was slim, clean-shaven and with that unmistakable beaming smile.

Wedding photos gave way to holiday snaps. The happy-looking couple stood in front of the Eiffel Tower; another of them at the Taj Mahal. She carefully prised out other photos which were slipped behind the mounted ones. More faraway places – her mother holding a cocktail, looking happy and carefree in a beach bar, palms lining the bay; another of her mother and Vincent sitting at what looked like a captain's table.

Lily smiled sadly. Her parents were happy once. She wondered if things might have been different for everyone if Vincent hadn't lost his brother all those years ago.

Next were photos of herself as a baby, a tiny bundle lying in a cot, followed by more baby shots, her mother cradling her in her arms. Then, Lily as a toddler on a blanket in the garden, crawling after a ball, her short hair fastened in little bunches, and more family shots taken at Tresor Bay.

Her earlier nerves were forgotten as she watched her family's lives unfold; the arrival of Alice – baby shots, and the two of them together, Lily hugging her toddler sister on a settee.

She touched a finger lightly to Alice's face, unaware of the tears streaming down her own. There were school photos (only one of them together – Alice's first year of school), and more of the family, including the same picture she had found in her parents' room.

Then nothing, just blank pages, a life cut short, a family story abruptly ended.

Oliver appeared at the car window, making her jump. She hadn't noticed him pull up.

'Whatever's wrong?'

'Nothing, I'm okay.' She rolled down the window. 'This is the album Mr Carne found. Here look, I'll show you.'

Oliver got in the front seat and turned the pages with interest.

'Just think, I may never have found this if I'd kept the desk.'

Oliver put an arm around her. 'I wonder why your mother hid it.'

'I have no idea,' she sighed. 'It seems she had quite a lot of secrets.'

'Do you still want to go to the aviary? I can manage, if you'd rather go home.'

'No, I'll come.' She smiled, wiping her eyes. 'Did you find any bird food in the stables?'

'Yes, there's masses over there, and the tubs in the aviary could do with topping up. If we go in my car, we could fit more in the back.'

He parked at the end of a narrow lane, overgrown with

brambles but wide enough to get through on foot. To one side was what remained of the kennels, a partially collapsed wooden construction. Around a bend, they walked into a large, sunlit clearing under a bright blue sky. To their left, a tumbledown drystone wall stretched the length of the stables. Between the two was once an impressive courtyard, its cobblestones now tufted with grass and covered with woodland debris.

'Gosh!' she said in surprise. 'I mean, it's totally neglected, but what a place!'

Oliver grinned and grabbed her hand. 'Come and see!'

The encroaching woods behind had partially reclaimed the low building; ivy and green-leafed climbers twisted and strained through broken roof tiles. Each stable had a gabled wooden front, giving the impression of a row of tiny terraced houses. Lily leant over the first stable door and peered into the gloom. Stacked in neat piles were at least twenty large plastic containers of pellets.

'You weren't kidding, there's a ton of the stuff!'

The next stable door was ajar. Its hinges creaked as she pushed it inwards, and a pungent smell hit them. An empty bucket and a long-abandoned broom lay in a puddle of stagnant rainwater. She ran her hand over the rough wooden doors as they wandered the length of the building.

Birds darted in and out of the stables and the fretwork of greenery that covered them. She stood back and looked around them. The stables were in the shade, nestled into the trees, but the courtyard and overgrown clearing were bathed in sunshine.

'I don't know if it's the promise of spring in the air, but this place feels almost enchanted.'

'I thought the same. Penwyth is certainly full of surprises.'

'We didn't come here much as kids. We were either in the gardens or messing about in the glasshouses. The kennels were out of bounds, and the family never used the stables. I guess it's stood empty for forty years or more.'

Later, back at the farm, Oliver looked through the album again. Lily's mother was attractive. She had big blue eyes, long, straight blonde hair, and rosebud lips. Alice resembled her, while Lily's eyes were green, her dark brown hair wavy and her features more delicate. To him, Lily had an ethereal beauty that seemed to glow from within.

Lily watched with interest as he pulled out a black-and-white photo concealed in the sleeve at the back of the album.

'Hey, what's this?' he asked.

The picture was of Joe and her mother. He was dressed in work clothes and a flat cap, her mother in a simple summer dress. They were arm in arm, looking relaxed and smiling fondly at each other. The stable wall behind them was solid (not neglected and crumbling as it was now), the cobblestones clean and shiny.

She turned to Oliver. 'That's why she hid the album.'

'Do you think that's where they used to meet?'

'It could be. It would have been the ideal place to leave notes for each other as no one ever went there. They look at ease together, don't they? Like they belong. It must have been exciting, having a secret love tryst.'

PART IV

Chapter 46

Douglas had just returned home with the new bike parts he had been waiting for.

'Look!' he said passing the latest copy of the *Lostmor Gazette* he'd picked up at Tasker's garage to Luke. 'We're famous, bro,' he grinned, revealing small, widely spaced teeth.

Luke read the front-page article:

Is Penwyth House cursed?

Some of our readers may be too young to remember the shocking family tragedy that occurred at Penwyth House.

On 17 June 1971, six-year-old Alice Sanders and her father, forty-two-year-old Vincent Sanders died after falling from the roof of their Gothic-styled mansion. The coroner later recorded a verdict of accidental death.

The late Elizabeth Sanders's surviving daughter, Lily, now thirty-three, is the sole beneficiary of the Penwyth Estate.

After a recent break-in at the house, Sergeant Weeks of the Devon and Cornwall Police gave the following statement:

Luke read the news item with interest. There was a picture of Lily Sanders as a young girl. It looked like a hastily acquired school photo. Was it the same woman he saw leaving the estate? Maybe. He was annoyed that he hadn't known about the groundsman, but it was too late now. He smirked at the fact Sergeant Weeks hadn't mentioned the gun theft – so as not to alert the public, he guessed.

He was pretty sure the groundsman hadn't seen their faces in the dark, and that the police had no clue who they were. Anyway, the break-in hadn't been a total waste of time – now, they were armed. Next time, he would research their chosen target more carefully – maybe a post office or a retail outlet, somewhere there was a guaranteed payout.

The following day, Douglas resumed work on the Triumph. Luke was glad of the peace; he needed to think. He had just torn off a few pages of the *Lostmor Gazette* to place in the hearth when he noticed a familiar name on one of the pages: Julia Sutton. He instantly recalled her long blonde hair and big blue eyes. He could picture her as clearly as if he had seen her yesterday. It had to be *his* Julia. How many Julia Suttons could there be in Lostmor? She had moved away with her family long ago, but maybe she had moved back. He smiled. Just the thought of seeing her again aroused him.

He read the two-line job advertisement with interest. She was looking for a part-time kennel hand at Fern Retreat. He folded up the page and slid it into his pocket, grinning cheerfully to himself. Dogs, eh? He had often wondered what happened to her. She had been a straight-A student, and he imagined her as a teacher or perhaps a lawyer. Her business venture surprised him.

Luke didn't like animals, especially dogs, but how hard could it be to look after a few mutts? For Julia, he'd wait a bit longer before beginning his prosperous life of crime.

A short time later, he cruised past Fern Retreat, hoping for a glimpse of her, but she was nowhere in sight. He didn't want to be spotted; he wanted to surprise her. He pulled in a bit further up the road and dialled the number on the advert. 'Oh hello, is this Julia Sutton? I'm ringing about the kennel-hand position.'

After a brief conversation, an interview was arranged. In a few days, he would finally see her again.

In the Black Dog inn, Lily raised her glass to Janet. 'Thanks for helping at the aviary.'

'No problem, I enjoyed it. It's such a magical place. And as for the house... Our visit may have been cut short, but it still left me speechless. I half expected to see Morticia Addams wafting down the staircase!'

Lily laughed. 'You are incorrigible.'

'Oh, I do hope so!' She grinned.

'What happened to the boxer dog?'

'Stanley? I had to keep him at the surgery overnight but he's fine now. He's a lovely old boy but partial to drinking out of the toilet. Unfortunately, it had just been bleached.'

'Oh poor thing. You know, you really should write your memoirs one day. It would make a fascinating read.'

'Hmm, maybe. Perhaps you should, too.'

'I think I'll stick to painting.'

The pub gradually got busier as Lily told Janet of her plans to move to Lostmor and open a new art gallery, before explaining about the retrieved family album.

'How wonderful! And how's Joe?'

'He's recovering well, but I've heard nothing more from the police. I'll call Sergeant Weeks tomorrow.'

'Hello!' said Timothy.

'Oh,' said Lily, 'what a nice surprise. Have you just got here?'

'Yes, I spotted you from the bar.'

'Why don't you join us? This is my friend, Janet.'

'Well, I don't want to impose,' he said politely.

'You're not,' Lily grinned, shifting slightly to make room in the booth.

Timothy sat. 'Do you hail from Lostmor, Janet?'

She shook her head and smiled. 'I've been here thirty years, but I'm from Devon originally.'

'Ah, a similar story to mine. I'm surprised our paths haven't crossed before. What brought you here?'

'I run a veterinary practice on the high street.'

'You must have some interesting stories.'

'Lily and I were just discussing that. She thinks I should write my memoirs.'

The three of them chatted about everyday things until the conversation turned to Joe and the police investigation.

'I've been helping Lily and her boyfriend, Oliver, look after the aviary until Joe's fully recovered,' Janet explained.

'Oliver?' Timothy asked.

'Oliver Bligh,' Lily added. 'He owns Bligh Farm, that's the contact address I gave you. Oh, and I've just leased a premise in Tresor Bay.'

'Is that for the art gallery you wanted to open?'

'It is indeed,' Lily smiled.

'Well, good luck with your new venture! That's wonderful news.'

Timothy knew nothing of Lily's recent discoveries regarding her mother's affair with Joe, or that he was her birth father. One day she would explain – when the time was right.

Just then, Oliver walked in. 'Hi, everyone. Sorry I'm late. The damn generator's playing up again.'

'Did you fix it?' Janet asked.

'I think so. I don't use it that much, but it comes in handy.'

'Oliver, this is Timothy.'

'Nice to meet you.' They shook hands. 'Would anyone like another drink?'

'I'm afraid I must be off,' Timothy replied. 'I have an early appointment with a new client, but it's nice to meet you too, Oliver. And you, Janet.' He beamed in her direction.

Lily gave him a quick hug. 'Thanks for all your help. I don't know what I'd do without you.'

'My pleasure.' He waved, heading for the door.

'He was sweet,' Janet remarked.

Lily gave her a knowing smile.

'What?' she said, looking slightly flustered.

Oliver ordered drinks at the bar. 'Hey, Marcus, how's things?'

'Can't complain. It's quite busy for March. Is it serious, then?' He nodded in Lily's direction.

'It might be.' He smiled. 'Her name's Lily. She's an artist. Paints landscapes, that sort of thing. She's opening up an art gallery in the bay soon.'

'I hope things work out for you,' said Marcus, passing him a tray of drinks.

Oliver rejoined Lily and Janet, squeezing his legs under the table. 'You know, I've been thinking about Douglas Holt. We should mention him to Sergeant Weeks.'

'Do you think he may be connected with the break-in?' Lily asked.

He shrugged. 'It's possible. He's certainly shifty and already proven he can be violent.'

'I've already given the sergeant a list of all the companies in and out of the estate, including Eastgate Skips. That's where you saw him driving the skip truck, wasn't it?'

'It was, but I think it's worth mentioning him by name. Just in case.'

'All right, I will. I was going to ring him anyway because I've not heard anything. I'll explain your previous run-in and about seeing him on the estate.'

A short time later, Janet said her goodbyes. Like Timothy, she too had clients early in the morning, albeit of the animal kind.

Lily gazed out at the sparkling bay. She remembered wistfully how nervous she had been driving to her first meeting with Timothy, and her shock at learning Penwyth House had never been sold. Things had indeed moved on since then. Through the window, she watched as the ornate Victorian streetlamps, which ran the length of the curved promenade, flickered on – all except for one, whose light flared then faltered repeatedly, like some frantic Morse code signal warning of danger.

Chapter 47

Arriving at Fern Retreat, Marcus and Horace were greeted by loud barking. Business was booming. He spotted Julia shutting one of the kennel doors. 'Hi!' he shouted over the din.

'Hi,' She smiled patting Horace. 'I was just about to exercise two guests, Bertie and Coco. Do you want to tag along?'

'Sure. I drove, so Horace could do with a run.'

'I'll grab Bella; she's in the house.'

They watched as the two border terriers ran back and forth after a ball, and Horace and Bella bolted, chasing each other's tails.

'Are things going okay?' he asked.

'Yes, great. I'm exhausted most of the time but I'm loving it. I have a couple of people coming this week about the kennel-hand position. One is a girl called Sarah. She grew up on a farm and is used to dogs. She's saving for university. The other is a chap. Think he said his name was Luke. He's local, says he's had mostly casual work but loves dogs and is looking for something more permanent. On first impressions, the girl sounds more suitable.'

'You never know, the guy may surprise you.'

'True. You can't always go by how people sound on the phone.'

He turned to face her and smiled. Her pale blue eyes were

completely mesmerising. 'I knew you'd make a huge success of this.

'When I asked you a moment ago if things were okay... I meant between us.'

She picked up a retrieved ball and swung the thrower for Bertie and Coco. 'You know that I think what you're doing is wrong, though I do understand why. The military may have trained you to kill, but defence during conflict is very different to killing for pure revenge, no matter how justified you think it is.

'The truth is, I thought I could handle this but now I'm not sure. Suppose you find this man – why not hand him over? I don't care what happens to him, but is he really worth going to prison for? Is that what Rose would have wanted?'

He paused before answering. 'Maybe not. But I can't do what you ask – I can't just hand him over.'

Her heart sank. 'Alright. What about us? Don't I mean anything to you?'

'Of course you do!' He drew her roughly to him. 'Julia, I love you. I don't want to involve you any more than I already have, but I promise that one day soon, this will all be over. Then we can do whatever you want; go wherever you like.'

Julia sighed. 'I have what I want right here. You... and this place, Fern Retreat. But what you're doing is jeopardising everything. And,' she said, breaking away from his embrace, 'even though I care for you, Marcus, I can't be with you while this is hanging over us. I need some time to think.'

Chapter 48

'Hello? Sergeant Weeks?'

'Hello, Miss Sanders. I trust you are well.'

'Fine, thank you. I wondered if you've made any progress finding Joe's attackers. I thought I might have heard from you by now.'

'Apologies. Nothing concrete, but it is early days. We're still trying to contact a few homeowners who are not currently in Lostmor – several have holiday homes near Penwyth Estate. It's possible someone may have seen a suspicious vehicle or persons on the night in question. Because the area is sparsely populated, anything or anyone out of place tends to stick in people's minds.'

'What about the blood results?'

'Mr Newman's only, and I'm afraid the fingerprints were also inconclusive.'

'So, you have no suspects or leads at the moment?'

'We are in the process of interviewing several known criminals in the area. It may seem as if nothing is happening, but I can assure you that this investigation is very much ongoing.'

'I understand. I'm very fond of Mr Newman, and he was attacked whilst in my employment, trying to protect my family home. So, it would mean a lot to be able to tell him that the people who hurt him so badly will be punished.'

'We are as eager as you to catch whoever's responsible, Miss Sanders.'

'This may be nothing, but Oliver Bligh asked me to mention someone called Douglas Holt. He works for Eastgate Skips.'

'Eastgate Skips? The firm you used at Penwyth House?'

'Correct. Douglas Holt also worked at Bligh Farm for a short spell. He turned out to be both lazy and unreliable – not that that makes him a suspect. But when Oliver said he was letting him go, he became violent, attacking him with a pitchfork.'

'Did Mr Bligh report the incident?'

'No. It was all over in seconds. Oliver diffused the situation and made sure he left the farm immediately.'

'That is unfortunate, but it doesn't necessarily mean he broke into Penwyth House.'

'Of course not, and it's only because he saw him again at the estate that he thought it might be worth mentioning.'

'You think that this might be some sort of vendetta?'

'Not really. If that was the case, why not target Bligh Farm rather than my property? I'm only speculating, but he could be an opportunist. Douglas Holt delivered the skip, realised the house was uninhabited, and maybe thought there could be something of value inside. So, he enlisted someone's help and decided to take a look for himself.'

'All right, it's worth checking. He will have already been questioned, so it's easy enough to check his alibi and see how credible it is.'

A few days later, Joe was discharged from the hospital with strict instructions to rest as much as possible. Although his ribs were painful, they were healing well. Even better news was that the sight in his right eye had continued to improve despite Dr Lake's initial concerns.

In anticipation of his homecoming, Oliver was at Edhen Cottage where he had stocked the fridge, chopped and stacked wood for the log store, and lit a fire.

Lily pulled up outside and Joe eased himself out of the car. 'It's good to be home,' he said, walking with the aid of a crutch.

'I hope you don't mind, but Oliver's inside warming the place up for you.'

'That's kind.'

'It's the least we could do.' She couldn't help feeling that what happened to Joe was somehow her fault. If she hadn't returned to Lostmor the attack may never have happened.

Every now and then, nagging doubts plagued her. Maybe she was the one who was cursed, not the house.

When Joe was safely inside and sat by the fire, Oliver said he'd go tend to the aviary.

'I wish I could go too,' said Joe.

Lily smiled. 'You'll soon be back with your birds. Don't worry, we're taking good care of them.'

She followed Oliver to the door. 'Thanks.'

He put his arms around her and kissed her on the lips. 'Tell him.'

She nodded. 'See you later.'

Back inside, Lily heated some soup for their supper and added more logs to the fire.

'I met up with Mr Carne from Lostmor Antiques not long ago. His men helped remove some of the furniture from the house. One of them found this hidden in an old desk.' She pulled out the treasured family album from a large shoulder bag.

'I didn't know there were any photos of your family. What a lovely surprise,' he said, turning the pages in wonder.

'I found a photo slipped into the back cover I want you to have.' Lily took a picture also from her bag and gave it to him.

Joe stared in disbelief at himself and Elizabeth, young, in love, and without a care in the world.

'Thank you.' Emotion caught in his voice. 'I remember taking this. I set the timer and only just got back to her before the camera flashed. I never got to see it.' Joe held the photo to his chest, and his sea-green eyes glistened with tears.

He looked at her hopefully. 'Do you know the outcome of the paternity test?'

'I've wanted to tell you for so long,' she said gently, 'but then you were attacked and so poorly. I couldn't seem to find the right time.

'Joe, you were right, Vincent was not my father. The test came back as a positive match with you. I've been told it's over 99% accurate. So, there is no doubt you are my biological father.'

Joe's voice quivered. 'My child, I can't tell you how long I've waited to hear those words.' He gently cupped her face in trembling hands and kissed her forehead. And they half laughed and cried as they embraced, as father and daughter.

Chapter 49

Luke arrived an hour early for his interview. Parked on the road, he watched a girl on a bicycle ride into Fern Retreat, then leave half an hour later. He checked his face in the rear-view mirror. He'd washed his hair that morning and tied it back in a ponytail. *Not too bad*, he thought, clean-shaven and wearing a fresh T-shirt and jeans.

He turned on the ignition and drove up the lane leading to the kennels. As he pulled up on the drive, there she was, smiling, walking fast towards him in Wellington boots and a puffer jacket. Her hair was still long but not as long as she'd worn it at school.

'You must be Luke. I'm Julia.'

'Yep. Nice to meet you.' He shook her hand and grinned his most charming grin.

She had expected someone a bit younger, someone nearer to Sarah's age. It was usually students who took the lower-wage jobs, trying to subsidise their college grants. This guy looked around her age.

'I'll show you around and then we can have a chat.'

They walked past the kennels to a crescendo of barking. Luke smiled and nodded and pulled sympathetic faces at the excited dogs. He tried to look interested, asking her how often she fed and exercised the dogs. She showed him the paddock, and then they returned to the reception hut where she greeted owners and took bookings.

'You know, you look familiar to me,' she said. 'Have you always lived in Lostmor?'

'I don't think we've met, but I was born and raised here.' He smiled salaciously. If anything, she had grown even more beautiful. He could imagine holding her, gazing down into those big blue eyes and kissing her soft, full lips.

'I can't pay much, and it's physically hard work. There's a lot of mucking out and exercising to do. Of course, it goes without saying that you need to enjoy being with dogs.'

He tried to focus. 'I understand about the money but it's a bit of a dream to work with dogs. So when I saw your ad, I thought, why not come along?'

He was beginning to enjoy himself but didn't want to overdo it. 'I expect you have other people to see, but I would be very interested in the job.' He tried to look sincere, with the right degree of humility.

'So what kind of work have you done previously, Luke?'

'Well, I'm not really a nine-to-five kind of guy. Ever since school, I've mostly worked outdoors, labouring or farm work.'

Julia studied his face. School... Of course, that was where she knew him from. 'You're Luke from West Hill High School, right? I'm Julia Sutton. We used to hang out in the library, in the third or fourth year.'

He feigned surprise and broke into a smile. 'Julia Sutton! I should have recognised your surname!'

'How have you been, Luke? Are you still an avid reader?'

'Wow, I can't believe this. Yes,' he lied. 'I read all the time. You?'

'Not so much these days. Can't seem to find the time, especially since opening up this place.'

'Didn't you move away with your family?'

'Yes, South Devon. I moved back not long ago.' She was beginning to remember a few more things about Luke. They were only ever friends, but he had shunned her after she started going out with another boy from school. At the time, she had been taken aback by his jealous behaviour. Their brief acquaintance had come to a sudden end. Though just silly teenage tantrums, he had upset her, and being quite naïve, she had not fully understood why. *This is all a bit strange*, she thought.

Sensing it was time to go, Luke slid off the stool where they sat in front of the counter. 'It's been nice seeing you again.'

'Well, thanks for coming. I've got your number, so I'll let you know in a few days.

'What is your surname? I can't quite recall.'

'Holt,' he smiled, waving once as he sauntered back to his van.

Chapter 50

Moving into Swan Song (as Hidden Treasures was shortly to be christened once the new signage arrived) went smoothly. Lily moved her belongings into the upstairs apartment before setting up her studio at the rear of the shop. Oliver helped, surprising her with a moving-in gift: a small ship crafted from aluminium, with a crescent moon and a trail of clouds drifting horizontally from the top of its mast. She adored it.

'We should celebrate!' he said, admiring the artwork she had hung so far, and the tasteful basket of white lilies and trailing orchids in the shop window.

'Well, that might be a bit premature. I'm nowhere near ready for opening!'

'But you've been working hard all day and... you did invite me to stay,' he said cheekily.

'True, but we have nothing here to eat apart from bread and butter. I nominate you to buy supper!'

'Cod and chips?'

'Splendid.' She smiled.

While she tidied up the shop for the evening, Oliver took Flynn for a stroll along the seafront, popping into The Tasty Plaice on his way back.

A few streets away, in the Black Dog inn, Marcus called Julia.

'Hi Julia, sorry. I know you said not to call but I just wanted to hear your voice.'

There was a pause before she replied. 'How are you?'

'Missing you.'

'Marcus, you're just making this harder.'

'I'm not going against your wishes. You asked me to keep my distance and I have. But it doesn't mean I care any less for you...'

'...It's not easy for me either.'

'At least tell me you're okay.'

'I'm fine. Busy.'

'How did the interviews go?'

'Sarah is starting next week. The other applicant wasn't really suitable.' She didn't mention that it turned out she knew him from school. Or that she remembered him as an odd kid, a loner. She couldn't explain why, but seeing him again, as a man, she had sensed something disturbing hidden behind the pleasantries.

But that encounter paled into insignificance, knowing what murderous thoughts were running through Marcus's head.

'Glad you've got some help sorted.'

'Is the pub busy? Are you working?'

'Yes but I'm on a break. I've just walked Horace and had some supper. One of my staff is off sick, so I'll be behind the bar till closing time.'

'Okay, well, I'm glad you're okay, but it's probably best you don't call me again, Marcus.' There was an awkward pause. She wanted to say more. She wanted to tell him how much she missed him too but it would only make things worse. 'Well, I'd better go check on the dogs. Take care,' she said, hanging up.

Marcus hung up and sat gazing at the television. The local news was on. A large mansion and a photo of a young girl flashed across the screen. He turned up the volume and caught the end of the report:

'... *the attempted burglary at Penwyth House, currently owned by Lily Sanders, ended in a brutal attack on the resident groundsman, Joe Newman.*'

Marcus switched channels. The weatherman pointed at a map of the UK and explained that a big storm was due to hit the southwest tomorrow night. Lostmor was covered in rain clouds and yellow zigzag symbols.

He switched it off; his mind was still occupied by the phone call he had earlier from Steve who had explained that Douglas could not possibly be involved with Rose's death because he was in police custody at the time. He was arrested the night before her fatal accident for being drunk and disorderly and not released until later the following day.

Marcus also learnt that Douglas and Luke's mother left the family household when her sons were still children. Social services became involved for a time due to school absences, but their father retained custody.

So, at this point, Marcus had nothing to link his daughter's death to the Holts apart from the wallet chain found in their garage that was missing a dragonhead link. The same link that Ellie found at the scene of the accident. And even though Douglas had a rock-solid alibi, what about his brother Luke? Marcus knew he couldn't let this go until he was certain neither was involved. It was time for a little chat with the Holts.

'Hmm, that was good,' said Lily, popping the last chip into her mouth.

Flynn, who'd had his share, sloped off to the lounge and curled up on the rug. Oliver cleared the dishes, then fetched champagne from the fridge as a surprise. He popped the cork and poured them both a glass.

'Oh, my goodness, cod and chips *and* bubbly! What more could I ask for?' she laughed.

'Here's to you,' he said, raising his glass. 'To Swan Song, which I'm sure will be an even bigger success than The Blue.'

Lily's face lit up. He thought she had never looked more radiant.

'I forgot to say – I called Sergeant Weeks and voiced your concerns about Douglas Holt. He's going to check his alibi for the night of the break-in. Other than that, he didn't have anything new to tell me. They're still investigating, but the fingerprints were inconclusive, and as suspected, the blood sample was Joe's.'

'That's a shame,' he said, putting his arm around her. 'How did things go at the cottage with Joe? Did you tell him?'

'Yes – after he asked me if I knew the result.'

'Really?'

She nodded. 'I still feel a bit overwhelmed; it was very emotional. We ended up laughing and crying together.' Her eyes glistened with tears of happiness.

'When I first returned to Lostmor, I thought I had no family left. Now, I've discovered my real father, and so much more about my mother. And,' she said, kissing Oliver softly on the lips, 'I found you.'

Despite all of this, that first night in her new home, Lily awoke suddenly from a terrifying nightmare. She turned to look at Oliver, who was sleeping peacefully beside her. She pushed back the quilt and pulled herself into a sitting position. Echoes of strange dreams chased each other around her head. She sat with her eyes closed, trying to slow her breathing, but voices called out to her: her mother chiding her over something, Alice giggling, Vincent shouting. Then, an enormous clap of thunder.

Her eyes sprang wide open. She stared unseeing at the bedroom window. The voices faded, replaced by a howling gale; the familiar sound of wind whistling down the chimneys of Penwyth House. She felt hot breath on her shoulder and slowly turned her head. Sitting beside her was the man she once considered her father. Vincent's distorted face leered before her, his words calm and clear, yet filled with an unsettling tension:

'Come to us, Lily. Join us – Alice and I – we miss you.' He smiled, but his mouth was just a black hole, moving like smoke. This time, she awoke for real, startling Oliver.

He stared at her with alarm, and she realised she was screaming.

Chapter 51
Friday 10ᵗʰ March, 1995

Douglas was angry with his brother. Luke's disappearance was nothing new. In the past, he had sometimes gone missing for weeks without a word of explanation. What bothered him this time was that just before dawn, he was woken by the roaring of his newly renovated Triumph Bonneville being ridden speedily away. His first thought was that someone was stealing it until he realised Luke was gone.

He had planned to take the bike out himself that morning. Luke had stolen his moment of glory after he had worked so hard to restore it. Douglas jumped into the van and accelerated at speed up the lane. He had no idea where his brother was, but he couldn't just sit at home seething with rage.

Ten miles away, cruising along the B road that connected Lostmor to St Oswald, Luke had to admit the Triumph was a pleasure to ride. Its 650cc engine purred like a cat, increasing to a satisfying throaty roar whenever he opened the throttle.

When he left Blackthorn Cottage earlier, he had driven at break-neck speed, skidding around all the bends. At one point a fox had streaked across the road in front of him. He swerved to miss it, screeching to a halt, only just managing to keep the bike upright. He was shaken. He remembered a time when a fox had run in the path of a truck he once owned. He had deliberately sped up and ran the creature over. This one stared briefly at him before hopping into the undergrowth.

Luke wiped his visor. An image of Rose momentarily popped into his brain, her dead body lying splayed across a car bonnet. What was the matter with him? He shook the image from his thoughts. It was Julia's phone call that had upset him. He'd been on edge ever since. She left a hasty message apologising, explaining she'd given the position to someone else – to the girl on the bicycle no doubt.

His first reaction had been to call her back and tell her exactly what he thought of her. But he was glad now he hadn't. Just because he failed to get the job, didn't mean he and Julia couldn't be together. Perhaps that was her plan. If she was his boss, it could complicate their relationship. He smiled despite the worsening rain. Everything was clear to him now. He turned the bike around and headed back towards Lostmor.

Marcus had been watching Blackthorn Cottage for a couple of hours. During active service, apart from the adrenaline-pumped moments of full-on armed combat, one was always waiting – waiting for orders, waiting for backup, waiting for the enemy. His patience was now rewarded when the now familiar transit van literally screeched out of the lane and onto the road taking the turn way too wide. He quickly started up the truck and followed. On either side of the road, trees swayed in the increasing wind, and it was starting to rain. A storm was blowing inland, as forecast. Even though Marcus had to drive fast to keep up with the van he was confident he hadn't been spotted. The rain was getting heavier by the minute and transits didn't have the best rear visibility.

Knowing there was a particularly steep descent just ahead, Marcus put his foot down, passed the van, then pulled in front of it at a forty-degree angle. Douglas had no choice but to swerve to avoid hitting the truck. With screeching brakes he left the road, landing in a ditch.

Marcus pulled up next to it, then checked the road for other cars. Before getting out, he reached for the Browning service pistol hidden in his glove box. He probably didn't need it but it reassured him to have it tucked in the small of his back.

He walked to the passenger side and peered in. The position of the vehicle meant the driver's side was now inaccessible. Marcus slid the door open and got in. Douglas was alone, holding his head with one hand and looking bewildered.

'You crazy fuck, you nearly killed me!'

Marcus stared at him, unspeaking.

'Who the fuck are you?'

'I'm Marcus Cole, Rose's father.'

Douglas could feel blood at his hairline. 'Who? Who's Rose? Look man. I'm fucking hurt! You have to get me out of here!'

'Do I?' Marcus said calmly, pulling out the gun from his belt.

'What's that for!' His voice was shrill, laced with fear. He tried to get away but the driver's door was jammed against the side of the ditch. 'I don't know who you think I am but you've got it wrong.'

'Okay, let's try again. Did you know my daughter, Rose?'

'Look, mister, I know your face. You run the Black Dog don't you? But I don't know any Rose. I swear.'

Marcus reached into his jacket pocket and pulled out the wallet chain. 'Are you telling me this isn't yours?' he asked, dangling it before him. 'I found it in your garage.'

Douglas stared at the chain. 'You stole it? That's not mine. That's Luke's.'

You mean your brother? Where is he? Where's Luke?'

'I dunno. He left early. Took off on my motorbike.'

Marcus looked at him thoughtfully. 'Tell me, what were you doing that night parked outside Oliver Bligh's farm?'

'What? Nothing.'

Marcus punched Douglas in the face. He shrieked as pain seared through his already throbbing skull.

'Tell me!' He raised his fist, about to hit him again.

'All right, all right! We never went near the farm. I knew Bligh, that's all. I worked for him, as a farmhand.'

'That doesn't answer my question.'

'We were keeping an eye on him. Luke and me had plans to break into a big mansion house nearby. We saw Bligh there once and wanted to see if he visited the place a lot. So we followed him for a while.'

Marcus stared at him. This sounded familiar. 'What place?'

'Um, Penwyth. Penwyth House.'

That was it. On the news, last night, a report of a break-in at Penwyth House and an assault on the groundsman. The owner was Lily Sanders. Lily... the artist; the woman in the pub with Oliver.

'So, it was you two who broke in? You attacked the groundsman?'

No reply.

Marcus pressed the barrel sharply against the side of

Douglas's head. 'Unless you want to be looking over your shoulder for the rest of your life, this little meeting never happened. Do you understand?'

He nodded vehemently, eyes wide with fear. Whatever his brother had done, he wasn't about to die for him.

The next blow – this time with the butt of the gun – knocked him out cold.

Chapter 52

By the time Luke returned to Lostmor, he was soaked through. Not that he was deterred; he just needed to speak to his girl, then everything would be okay.

It was early afternoon, and Julia was in the paddock throwing a ball for a group of dogs. Her hood was turned up against the wind and driving rain. The gate behind her shook and rattled, and she watched as a string of bunting, wildly flapping overhead, flew off and lodged in a solitary tree by the house. Storm clouds were rolling in fast, and the moist air was thick with salt. Overhead, gulls shrieked their warning of the incoming gale as they lurched and tumbled in its current.

She called the dogs back and clipped them to their leads. Back at the kennels, she dried Ralph, a young boisterous Labrador, and two cocker spaniels, Treacle and Posy. She refilled their bowls and settled them all down as best she could. Even though they were warm and sheltered from the storm, she was worried they would be frightened if it worsened. She envisaged moving them into the house for the night where they would be less stressed.

For the first time since opening Fern Retreat, she realised how exposed to the elements it was. As she rounded the corner to the house, she was surprised to hear Bella barking inside. Directly outside the front door she saw a large motorbike parked. She looked around, but there was no one in sight. She glanced in the window – a man was sitting at her kitchen table, looking down at a mobile phone.

What was happening? Was she being burgled? Whoever he was had walked straight into her house!

She reached into her pocket for her phone, but she didn't have it. She silently cursed herself.

She dared to look closer, realising who it was with a sickening feeling in her stomach.

Luke Holt.

Muddy water sprayed out from under the truck's wheels as Marcus drove at speed along the uneven lane to the Holts's place. He passed the bungalow, turned around in front of the garage, and jumped out.

The darkening sky gave its first low grumble, and tar-black clouds released another deluge of rain. He lifted the overhead garage door a fraction. No bike. No one was there.

He ran to the bungalow. The front door was locked, but the simple Yale mechanism was no match for a quickly aimed boot. It swung open. Marcus scanned the gloomy interior and what narrowly passed as a living space. Rubbish piled up everywhere – what he expected. Empty beer cans littered the floor, and blackened ash from the now dead fire spilt onto the hearth rug.

He pushed open the door to a small bedroom. Clothes covered the floor. A bedside table held a photo frame. It was the first sign of anything remotely personal – an image of a man standing proudly before a classic old Norton motorbike. A small boy with thick hair who looked like Douglas was perched on top of the bike, his chubby legs dangling over the edge.

The second bedroom was tidier; clothes folded in a pile on an old dining chair. He sat on the bed and reached for the wastepaper bin next to it. He sifted through its contents: mainly food wrappers and empty cigarette packets. On finding a screwed-up page torn from a newspaper, he flattened it out. It was part of the jobs section of a local paper.

Marcus sighed. He still didn't know if Luke had anything to do with Rose's death but he did know a lot more about his character. Just like Douglas, he was a second-rate thief and probably violent too. He remembered the news report saying the attack on the groundsman was brutal which had to be one or both of the brothers' handy work. Now he wouldn't be satisfied until he had looked Luke in the eye and told him he was Rose's father. How he reacted would tell him everything he needed to know. Unfortunately, he had no idea where he was. He would have to wait for Luke to return or go in search of him.

He pulled out the chain and looked at the dragon heads again. Could Luke be who he was looking for? What could his daughter have seen in someone like him? He was trash, just like his brother. Perhaps that was why? Rebecca had said Rose was rebelling. So, she took up with someone older than her, someone reckless, of whom she knew her parents would disapprove.

He looked closer at the piece of newspaper, skimming the jobs. Halfway down, he saw Julia's advert for a kennel hand.

He thought back to Tom showing him the *Lostmor Gazette*; the news item and photo of Julia advertising the kennel, and his first visit there with Horace. He could picture her now, standing in her wellies with a big welcoming smile, her long blonde hair tied in a loose ponytail.

Why had Luke torn out the jobs section? What had Julia said the names were of the applicants? One was called Sarah; she got the job. What was the other name? It was a guy... a guy called Luke.

He grabbed his phone and dialled her number. It went straight to answerphone. He tried three times, but there was no reply. It could be a coincidence – another Luke. Except his gut was telling him otherwise.

He ran to the truck as fast as he could.

Chapter 53

Julia slid back from the window and tried to think what to do. She could confront Luke, ask him what the hell he thought he was doing walking into her home uninvited.

The fact he was in her kitchen was deeply troubling. What if he didn't apologise and leave? She should run to the road – he hadn't spotted her yet. Then she could keep going until someone drove by. Her heart was racing, but she tried to calm herself. She could hear Bella still barking. She was shut in somewhere.

'Julia!' – he appeared from nowhere – 'there you are. What are you doing out here in the rain? Are you coming in?' He was grinning from ear to ear. 'I've been waiting for you.' His hands hung loosely by his sides, and long, wet strands of hair clung to his face. His behaviour scared her, and she instinctively tried to humour him.

'Luke! What a surprise.' She half smiled, hoping she sounded convincing. 'I've been in the paddock but got rained off. Is that your bike?'

'Kind of,' he said cheerily. 'I borrowed it.' He gently touched Julia's back, directing her through the open door.

'I can hear Bella,' she said casually.

'Hmm, she wouldn't stop barking, so I shut her in your bedroom. Don't worry,' he said amiably, rolling his eyes, 'I know how you are about dogs. She's fine. Let's sit, shall we?' He pulled a dining chair out for her.

'Oh, let me take your coat. You're soaked.'

She slipped off her coat and sat. On the table were two glasses and a bottle of wine he had taken from the fridge. He sat down beside her.

'How about a drink?' Without waiting for a reply, he poured them both a large glass. He smiled affectionately. 'I'm sorry to turn up unannounced like this, but you don't need to be nervous. I just need to talk to you – about us.'

He really is batshit crazy, she thought.

She had to find a way out of this. She glanced at the wall clock. It was still early, only 2:30 but she wasn't expecting any visitors. No one was coming to her rescue.

Luke casually pulled out her car keys and phone from inside his leather jacket pocket. 'Someone called Marcus seems keen to get hold of you. He's rung three times.'

Her heart sank. He had already crossed the line. Now showing her that he'd taken her only means of escape and communication, suggested something worse. But there was a glimmer of hope: Marcus was trying to contact her, quite urgently it seemed.

'Marcus? Oh, he's just a client. I look after his dog sometimes.'

'I see.'

'Is this about the job?' she said, changing the subject. 'I'm sorry. Perhaps we can talk about another role for you?'

'That's exactly what I had in mind.' He turned his chair to hers and gently touched her face.

Julia put her hand on his and then slowly removed it. She

took a sip from her glass. 'To us,' she said.

He joined her, taking a large swig. Outside, rain lashed against the glass, making the sash windows judder. Maybe she could cook something for them? That would waste some time.

'Are you hungry?'

'Hmm, no,' he replied, his heavy-lidded eyes scaling her body up and down.

'Okay, well I am. Do you mind if I make something?'

'Let's finish the wine first. I admit I was disappointed by your message. But then I got to thinking. We go way back, don't we?'

'Yes, we do.'

'I wanted to apologise for how I treated you back then.'

'We were friends, weren't we?'

'Yes, but I got upset over one of your friends – Josh.'

'I don't remember him. It was such a long time ago.'

'It doesn't matter now,' he said, placing one hand on her thigh.

Julia tried to rise, but he firmly touched her shoulder.

'Don't be so jumpy! We're celebrating, after all.'

'What are we celebrating?' she asked in a shaky voice.

'You and me, of course! It's okay that you gave the kennel job to someone else. You did find someone, right?'

'Yes.'

'Well, that means you'll have more time,' he said cheerily.

Julia was perplexed, trying to work out where this was going. 'To do what?'

'To spend with me, silly! We can get to know each other again; talk about books, just like we used to.' He drained his glass and lifted Julia's to her lips. 'Drink,' he said softly.

She reluctantly did as she was told.

He reached for the bottle, refilled their glasses, and then casually walked to the window. He looked out at the rain, his expression bland.

'Are you sure Marcus is a client?'

'Yes. He's probably phoning to say he's on his way to pick up his dog, Ralph.'

'You know, I was waiting quite a while for you to come back from the paddock, and I had a little wander. Your appointment book in the hut looks busy. Funny, I didn't see a client called Marcus. I could have sworn good old Ralph was being picked up tomorrow by Caroline.'

He turned to face her. Something dark and unreadable flickered across his features.

He was still by the window, and she was much closer to the door than he was. Impulsively, she leapt for the door handle. But he pre-empted her. He got to her in seconds. Grabbing her from behind, he threw her headlong back into the room. As she landed, her head hit the brick edge of the inglenook fireplace. She heard a strange whimpering noise leave her throat. Dazed, she felt the side of her head. It was sticky. She tried to focus, but the room was spinning.

Luke pulled her roughly to her feet and sat her firmly back on the chair. He knelt in front of her and tugged at her jeans. Ripping her leather belt off, he used it to bind her wrists behind her. She wasn't sure what was happening. Pain was blooming in her temple as she struggled to stay conscious.

'You shouldn't lie to me, Julia,' he hissed. 'You're seeing this Marcus, aren't you? I hoped we could start afresh, but now you've spoilt everything.'

His face was inches from hers. She could smell sour wine and tobacco and felt nauseous. He grabbed her chin and moved her face from side to side. 'Shit, you're a mess. You shouldn't have made me do that.'

She tried to speak, but the words wouldn't form. Her whole face felt numb.

'Why do you keep whoring yourself out to other men?' he whispered. 'If that's what you are, a whore,' he sighed, 'then I guess I'll have to treat you like one.'

Walking to the units, Luke slid a kitchen knife out of the wooden block, then came back and knelt in front of her. He turned the knife's edge in his hands and smiled. He used the blade to roughly flick the top button off the front of her shirt.

'You know, even when you're a mess, you still look sexy.'

She managed to whisper, 'Please don't. You wanted to talk.'

He slid his hand inside her shirt. Julia cringed at his touch but stayed silent.

'Talking's over,' he said softly, sliding her chair closer.

Her phone lit up on the table and then pinged: she had a voicemail. Cursing, Luke picked it up – Marcus again. He was going to discard it but had second thoughts. He listened to the recording, then put her phone in his pocket.

'Well, it seems your hero is on his way. I guess playtime will have to wait. Still, nice of him to forewarn me.'

Chapter 54

Marcus drove as fast as he could towards Fern Retreat, his mind racing.

Douglas Holt had recognised the chain as his brother Luke's, and the dragonhead link Ellie found was from an identical chain.

Someone called Luke had applied for a job working for Julia. And as he had just found the job advertisement in Luke Holt's bedroom, surely it was one and the same person. Coincidence? He didn't believe in them.

Did Luke somehow know Marcus was pursuing him? And that Julia was his girlfriend? It made no sense. If he knew he was Rose's father, surely, he would be running in the opposite direction.

He gripped the steering wheel harder. One thing he did know was the Holts' capacity for violence, and, he thought grimly, Julia had no idea how dangerous Luke was.

He stared ahead and prayed that he was wrong, that he was overreacting.

Luke dragged Julia to her feet. He pushed her outside and shoved her against the wall while he kick-started the motorbike.

Waving the kitchen knife, he shouted at her to get on. She was so weak that she slid to the ground.

'Fuck!' He lifted the bike onto its centre stand and dragged her to it. 'Get on!'

'Can't,' she managed to say.

'Shit,' he muttered, unfastening the belt around her hands. He kicked the bike off its stand, lifted her on, and then scrambled on too.

She looked in danger of passing out.

'Don't try anything. Hold on to me. We're not going far, just to my place. Then I'll clean you up.'

She clung to him to protect herself from the driving rain, terrified of falling off. Luke rode into the lane. She was instantly soaked through, the sluicing wind and biting cold shocking her back into full consciousness. After a few minutes, the pain in her head started to fade to a dull throb. She thought she saw lights coming towards them.

Luke switched off the headlight and quickly pulled into a passing point, where bushes partly concealed them. He grabbed her hair and pulled her head down in an attempt to hide her. A new wave of pain screamed in her temple. When the vehicle passed, he let go.

They were straddling the bike, its engine still running. He turned slightly, still holding the knife.

'You have to hold on tight!' he shouted through the rain. He switched the headlight back on, geared up, and accelerated.

Julia wasn't sure for how long they had ridden – maybe five minutes. The road looked wider, and the hedgerow had receded. She guessed they were in open pastureland and approaching the cliffs.

Travelling from the opposite direction, Marcus had glimpsed a headlight that had then strangely disappeared. He slowed a little at a passing point. Peering through his windscreen, he spotted the end of a stationary motorbike half hidden in a thicket. Why would someone on a bike stop in this weather? It had to be Luke, and he was not far from Fern Retreat.

But by the time he'd reversed back, the bike had gone. To change direction, he had to make a frustrating four-point turn. He switched to full beam and accelerated fast.

A few minutes later, he saw a rear light. He sped up. It wasn't easy trying to keep up – the bike sped up too as the road widened. But even from a distance, he could see there was a woman riding pillion. She had no helmet or coat and was swaying precariously. He pressed the pedal to the floor, slightly narrowing the gap.

It was Julia.

He was horrified.

Marcus had thought nothing could ever scare him more than Rose's death, but now by some sick twist of fate, he was watching history repeat itself and powerless to stop it.

Fearing for her life, he pulled back, hoping the bike would slow too. It made no difference.

He continued to follow, trying to keep the bike's rear light in view.

Luke was hunched low over the tank. He shoved the knife into his back pocket, so he had better control. He knew they were being followed and guessed it was Julia's boyfriend. It must have been him in the truck that passed them earlier.

The night was not going as planned.

Julia knew it was Marcus, too. She had to try to stop the bike. They might crash, but at the speed he was going, it was just a matter of time before they came off anyway. Her hands were so cold she could barely move them, but she let go of Luke with one to try and grab the knife — just as he took a sudden bend too fast.

The bike wobbled and he lost control. They left the road, bumping onto uneven grassland. Luke threw himself off seconds before the bike connected with a large log. On impact, Julia was thrown onto the grass.

Luke landed headlong in some brambles, his head and shoulders trapped. He groaned and screamed with pain as dozens of tiny barbs tore at his face. Desperate to break free, he ripped his way out, leaving clumps of his hair behind. He stood, swaying with the effort.

'Julia!' he yelled.

The fallen bike's headlight illuminated where she lay, motionless. He scrambled to her and pulled her onto her back.

Julia came to and was filled with fear at the sight of his ruined face looming over her.

'Julia,' he hissed. 'You have to get up. We have to go.'

'Can't,' she gasped. She could hear the sea raging below. They were close to the edge.

Luke glanced back up the road. He could see headlights approaching fast. He pulled the knife from his back pocket and held it to her throat.

'Get up or I swear I will cut you,' he seethed.

She couldn't fight anymore; everything hurt. She was falling into a dark, quiet place and welcomed it.

But just before she passed out, she vaguely heard Luke

scream and then Marcus's voice as he gently lifted her into his arms.

He was unsure what injuries she had suffered but she had a nasty cut to her temple and felt ice cold to the touch. As he carefully laid her across the backseat of the truck and covered her with a blanket, he looked up and was shocked to see Luke's blood-streaked face pressed against the opposite window. A moment ago he thought he had knocked him out cold.

Marcus got out slowly and closed the truck door. Luke staggered back a step smiling.

'You must be Marcus.'

'And you must be Luke.' Marcus walked around the back of the truck to face him. He could see he had the knife in his hand which he must have retrieved from the ground.

'How do you know who I am?'

'Because I've been looking for you.'

'I thought you were here for Julia.'

'I am. But I'm also here for you.' Marcus pulled out the wallet chain and threw it at him. 'This is yours I believe.'

Luke slowly retrieved it from the ground with his free hand and regarded it curiously. 'Where did you get it?'

'Your garage. Look, I even fixed it for you. Courtesy of a little girl called Ellie. Does her name ring a bell?'

'I've no idea what you're talking about.'

'All right. How about Rose... Rose Cole?'

Luke's smirk dissolved. He used his sleeve to wipe blood from his eyes and tried to think straight. He thought he was the only person alive who knew about him and Rose. 'Are you the police?'

'You wish. Rose was my daughter.'

Luke fidgeted. 'You're her father? And you're seeing Julia? *My* Julia?'

Marcus stood, unmoving in the rain. 'You don't get to ask any more questions.' He drew his gun.

Luke's eyes widened. 'It wasn't my fault!' He blurted out. 'What happened to Rose... it was an accident!'

'Quite accident-prone, aren't you?' he replied, nodding at the motorbike.

'I loved Rose, and she loved me,' he said defensively, eyeing the gun.

'Don't say her name,' he scowled. 'You are not worthy. You took her life; just threw it away. And then, being the lowlife that you are, ran off, leaving a little girl and her injured grandmother alone.'

'No!' He yelled. His head felt like it was going to explode and he staggered to stay upright in the driving rain. 'Like I said, it was an accident. There was nothing I could do. I'm sorry. I panicked. I shouldn't have run.'

'You could have come forward later. That might at least have given Rose's mother some closure for losing her only child. *Our* only child.'

Luke said nothing.

'Why did you kidnap Julia? Where the hell were you taking her?'

Again, no reply.

'Is this what you do? Prey on women? Are there others that you've hurt? Killed?'

'No! We know each other. Long before you ever came along.'

'I don't believe you.'

'It's true. We went to the same school.'

'Jesus, what is this, a high school crush?' he mocked.

Luke gazed at Marcus with wild eyes.

'Oh, Christ, it is, isn't it? That's why you applied for the kennel-hand job.'

'I love her!' he shrieked.

'I can't listen to any more.' He raised the gun.

Knowing he had nothing to lose, Luke leapt at him, wielding the knife and screaming like a banshee. Tempting though it was to shoot him, Marcus resisted. Instead, he punched him hard in the gut. Luke reeled. He let go of the knife and dropped to his knees. Marcus dragged Luke to his feet with one hand and still pointing the gun at him nodded at the motorbike. The engine was still running.

'Pick it up and get on,' he demanded.

'What? Why?' he stammered in confusion. 'Are you letting me go?'

'In a manner of speaking,' he smiled. 'You're going to get on it and drive in that direction.' He waved the gun toward the cliff edge and sea beyond. 'If you don't, I'll shoot you dead.'

'You're fucking crazy!'

'You better believe it,' he said, taking aim.

Luke glared at him, his long, sodden hair half covering his shredded face. With a supreme effort, he dragged the bike upright and swung his leg over. He jutted his chin up and laughed defiantly. Whatever he did next, he knew he was dead.

'I'll be seeing you.' He squeezed the clutch lever and accelerated.

Marcus watched him go. The engine screeched as the bike shot over the edge, dropping into the raging black water below.

Chapter 55

Lily had enjoyed getting Swan Song ready and celebrating with Oliver, but she felt ragged and unsettled after her terrifying nightmare.

'I know you didn't want to talk about it last night but what were you dreaming about?' he asked, passing her a strong black coffee.

'Nothing,' she replied, savouring the bitter taste. She needed energising.

'Lily, you were screaming.'

'I'm sorry for startling you.'

He looked perplexed. 'Do you need any help today?'

'Thanks, but I can manage. I'm just unpacking if you need to go.'

'All right, well I think I'll head home, then. The storm's getting worse. I'd better check that everything's covered up in the barn. These high winds are expected to last throughout today and tonight.'

'Um, this may seem a strange thing to ask, but do you think you could come with me to Penwyth House tonight?'

'I can, but why?'

'Because I'm so close to remembering what happened there. I know my parents argued that night... The rest is in here.' She tapped her head. 'Maybe if I go up on the roof while there's a storm, it might trigger something.'

'You look tired. Can't it wait? Storms come and go all the time here. We could go another night.'

Her eyes implored him to agree. 'I need to try. I could go on my own; I'll be fine. And I won't disturb Joe. He won't even know I'm at the house.'

'That's what you dreamt about last night, wasn't it?'

She nodded. 'Memories still haunt me. They have for years. I've tried to walk away from my past, but it hasn't worked. That's why this is important to me. Returning to Penwyth has helped me recall things. I can't give up now.'

He threw his hands up in exasperation. 'I don't think you should go on the roof at all. It's not safe, and you definitely shouldn't go alone. But I know what this means to you, so I'll come with you. But if it's too dangerous, we walk away. Agreed?'

When they pulled up outside Penwyth House later that night, the deluge of rain that had fallen all day had finally stopped. Still, a strong gale screeched around the mansion's walls, rushing inland like some unleashed demonic force.

Lily gazed up at the roof. It was too dark to see the familiar chimneys and spires.

'Come on,' said Oliver. 'Let's get inside before something falls on us.'

His torch cast an eerie light around the hallway, shadows jumping out at them. The old house creaked and groaned so much, he thought the whole place might be lifted up and carried away.

'I don't think we should go up there. The gale is too strong. Half the roof's probably missing.'

Lily stopped at the bottom of the stairs. 'If it looks too risky, I could at least stand at the entrance.'

'Okay, but we stay together.'

As they reached the top landing, the entire house seemed to vibrate, making the chandelier's crystals tinkle.

'This way.' She placed one foot on the bottom stair leading onto the roof. The last time she had stood there, she had heard Vincent whispering in her ear and had fled. As she began to climb, she saw something blue on the ground behind the slatted stairs that she hadn't noticed before.

'Look, it's Hoppy! Alice's favourite toy. She must have dropped it that night.' She picked it up and held it close to her chest as they kept climbing.

Strangely, she felt nothing apart from the eeriness of being in the dark and the sounds of the storm – no flashbacks and no gut-wrenching feeling of dread.

At the top, she banged hard on the horizontal metal bar. It budged slightly, another shove, and it opened.

'You okay?' he asked.

She nodded as they looked in awe at the carnage outside. A small chimney near the entrance had fallen and lay half submerged in rainwater; broken bricks and tiles littered the floor.

'We won't be able to see where we're standing in all this water!' He shouted above the wind. 'Only go a few steps!' In the distance, thunder rolled inland. 'Stay low or we'll be blown away!'

They moved carefully through the debris. She peered at the spot where Vincent and Alice had stood shortly before they had fallen and edged towards the turrets on the far ledge. Oliver grabbed her arm just as a powerful gust of wind hit them. They had no choice but to hunker down. Thunder rippled across the sky, this time closer.

'We have to go back! It's too dangerous.'

She nodded her agreement. Seconds later, white-hot lightning lit the entire sky like a camera flash. They watched a silent pattern of light crisscross downwards, followed by an eruption of noise. One of the two large turrets was struck and partially collapsed, falling onto the drive below. A sonic boom exploded overhead as though the sky was being ripped in two. They had no choice but to wait until the chaos stopped.

A short time later, when things had quietened and the storm moved away, he shone the torch over the charred remains of the collapsed column. The air was alive with static electricity and filled with the pungent smell of ozone. They looked at each other in disbelief.

When they were safely back inside, he asked, 'Did it help being out there?'

'No.' She sighed. 'I'm sorry, I really hoped it would. At least I found Hoppy.'

Come on,' he gave her a hug. 'Let's get out of here.'

Downstairs, Oliver opened the front door. 'Why don't you wait here for a minute? There's rubble on the drive. I'm hoping the car didn't get hit as it's parked further back. I'll just check, then I'll come back for you.'

She stood waiting, watching through the window. Glancing down, she noticed the window seat. She had often sat there as a child. She shone the torch on it. Underneath it, she remembered, was a small storage space. Lifting the lid, she saw something inside. She pulled out the object that had laid there unnoticed for decades and her heart leapt into her throat. It was the face of her nightmares: an African mask.

Seeing it instantly jolted her memory. The mask used to sit on the windowsill. The final piece of the jigsaw slotted into place.

And someone was calling her...

June 1971

Lily stood in the doorway on the roof of Penwyth House. She watched as Alice ran through the storm to her father. He swept her up in his arms, swaying in the wind and the rain.

'Lily! Come here!' Vincent gestured towards her, his voice half lost in the storm.

She stared at them, silhouetted by lightning in the night sky.

'Lily!' her mother called from below. 'What are you doing up there? Come down!'

'Daddy and Alice are up here! Mummy, they are at the edge, and he's calling me.'

'No! No, Lily.' Her mother was looking up at her from the bottom of the stairs. 'You come here right now. Do you hear me?'

Lily climbed back down the stairs. She could still hear her father shouting.

Her mother grabbed hold of her.

'Listen to me. Go and wait for me in the hallway. Okay?'

Lily solemnly nodded.

Her mother's face was deathly white. 'Go! Go now!'

She ran down the main stairs as fast as possible and waited breathlessly. After what seemed like an age, her mother came running down. She looked terrified.

'Where's Daddy and Alice?'

Her mother didn't answer. 'I have to fetch Joe. You stay here, okay? Your father's been drinking and needs help. Don't worry, Joe will know what to do. Promise me you'll stay here.'

Lily's eyes grew wide with fear. 'I promise.'

Her mother flung the door open and ran out into the storm. Lily wandered to the window and picked up the African mask from its stand on the sill. She ran her fingers over its narrow eyes and the grooves of its harsh features. Then something dropped right in front of the window. She slowly put the mask down.

With feet like lead, she walked through the front door, down the steps, into the rain and stared at the crumpled heap on the floor. Vincent was still alive and reaching out to her. A trail of blood trickled from the side of his mouth. She could see one of Alice's hands motionless, protruding from underneath her father's broken body.

'Daddy! What do I do?' she sobbed.

He tried to speak. She knelt beside him, putting her ear close to his mouth. 'Why did you run away, Lily?' he said with effort. 'You should have come with us,' he smiled. He exhaled one last time, then his hand flopped to the ground.

Lily heard a man yell her name and she got to her feet. Her

mother and Joe were running towards her.

March 1995

Oliver appeared in the doorway. 'That's a relief. It's okay, the car's not touched.' He saw her face, drained of colour, and his expression turned to that of concern. 'Lily? What is it?'

She dropped the mask on the floor. 'He jumped,' she said flatly. 'It wasn't an accident. He jumped.'

Chapter 56

'Here, take a few sips.'

Julia swallowed some water and tried to ignore the searing pain in her shoulder. 'Luke?' she asked Marcus with a trace of fear in her eyes.

'He's gone.' He looked closer at the gash to her temple. It was deep but had stopped bleeding. 'It's over,' he reassured her. 'Try and relax. We're leaving. I'm taking you to the hospital.'

He drove carefully to St Oswald, not wishing to worsen her pain. Despite her injuries, he felt a huge sense of relief wash over him. She was alive. She was going to be okay.

The severity of the storm meant a busy evening for the A&E department. The staff looked up in surprise when they saw a man carrying a woman into reception wrapped in a blanket. A trolley was quickly brought out, and Julia whisked away while Marcus was dispatched to the waiting room.

Two hours later, a woman in scrubs emerged. 'Hello, I'm Dr Williams. And you are?'

'I'm Julia's boyfriend. How is she? Is she going to be okay?'

'She has a nasty head injury, but the MRI shows no trauma to the brain. She also has a fractured collarbone and some superficial cuts. As well as bruising to her wrists. We'll need to keep her in for a few days.

'Your girlfriend has given us some details about what

happened.' She regarded Marcus with concern. 'Under the circumstances, I wonder if I could ask you to explain in your own words.'

So, as he and Julia agreed on the way to St Oswald, he recounted their version of events for what happened that evening.

The doctor nodded. 'Julia told me that a man forced her to leave her home and go with him.

'That's right,' he said, grimly. 'I was on my way over to see her anyway. She's just opened a dog kennel in Lostmor. The place is remote and wide open to the elements. She wasn't answering her phone and I was concerned for her and the dogs with the storm being so bad. It was pitch black and I was not far from the kennels when I saw a motorbike on the road. As I passed it, I noticed a woman on the back. She had no helmet on, not even a coat and was completely drenched. I was horrified when I realised it was Julia.'

'So what did you do? What happened next?'

'As soon as the biker saw me he drove off at speed. I followed him but I had to turn the truck around first and the lane was narrow. All I know is by the time I caught up. Julia was lying unconscious on the ground not far from the cliff edge.'

'And the man on the bike?'

'No idea. I couldn't see him or the bike anywhere around. All I was thinking about was Julia. When I saw her lying there, I thought she was dead. When I realised she was unconscious and not knowing the extent of her injuries, I knew I had to get her help as soon as possible so I drove her straight here.'

'Couldn't you have called for help? An ambulance? The police?'

'An ambulance would have taken too long to reach us. Especially in this weather. It took me an hour to get here as it was. As for the police. Sorry, I should have called them. I wasn't thinking straight. I was so worried about Julia.'

'Well, we have notified them about the kidnapping. Obviously they will want to talk to you both as soon as possible. I understand from Julia that she knows this man?'

'Luke Holt. Yes. He turned up for a job she had advertised helping at the kennels. She recognised him from high school.'

'So do you have any idea why he did this?'

Marcus shrugged and shook his head. 'On the way here she told me he had a crush on her back when they were kids. But she hadn't seen him since. Not until he showed up for that interview. She gave the job to someone else and that was that. Until tonight... when the crazy bastard broke into her home and threatened her! Sorry... it's just she could have died out there.'

'I understand.' She studied his face, then gave a brief smile. 'It's lucky you turned up when you did.'

'Do you think I could see her now, Doctor?'

'Only for a moment. She's just been given a sedative and needs to rest.'

Julia's head was bandaged and her right arm in a sling. She was hooked up to a monitor and a saline drip. Marcus was used to hospitals (albeit military ones) as both a patient and visitor. As a result, he disliked being anywhere near them – too many bad memories. Images of men he used to know, their bodies mutilated and broken, still haunted him. He was one of the lucky ones. A skilled medical team had saved him, but it was too late for many, including Jack.

He sat close to Julia holding her grazed hand. She turned her head and opened her eyes momentarily.

'Bella...' she mumbled.

'Don't worry, my love. I'll take care of everything. We can talk in the morning.' He squeezed her hand, as she drifted into a heavy, dreamless sleep wishing he could stay.

Fern Retreat had taken a pounding, and several fence panels at the front of the property were down. Marcus swung the truck into the drive, having first picked Horace up from the Black Dog inn. 'Stay here boy. I'll be right back.'

He stepped onto the porch. The front door was wide open, and rainwater had soaked the entrance. He picked Julia's belt up off the ground. *What the hell happened here?* he thought, looking around apprehensively. Inside, a chair was overturned; Julia's car keys and a bottle of wine with two glasses on the table.

'Bella?' he called. He could hear the dog howling. He took the stairs two at a time. She leapt at him enthusiastically as soon as he opened the bedroom door. He quickly checked the other bedrooms; nothing seemed disturbed.

Back downstairs, he cleaned up. The Aga was cold, but a big Victorian-style radiator was piping hot. It would soon warm the place.

He noticed blood on the brickwork. Julia had said she hit her head on the fireplace when struggling to get away. He sighed. It looked like she'd put up a fight.

Marcus grabbed the torch by the door and went back

outside. It was only ten o'clock, but it felt later. Fatigue was setting in. Overhead, lightning zigzagged across the sky, shortly followed by deafening thunder. He crossed to the kennels.

Ralph was sat in the corner, refusing to move. Marcus comforted him, persuading him to come out on his lead. He did the same with Treacle and Posy, who were huddled together. Next, he fetched Horace and settled them all with Bella in the kitchen.

Now exhausted, he lay down on the couch in the lounge. He didn't want to sleep upstairs without Julia.

The lightning gradually faded away, and the thunder became a distant rumble. He closed his eyes and drifted off to sleep within seconds.

The following morning, he was greeted by sunshine and clear blue skies. He fed and exercised the dogs in the paddock, noticing two sheets of corrugated iron had blown off a lean-to, damaging the fencing he and Julia had erected.

He phoned Susie, whom he'd already told he had an emergency when he'd picked up Horace. She was her usual amenable self. She reassured him she and Andy could cover for a few more days, and Bernie, the chef, was in all week. Marcus thanked her and hung up. Next, he called the owners of Ralph and Treacle and Posy, asking if they could pick them up by late afternoon. He also contacted any clients booked for the next week, apologising for cancelling and briefly explaining that Julia had been involved in a motorbike accident.

Once the dogs' owners had picked up their pets and gone, Marcus left Bella and Horace asleep in front of the Aga. He grabbed his car keys, keen to get to the hospital. On the drive, he glanced at the reception hut and noticed the security camera above the door. With everything going on, he'd forgotten about it. Instead of going to his car, he unlocked the hut and set about checking the video footage...

A short time later at St Oswald Hospital, Marcus was pleased to see Julia sitting up in bed, sipping tea. He kissed her gently on the cheek then pulled up a chair.

'It must be quite a bump,' he said, looking at her bandaged head.

'It doesn't hurt much now I've had painkillers. How are the dogs?'

'They're all fine. Bella and Horace are back at the house, Ralph and the terriers have been collected, and I've cancelled your bookings for the next week. And there's no need to worry – everyone I spoke to was more concerned about you than their booking.'

'What did you say?' Her face was cut and bruised, and her brave blue eyes were melting his heart.

'I told them you were in a motorbike accident. Nothing else.'

'And the hospital staff?'

'As we agreed.'

She looked at him curiously. 'How did you know I was in trouble?'

He took her hand. 'It can wait. Plenty of time to talk when you're better.'

'I may look like I've been hit by a bus, but I'm okay, thanks to you. So, tell me, how did you know?'

Marcus got up, closed the door and returned. He told her about his assault on Douglas and everything that followed.

Julia then recounted the incident with Luke, her voice breaking as emotion got the better of her.

'It's okay. You were brave to face up to him. That madman nearly killed you!'

'Apparently, the police came yesterday when I was sedated. The nurse told them they'd have to come back.'

'It's to be expected. They'll want to question us both.'

'Marcus,' she whispered, glancing at the closed door. 'He is gone, isn't he?'

In a lowered voice, he replied. 'He's gone. No one could have survived that. There's something else you should know. The security camera. Above the reception office.'

'I forgot all about it.'

'Me too, until this morning.'

'It's directed at the house. Have you replayed the tape?'

'Yes. It shows everything that occurred between you and him outside the house. From the moment he enters your home uninvited until later when he drags you out and manhandles you at knifepoint onto his bike. I could see that he had hurt you and that your wrists were bound... It wasn't an easy watch.'

She squeezed his hand. 'If the police have any doubts about our story, this proves he kidnapped me.'

Marcus nodded. 'Without a doubt.'

<h1>Chapter 57</h1>

'Hello, Miss Sanders. It's Sergeant Weeks. I have some news regarding the break-in at Penwyth House.'

'Oh?'

'We have someone in custody.'

'Who?'

'Douglas Holt. Mr Bligh's instincts were right about him. He has a police record, although only minor offences until now.

'Oddly, a colleague and I were on our way to the Holt residence when we received a radio request to attend a car accident en route. Someone reported seeing a van in a ditch. When we reached the scene, we realised the driver was still inside the vehicle and that it was none other than Douglas Holt. He had suffered some minor injuries, so we weren't able to question him until later. However, when we did, he voluntarily confessed to the burglary, the assault on Mr Newman, and to stealing the shotgun, which we have since retrieved from his home.'

'Well, that is very good news. What about his accomplice?'

'Mr Holt claims he acted alone. However, I appreciate that Mr Newman is positive he was confronted by two people that night at Penwyth House. Douglas previously stated that he had spent the night of the burglary at home with his brother

Luke when questioned by police. So we are very keen to speak with his brother and actively looking for him.'

'And Douglas has no idea where he might be?'

'He says not. Apparently, he often takes off for days without a word.'

'Do you think he's telling the truth?'

'I'm not sure. His confession was a little unusual. It's not often our job is made so easy. It's as if it meant nothing to him. If I'm honest, he seemed scared, but of what or whom, I don't know.'

'Will he remain in custody?

'For now, yes.'

'Does his brother have a criminal record, too?'

'No, but as I said, he is wanted for questioning. We'll find him; he'll turn up sooner or later.'

'I hope so. I can't tell you how relieved I am that you've made an arrest. And Joe will be too. Does he know yet?'

'I was on my way over there to tell him in person.'

'I'm seeing him tomorrow. If you like, I can let him know.'

'Fine, if you're happy to do that. In that case, could you also inform him that his shotgun will be held as evidence until the accused appears in court? In the meantime, he will need to come to the station to identify the firearm – when he's feeling up to it, of course.'

Joe was sitting outside his cottage when Lily pulled up. He carefully rose to greet her. She was pleased to see his face healing nicely, and that he was moving more easily.

'Come on in.' He smiled.

She noticed the photo she had given him, proudly placed next to the one of her mother. 'You look so happy together.' She picked it up.

'And young!' he added.

She laughed. 'You seem better. How are you feeling?'

'My jaw doesn't ache as much. I can manage more than just soup through a straw now, thank heavens! Ribs are still sore, but I'm getting there.'

'And your eye?'

'I've got a follow-up next week, but I think the right one is better. I can see well enough to take care of the aviary now.'

'Have you been there yet?'

'Yes, and I bumped into your friend, Janet. Nice lady. We had a pleasant chat by the waterfall. I thanked her for all her help.'

'I know how much your birds mean to you, and we can still help out. You only have to ask. While you were in the hospital, Timothy drew up papers for a change in ownership of Edhen Cottage, and the surrounding land we mentioned. I've already signed. We can go through them together, or I can leave them with you to look at?'

He smiled. 'You know I trust you. Where do I sign?'

As a formality, she showed him the deeds outlining the property's boundaries. 'Congratulations. It's official!' Lily declared when he'd added his name. 'Edhen Cottage is yours and always will be.'

They hugged.

'Thank you. I really couldn't ask for anything more,' he said.

'I have some more news… about the people who attacked you.' She relayed what Sergeant Weeks had told her.

'It's a relief one of them's been caught. Do you think his brother is involved?'

'We'll have to wait and see. But the police are adamant that they will find him. They assured me it's only a matter of time.'

'I hope so. I just want to put this behind me.' He sighed. 'What's next for you, Lily? Will you stay in Lostmor?'

'Yes,' she said, taking his hand. 'Everyone I care about is here. Why would I leave?'

He was relieved he wasn't about to lose her again.

'I still have my apartment in Bristol, but it's only rented. I've opened an art gallery in Tresor Bay and I'm renting the apartment above it.'

'And Oliver? You like him a lot, don't you?'

'Yes.'

He smiled. 'I'm happy for you. He seems a good man. And what about Penwyth House? Is it going up for sale?'

'Actually, not for a while. I've decided to renovate it first.'

He looked surprised. 'What made you change your mind?'

'It was my home once; it just feels like the right thing to do. But it may be noisy around here for a while!'

'That's okay. The place has been too quiet for too long! Besides, I'm glad it's you restoring it and not some stranger. I've done my best with the estate, but it's time the house was returned to your care, Lily.'

'I will do my very best. I'll also be installing some long-overdue security cameras and fixing the entrance gate.

'You know, the day I found you, I was driving to Edhen Cottage and only stopped because there was this seagull on the drive in front of Penwyth House blocking my way forward. He just wouldn't budge so I got out to try and shoo him out of the way. That was when I noticed broken glass and opened up the house. It may sound crazy but I think he knew you were in there and that you needed help.'

'That must have been Mike. Fixed his claw when he was a chick. My word, that is something, isn't it?' He laughed. 'He flies in now and then.' He paused for a moment, gazing at Lily with his sea-green eyes. 'How about you and I visit Alice sometime soon?'

Lily smiled and nodded. 'Yes, I would like that. I would like that very much.'

Her headstone simply read:

Alice Sanders
1965-1971
Forever in our hearts

Lily placed Hoppy on top of Alice's grave. She and Joe stood quietly together under the cedar tree. 'I miss you,' she whispered to her sister.

She turned to her father. 'I finally remembered what happened that night. You were there, weren't you?'

'I was too late,' he said sadly. 'There was nothing me nor your mother could do. It was just a tragic accident.'

What was there to gain by telling him the truth now? It would only upset him to know Vincent had whispered in his little girl's ear that she should have died, too.

They held hands and gazed out to sea, lost in their thoughts. Above them, a gentle breeze rustled the leaves, bringing the promise of spring.

Chapter 58

'It seems strange being a customer in the Black Dog inn,' said Marcus, spotting Tom in his usual corner. 'I may forget in a minute and start pulling pints!'

Julia laughed, her fingers lightly touching the now-fading scar on her temple.

'Does it bother you?' he asked referring to her injury.

'No, not at all.'

'What about your shoulder?'

'No pain, or even discomfort. I threw balls for the dogs overarm today instead of relying on Sarah to exercise them. The hospital did say I should be back to full strength in three months, so I can start helping out more now. We're lucky Sarah turned out to be such a diamond. I'm going to miss her when she goes to university.'

'She's been a great help. And offering to doggy sit tonight was thoughtful. I guess we'll have to advertise for someone else in September.'

'I'll be more selective with the interviewees this time,' she said wryly.

Since Julia's discharge from the hospital, Marcus had stayed close. He took no pleasure in what he had done, but nor did he have any regrets. If he had handed Luke over to the police, he would one day be released. This way, he could rest easy at night.

Inevitably, a police investigation ensued. Luke's fingerprints were found all over Julia's kitchen. The security footage at Fern Retreat backed up her account of Luke breaking into her home, assaulting her and subsequently kidnapping her. The kitchen knife that he used to threaten her with was discovered at the scene of the accident. Investigators found tyre tracks all over the crash site. It was concluded that the motorbike was travelling too fast and that the extreme weather conditions probably contributed to him swerving off of the road. As Julia was knocked unconscious and at that point, no other witnesses were present the police report suggested that Luke either fled the scene on his motorbike. Or, as Sergeant Weeks suspected, drove over the cliff edge having completely misjudged how close to the edge he was. He remembered only too well a tragic incident two years earlier when a car had gone over the edge, again at night and in poor weather conditions. Only in that instance, a body was found in the water shortly after. This particular case was more baffling. Tyre tracks were shown leading to the edge just yards from the road but because of the amount of rain that continued to fall that night it was hard for the police to predict an exact trajectory for the bike. He believed it was entirely possible that Luke was injured possibly concussed. In his confusion and panic to leave before Julia's body was found and himself subsequently arrested, he literally accelerated away in the dark, accidentally plunging to his death.

As for Julia, Marcus was concerned that Luke's assault on her, the kidnapping and the injuries inflicted on her when she was thrown from the motorbike may have some lasting impact.

But he need not have worried. All she wanted was to get back to normal. He had witnessed post-traumatic stress disorder before, and she showed none of the signs. Instead, as the weeks passed and she gradually recovered, she told him she loved him and asked him to move in with her. He had not hesitated. He had taken her in his arms and told her he loved her too. Not long after, he resigned as landlord of the Black Dog inn.

Julia looked at Marcus's face, his features now so familiar to her. The haunted look he had worn all those months ago was gone; in his eyes, she saw only kindness.

Marcus felt a firm hand on his shoulder.

'It's been a while. How are you?'

He got to his feet as he shook Oliver's hand and smiled at the woman beside him. 'I'm good,' he replied. 'I'm not sure you've met Julia. Julia, this is Oliver. And you must be Lily.'

'Yes,' she replied. 'I know your face. You used to work here!'

'For my sins, yes.' He grinned. 'You're welcome to join us.'

Julia shoved along and beckoned for Lily to sit next to her. 'Thanks!' she replied, Oliver taking the seat opposite.

'What are you up to now?' he asked Marcus.

'I'm helping Julia run Fern Retreat.'

'And how's Horace?'

'Having the time of his life,' Marcus replied. 'His days are spent tearing around the paddock with the other dogs. And he's taken a shine to Bella, Julia's springer spaniel.'

'I remember Horace,' said Lily. 'A big soppy Labrador.'

'That's him.' Julia smiled. 'What do you do, Lily? Do you work in Lostmor?'

'Yes, not far from here. I run an art gallery called Swan Song. Do you know it?'

'No, I'm afraid I rarely get a chance to go anywhere since I bought Fern Retreat. We're only here tonight because our kennel-hand offered to doggy sit!' She laughed. 'Not that I'm complaining – business is booming. And it's easier now that I have help.' She glanced happily at Marcus, who was chatting to Oliver about his farm.

'My family moved away when I was a teenager. I only moved back to Lostmor this year.'

'Well, Julia, I guess that makes us both second-timers in Lostmor! I was born here but moved away with my mother when I was young. I recently moved back from Bristol.'

'Did you come here to open your art gallery?'

'Um no, that came later. I inherited a property here, but then also met Oliver by chance when I found his dog – a Jack Russell called Flynn – up on the coastal road.'

Julia looked at her curiously. She had only met Marcus because he had brought Horace to Fern Retreat. 'It sounds an interesting story!'

'Lily, do you want a refill?' Oliver asked. 'Can I interest anyone else?'

'I'm interested,' said Marcus, 'but we told Sarah we'd be back by ten.'

'Some other time, then?'

'Why don't you and Julia join Lily and me for supper at the farm one evening?' Oliver suggested.

'That would be lovely.' Julia grinned. 'Perhaps you can tell me what happened after your encounter with a certain Jack Russell.'

Oliver laughed. 'That may take some time!'

Chapter 59

'That was a busy afternoon,' Julia said over dinner at Fern Retreat. 'Lots of people collecting dogs. At least tomorrow's pretty quiet.

'They were a nice couple, in the pub last night.'

'Oliver's a good bloke,' he replied, stroking Horace's head under the table.

'How do you know him?'

'I met him when I was the pub manager. He came in once a week and usually sat at the bar. He used to chat about the farm, you know, the usual stuff. I saw something on the news a while back about his girlfriend, Lily Sanders. I think her family has a troubled past. She recently inherited a big old mansion house and estate on the edge of Lostmor.'

'Goodness. Some people do have interesting lives!'

He omitted to mention the attempted burglary and assault involving the Holt brothers at Penwyth House. Some other time... If they did go to Oliver's for supper, he would forewarn her in case the subject came up. Otherwise, there seemed little point in bringing up their unwelcome names.

'I wouldn't say ours are exactly run-of-the-mill,' Marcus added.

She reached for his hand across the table. 'What if I were to tell you that our lives are about to get much more interesting...'

She paused.

He gasped. 'You're pregnant?'

She nodded. 'I know we haven't even talked about children but yes, I am.'

He rose, quickly pushing the kitchen chair back. Julia got up too and wrapped her arms around his neck.

He looked at her with tears of joy in his eyes. 'I could not be happier,' he whispered.

'Are you sure? Things have moved quickly between us, and we're so busy with the kennels...'

'True, things have happened quickly. But I'm glad. I love you. I only want to be with you. And our baby.' He smiled, gently placing a hand on her tummy. 'We can always hire more staff to help with the dogs. And we don't have to worry about money; twenty-two years in the army and not a lot to spend it on has left me financially secure.'

'That's good' – she smiled fondly and kissed him – 'because it's twins!'

At Bligh Farm, Oliver sat on Lily's bench gazing at the horizon. It was a warm summer evening. The long daylight hours lingered into twilight, and gentle waves glittered like sequins beyond the cliffs.

'There you are,' Lily smiled, sitting beside him. 'I have something to show you.'

'You do?'

Lily handed him the photo of her grandparents, Alfred and Jeanie. 'Remember this? I took it out of the album to frame it – look what I found on the back.'

Oliver turned it over. 'It's a recipe… for whisky!'

She nodded. 'This is my family's legacy, the ingredients for the finest single-malt Cornish whisky ever produced! And as far as I know, the only one in existence.'

He looked at her with surprise. 'This is unbelievable! It begs the question what will you do with it?'

'I'm not sure yet, but it's another piece of Sanders's history reclaimed. Imagine, a handwritten recipe found just by chance.'

'The gods are moving those chess pieces again.'

'Perhaps.' She laughed. Her long hair fell gently over her shoulders, and he thought she had never looked more beautiful.

Above them, birdsong floated down in the evening air – skylarks. He couldn't remember the last time he'd heard skylarks. He leant in gently and kissed her. 'Looks like it's your move.'